CADIAN BLOOD

'I AM HAVING absolutely no fun today,' Darrick hissed, pulling out a chunk of shrapnel from his thigh. He looked up from where he lay. His men – those that still lived – were rousing. Too experienced to rise fully and face enemy fire, they crawled through the shredded furniture, finding cover wherever they could. Las-fire was already flashing at them from the Kathurite positions across the chamber.

'This is Alliance, captain.' Darrick reached out bleeding fingers to pull his fallen lasgun closer. He'd carried that weapon since he'd been a Whiteshield over twenty years ago. Not a chance in hell he'd leave it here, no matter how battered it was. His fingertips snagged the strap, and he dragged on it. The rifle bore a palette of fresh burns and new scratches, but otherwise looked fine. He guessed it would still fire. 'Alliance: Broken,' he repeated.

'Acknowledged. *Cruor* inbound. Hold in the name of the Emperor,' was Thade's curt reply before cutting the link.

Easier said than done, thought Darrick.

In the same series

· IMPERIAL GUARD ·

THE IMPERIAL GUARD OMNIBUS
by Mitchel Scanlon, Steve Lyons and Steve Parker
(Omnibus contains the books FIFTEEN HOURS,
DEATH WORLD and REBEL WINTER)

DESERT RAIDERS
Lucien Soulban

ICE GUARD
Steve Lyons

GUNHEADS
Steve Parker

· GAUNT'S GHOSTS ·

*Colonel-Commissar Gaunt and his regiment, the
Tanith First-and-Only, struggle for survival on the
battlefields of the far future.*
by Dan Abnett

The Founding
(Omnibus containing books 1-3 in the series:
First and Only, Ghostmaker and *Necropolis*)

The Saint
(Omnibus containing books 4-7 in the series:
Honour Guard, The Guns of Tanith, Straight Silver
and *Sabbat Martyr*)

The Lost
Book 8 – TRAITOR GENERAL
Book 9 – HIS LAST COMMAND
Book 10 – THE ARMOUR OF CONTEMPT
Book 11 – ONLY IN DEATH

Also
DOUBLE EAGLE

A WARHAMMER 40,000 NOVEL

CADIAN BLOOD

Aaron Dembski-Bowden

*Dedicated to Mum and Dad, because they'd kill me
if I didn't.*

A BLACK LIBRARY PUBLICATION

First published in Great Britain in 2009 by
BL Publishing,
Games Workshop Ltd.,
Willow Road, Nottingham,
NG7 2WS, UK.

10 9 8 7 6 5 4 3 2 1

Cover illustration by Hardy Fowler.

A CIP record for this book is available from the British Library.

US ISBN13: 978 1 84416 771 5

Distributed in the US by Simon & Schuster
1230 Avenue of the Americas, New York, NY 10020, US.

See the Black Library on the Internet at
www.blacklibrary.com

Find out more about Games Workshop
and the world of Warhammer 40,000 at
www.games-workshop.com

Printed and bound in the US.

IT IS THE 41st millennium. For more than a hundred centuries the Emperor has sat immobile on the Golden Throne of Earth. He is the master of mankind by the will of the gods, and master of a million worlds by the might of his inexhaustible armies. He is a rotting carcass writhing invisibly with power from the Dark Age of Technology. He is the Carrion Lord of the Imperium for whom a thousand souls are sacrificed every day, so that he may never truly die.

YET EVEN IN his deathless state, the Emperor continues his eternal vigilance. Mighty battlefleets cross the daemon-infested miasma of the warp, the only route between distant stars, their way lit by the Astronomican, the psychic manifestation of the Emperor's will. Vast armies give battle in His name on uncounted worlds. Greatest amongst His soldiers are the Adeptus Astartes, the Space Marines, bio-engineered super-warriors. Their comrades in arms are legion: the Imperial Guard and countless planetary defence forces, the ever-vigilant Inquisition and the tech-priests of the Adeptus Mechanicus to name only a few. But for all their multitudes, they are barely enough to hold off the ever-present threat from aliens, heretics, mutants – and worse.

TO BE A man in such times is to be one amongst untold billions. It is to live in the cruellest and most bloody regime imaginable. These are the tales of those times. Forget the power of technology and science, for so much has been forgotten, never to be relearned. Forget the promise of progress and understanding, for in the grim dark future there is only war. There is no peace amongst the stars, only an eternity of carnage and slaughter, and the laughter of thirsting gods.

PROLOGUE
The Way a World Dies

I

AT FIRST THERE was silence.

People died, but there was no outcry. The bodies rested in noiseless repose in tower habitation spires; in the prayer rooms of great monasteries; in gutters by the sides of streets. The deaths went unnoticed. This was a world that saw ten million new pilgrims each month – it was no stranger to off-worlders making planetfall only to die soon after.

The shrineworld of Kathur, named for the saint himself, was a beacon of faith and hope for the people of Scarus Sector. Faith flared or withered for those who came to tread the holy soil of this blessed world, seeking affirmation for lives lived without meaning. Hope flowered or died for those who landed here seeking to touch the relics of a long-dead saint and be healed of injury or illness.

When people began to die there was no planet-wide panic, no ringing sirens wailing across cities, and no distress calls to nearby worlds, crying of a devastating disease. The sickness spread, tearing through the population, but to those who watched for such things, it was just a spike in the numbers. These things happened from time to time.

A plague brought from off-world, the world's leaders said. Faith will scourge the taint from the righteous and pure.

No warnings. No panic.

Silence.

II

THE SILENCE DID not last long.

At the dawn of the outbreak's second week, there were too many dead for the funeral priests to haul into the consecrated incinerators, and the Ecclesiarchy governors realised their planet was suffering no natural plague. The death toll was catastrophic, and the Kathurite acolytes traditionally tasked with funerary rites walked the streets in gangs, losing the battle to do their simple duty.

The initial astropathic cries for help reached out from Kathur. Several hundred psykers worldwide screamed their pleas into the warp, begging for assistance. Imperial forces in the sector responded to the cries for aid in impressive time: Scarus was forever the Archenemy's ripest target, and the Emperor's servants never relaxed their vigilance here. Fleets of ships powered up their engines and broke into the warp, chasing the source of the psychic screams like bloodhounds pursuing the scent of prey.

The stream of comm-channel messages and psychic transmissions from Kathur told of a plague without end, of millions already dead, of a planet dying.

The Imperium was no stranger to the Curse of Unbelief. Even now, the plague wracked dozens of worlds across Segmentum Obscurus – but Kathur was the anomaly, the one world that broke the pattern of infection. The other infected worlds stood on the rim of the Warmaster's Black Crusade. Kathur, however, was far from the Great Eye and the systems drowning in the tides of battle.

All this death made no sense. There was no spaceship of the Archenemy to spread the taint, no touch of heresy detected among the populace, and no sign of Chaos in the planet's rule.

But it *was* the Curse.

The Curse of Unbelief ripped across the shrineworld now, taking those who lacked true faith in the God-Emperor. It rotted flesh and turned organs putrescent while the victims still lived. Many turned to suicide rather than decay in agony. Riots broke out over the planet. Funeral pyres burned endlessly, the streams of black smoke choking the sky around the largest cathedral-cities.

The Adeptus hierarchs receiving the first wave of communications from Kathur ordered the planet cut off from the Imperium at the first signs of the Curse of Unbelief. Assembled in the heavens above the doomed world, a mighty fleet coalesced over the course of several days. They did not come to save the people – they came only to stop the population evacuating. The taint, the fleet-captains knew, must never be spread. On the command decks of Imperial Navy vessels stationed in high orbit, stern-faced inquisitors oversaw the blockade's management.

No vaccine had ever been found to ease the sufferings of the afflicted. In the words of Inquisitor Caius, as he stood on the bridge of the Gothic-class vessel *In His Name*, 'We consign these souls to oblivion, for mercy now would damn us all.'

The blockade of Imperial Navy vessels hung in the reaches above Kathur, enforcing the quarantine with lethal vigour. Thousands of the Emperor's citizens died under the anger of Imperial guns as the blockade vessels fired on any ship fleeing the planet. It wasn't long before the attempts ceased. The people on the surface were either too ill to make the journey, or already dead.

Bizarrely, pilgrims sought to make planetfall, still wishing to walk among the cathedral-cities of the saint's world and receive the blessing of Saint

Kathur. Any attempts by pilgrim vessels to reach the surface were deterred by stern threats and the weapons batteries of Cobra-class destroyers. Such warnings, a barefaced presentation of the Emperor's might, were enough for most ships. A single vessel had been filled with souls pious enough to run the blockade. This ship, a wallowing barge little more than a cargo hauler and packed with three hundred pilgrims, ultimately did make it down to the surface of Kathur. What remained of the ship after its brief encounter with Imperial Fury fighters flamed through the atmosphere and crashed into the western ocean.

Inquisitor Bastian Caius of the Ordo Sepulturum stayed in vox-contact with the Enforcer Marshal of Kathur, a man by the name of Bannecheck, until the very end of Imperial control. The commander of the planet's Enforcers remained in touch with the inquisitor for seventeen days, describing the scenes of carnage and plague ravaging the surface as his men tried to retain order. Every word was recorded. Each syllable of his rhythmic cant, distorted as it was by vox interference. Through this crackling monotone, Caius learned of the erosion and breakdown of Imperial rule.

On the third day of contact, the marshal reported cults rising among the dwindling Kathur Planetary Defence Force, and of cultists within being spared the curse's death. The *Dictate Imperialis* was broken, the Emperor's Law abandoned. By this time, the global law enforcement force was already effectively destroyed. It fell to the elite Enforcers to take to the streets, slaughtering cultists in a series of brutal raids on hidden strongholds.

Despite initial successes, they were doomed to fail.

On the sixth day, chanting rose from temples across the planet – no longer in praise of the Emperor, but now pleading to the Ruinous Powers for mercy. Control across the planet was under threat, with the capital city of Solthane standing out as the final bastion of Imperial order. The Enforcers entered the cathedral districts of Solthane in unprecedented force, leading the shattered remains of still-loyal PDF and the still-living law enforcement officers. Their objective was to quell the rising cults across the planet in a decisive and damning half-week of fighting.

Bannecheck reported losses among his forces of ninety-three per cent on the morning of the ninth day. The cults' numbers were far greater than had been initially surmised. Those that were not already well-armed by the PDF defectors overcame Enforcer assault teams by sheer weight of numbers. The marshal produced evidence, in both audio and pict form, of his men dragged down and eaten by plague victims in some districts, and falling under fire from hordes of cultists in others.

Caius looked at other grey, blurry picts beamed up from the surface by Bannecheck. Here an Enforcer team's Repressor tank flamed in the street; there a horde of plague victims surrounded a monastery filled with dying citizens.

Too many of the dead had not been destroyed. The still-living population were paying for the failure of the funereal priesthood now.

On the eleventh day, reports became increasingly choppy and erratic. The swelling cults claimed whole districts of the dying cities, each member saved from death by their new allegiance. Chaos emanations wreathed the planet, eroding all reliability in astropathic contact and paining all psychically-gifted souls aboard the blockade fleet vessels. The ships' Navigators and all present inquisitors had a lifetime of training to resist such invasive psychic agony, but they still suffered. The touch of Chaos infected many of those without psychic talents: incidents of homicide and apostasy broke out aboard the destroyer vessels. These were quickly crushed by inquisitor-led purges, though the Cobra destroyer *Terra's Spite* was lost when the unrest within the ship's bowels led to explosions in the enginarium. Three hundred souls lost, and the wreckage rained on the cathedral cities below – a storm of fire from the heavens.

The inquisitors ordered the blockade into a higher orbit after the shipboard purges were complete. Kathur was now an unholy beacon within the warp, and proximity to the foulness sweeping the planet was deemed a moral threat to the Naval crews. Small clusters of destroyers orbited the planet in shifts, then broke away to allow others their turn. No captain wished to risk his men becoming tainted by the Archenemy's emanations rising from the doomed world below.

On the seventeenth day, the horde of curse victims besieging the Enforcer precinct headquarters battered down the final barricades, and the handful of still-living black-armoured peacekeepers fell. Inquisitor Caius recorded the Enforcer Marshal's final words for Ordo Sepulturum records.

'We will stand before the Throne and we will not flinch before His judgement, for we die doing our duty.' The inquisitor could hear the moistness of the man's lips in each word. The marshal had been dying, coughing up mouthfuls of diseased blood. He finished with a strained *'The Emperor protects.'*

In truth, there had been more, but Caius deleted the man's final oaths cried in agony and the wails of the plague victims in the room. Some stories didn't need to be told.

With the blockade in place, there was talk of *Exterminatus*, of bombarding the world from space in the name of the Emperor. Such discussion was quickly quenched. Orbital bombardment would not be sanctioned: the damage to the planet's precious architecture, as well as the loss of so many relics, would be the gravest sin. To use virus bombs would destroy all hope of resettlement for months to come, without guaranteeing the final deaths of the plague victims. To use cyclonic torpedoes would ravage the planet on the tectonic level – blasphemy beyond belief.

So Kathur was allowed to die.

* * *

III

PREPARATIONS WERE MADE on worlds elsewhere in Scarus Sector. The talk of outbreaks, quarantines and blockades became plans for invasion. Weeks passed before these preparations bore fruit, but for all its slowness, the Imperial war machine was a relentless beast.

How did this happen?

The question raged through the orbiting fleet, and through the echelons of Imperial rule that were even allowed to become aware of the situation. Nothing made sense. No response seemed without myriad flaws. The shrineworld was precious beyond reckoning, yet had fallen without cause. Elsewhere, under the shadow of the Warmaster's new crusade, all worlds falling to the plague had been besieged, assaulted, or otherwise corrupted by the mass presence of Archenemy vessels.

With Kathur, there had been nothing but silence.

At last, it was decided. Regiments of Imperial Guard were withdrawn from the greater war effort around the Eye of Terror, and assigned as the vanguard to a larger force of conquest. This blasphemy would not be tolerated. This desecration would not be allowed to stand.

In the heavens above the shrineworld, a small fleet of hulking ships drew close, falling into a restful orbit. The blockade of destroyers scattered to the warp, leaving their ward in the care of these new arrivals, the troopships of the Imperial Guard.

One other vessel of note broke from warp space and glided into orbit alongside these monumental troop transports: a strike cruiser of the Adeptus Astartes, black as death in the night, bearing the marble corvid sigil of the Raven Guard. The fleet drew close to the planet, casting colossal shadows as the great ships blocked out the sun on the world below.

The Kathur Reclamation was underway. The Imperium of Man had come to take back its holy world.

Among the silent cathedrals and towering monasteries on the surface, the months-dead population sensed the presence of the Emperor's servants. They looked up, staring, waiting.

As the first troop transports came through the cloud cover, all over the planet a great cry was raised. The voices of fifty million dead men, women and children rose to the sky in a long and tortured chorus.

Words of Truth

The Eagle & Bolter

The Kathur Reclamation has commenced!

The following regiments of His Most Glorious Majesty's Imperial Guard and supporting forces are committed to retaking the shrineworld from the hated Archenemy:

Vednikan 12th Rifles
303rd Uriah
25th Kiridian Irregulars
Janus 6th
3rd Skarran Rangers
Hadris Rift 40th Armoured
Cadian 88th Mechanised Infantry

Half a company of the Emperor's beloved Raven Guard Astartes Chapter.

Agents of His Divine Majesty's Holy Inquisition – the Ordo Sepulturum.

Reports from Lord General Maggrig sent directly to the *Eagle & Bolter* cite that the initial troop landings are complete with minimal casualties and all resistance to date utterly destroyed. The main force of the Reclamation is due to arrive in several weeks.

The 25th Kiridian Irregulars are to be commended for their valiant defence last week of a vital communications tower in the capital city of Solthane. The Kiridians fought a heroic battle lasting several days, ultimately defeating the diseased dregs of the Kathur Planetary Defence Force (the so-called 'Remnant') assailing their position. Casualties were light.

The Janus 6th has pressed deep into enemy-held territory, securing a monastery dedicated to the Holy God-Emperor. Even as we go to press, they crush all remnants of the PDF that seek to oust their successful beachhead in Solthane.

The Cadian 88th Mechanised Infantry, proudly boasting a captain bearing the Ward of Cadia medal for his valour in the opening engagements of the Thirteenth Black Crusade, is tasked in the coming days to assist in the Janusians' defiant infiltration.

Forward, the Janus 6th!
The Emperor protects!

Part I
Curse of Unbelief

CHAPTER I
Unbroken

'We're the Cadian Shock. In our veins beats the blood of a thousand generations of the Imperium's most devoted guardians. We'll never again see blasphemy as black as that which we face on this world. Take solace in that, sons of the Emperor. After this war, no duty will ever seem as dark.'

– Captain Parmenion Thade,
first day of the Kathur
Reclamation

Solthane, Capital city of Kathur

'THE JANUS 6TH is dead.'

Vertain sat in his Sentinel's creaking cockpit seat, monitoring the walker's primitive scanner displays and staring out of the vision slits in the vehicle's armoured front. Several hundred metres in the distance, through the buildings either side of the street, he saw the monastery burning. A pillar of orange rage and black smoke choked the sky, and he couldn't even report it to those who needed to know.

As recon missions went, this one was looking to end pretty badly. Vertain looked at his auspex display again, checking where the rest of his patrol group was. It looked fine. It felt like they were screwed, because Vertain was damn sure this night was going to end in bloodshed, but tactically speaking, his Sentinel squadron were in perfect formation as they stalked and scouted the abandoned streets.

Ahead, the colossal monastery still burned. The captain had warned about this, damn it. He'd said the Janus 6th was walking into their deaths.

And now the vox was bitching around again. Nothing ever worked right on this damn planet. The city's silence amplified the rattling clank of his Sentinel's ungainly stride, and that didn't exactly help Vertain's hearing, but the comms being screwed to the Eye and back were the main issue. Vox-ghosts, lost signals, channels slipping, vox-casters detuning... Hell, they'd seen it all on Kathur so far.

'Insurgency Walker C-Eighty-Eight Primus-Alpha,' the voice came over the vox again in a tone of agonising calm. 'Repeat, please.'

This was a problem. The only half-reliable vox-channel Vertain had been able to use through Kathur's interference was a route back to main headquarters. Main headquarters was three dozen kilometres away in the wrong direction. Help wasn't coming from there, and they weren't the ones that needed to be told about this development just yet – even if they couldn't already tell from orbital surveillance. Other ears needed to hear it now.

To make matters worse, they apparently had an idiot manning the forward recon channel tonight. So far Vertain had managed to relay his ID code, and that was about it. He'd been trying for over five minutes. Interference or not… You'd think they could've boosted the signal by now. *I'll bet a year's pay this bastard isn't Cadian.*

'This is Scout-Lieutenant Adar Vertain of the Cadian 88th. I am leading the recon mission to assess the progress of the Janus 6th. Put me through to Captain Parmenion Thade.' He spilled out the rough coordinates where the rest of the regiment was based in the city for the night.

'Repeat, please.'

Vertain brought his walker to a halt. It stood in the dead street, juddering as its engine idled. The spotlight beamed forward into nothingness, slicing into a dark alley between two silent buildings. This city was a tomb.

'In the name of the Emperor, the Janus 6th is up to its neck in it. Get me a vox-link to my captain, immediately.'

'Insurgency Walker C-Eighty-Eight Primus-Alpha. Your signal is weak. Repeat, please.'

Vertain swore, and killed the link. 'I hate this planet.'

Control sticks gripped in gloved hands, Vertain pushed forward and set the noisy Sentinel clanking ahead in a slow stride of graceless machinery. The searchlight bolted to the cheek of the walker's pilot pod tore left and right in the darkness, cutting a harsh white glare through the deserted streets.

Abandoned buildings. Bodies here and there. Nothing but silence.

Vertain was unshaven, as if he'd spent so much time hiding within his Sentinel's cockpit that he'd not had the opportunity to shave in a week. This wasn't too far from the truth.

'Vertain to Dead Man's Hand. Acknowledge signal.' Four voices came back in turn as each member of the Sentinel squadron voxed to their officer. No one was dead. That was something, at least. 'Form up in parallel streets and proceed to the main plaza ahead. Stalking pattern: Viridian. Tonight we're the Emperor's eyes, not his fists.'

'Acknowledge pattern: Viridian,' came three of the four voices.

'Copy that. No heroics,' came the last.

The Sentinels, scattered but each within scanner range of all four others, strode towards the burning monastery. Occasional gunfire rang out as they annihilated small groups of plague-slain, destroying the tainted dead that clung to false life, roving the streets in packs.

Splayed claw-feet of battered, blessed iron stomped on the smooth stone roads. Vertain rode with the gentle side-to-side motion of his Sentinel's gait, as familiar to him as standing in his own boots.

The capital city Solthane was built in worship of the Emperor and His great saint, Kathur. Its one purpose was to look beautiful: a purpose hundreds of planetary governors and ranking Ecclesiarchs had been building on for thousands of years as new shrines, places of pilgrimage, monuments and chapel-habs were erected. All sense of the original layout was centuries lost, buried and distorted in the ever-expanding mass of new construction.

Solthane now, torn back metre by metre by the Imperial Guard, was a labyrinth of winding and meandering streets populated only by abandoned traders' carts still filled with cheap wares and false relics. Deserted promenades were punctuated by marble statues depicting Kathur, lesser saints, and the nameless Raven Guard heroes who had originally served in the war to take the world, ten thousand years ago in the Great Crusade. Shortcut alleys twisted in the shadows of the towering chapel-hab blocks, all of which were encrusted with granite angels staring down at the dead city.

In his opinion – and as lead scout for the Cadian 88th, his opinion counted in every planning session he bothered to speak it – Vertain believed the chapel-habs were the worst aspect of the city's current state. The habitation towers dominated the skyline, thrusting up at random wherever there had been space to house the vast numbers of pilgrims forever moving through the city. Solthane was beauty turned to ugliness in its rich excess, and it gave enemy troops a million places to hide. The chapel-habs now stood as great apartment spires filled with the dead. No regiment wanted to draw the duty of cleansing those places, seeking out agents of the Archenemy lurking among the plague-slain. No one wanted to risk walking knee-deep in bodies only for the plague-slain to rise again.

Ahead of Vertain, the monastery burned, filling his viewing slits with orange warmth. His scanner choked in bursts through static, but he could see the walls lining the edge of the holy site's grounds rising up at the end of the street. His walker stomped closer, iron feet thudding onto the stone road. No enemies were visible outside the thirty-metre high walls, but at this range Vertain could hear the faint crack of countless lasguns and the heavy chatter of bolt weapons. The Janus 6th was fighting a losing war within the temple grounds. He clicked his vox-link live and was about to try for the captain again, when another voice crackled over.

'Sir, I've got… something.'

The vox was hellishly distorted even at close range, so the other pilot's voice was garbled, rendering the speaker unidentifiable. It took a glance at the scanner display to see Greer's placement beacon flashing. He was three streets to the west, close to the front gate of the monastery's grounds.

'Specifics, Greer,' said Vertain.

'If I had specifics, I'd give you them. My vox keeps detuning to another frequency.'

'You told me Enginseer Culus fixed that two nights ago.'

Now was not the time for instrument failure. The enemy could easily pick up stray vox on insecure frequencies. Greer's instruments had been the subject of repeated repair since he'd taken a rocket hit on the cockpit pod a year ago, fighting heretics in the cities of Beshic V. The scorched and twisted metal that had blackened his walker's cheek was gone, but the missile's legacy remained.

'He *did* fix it. I'm saying it's shaken loose again. I'm hearing… something. I'll pulse the frequency over. Listen for yourself.'

'Send me the frequency.'

'Can … hear … at?' Greer asked in a surge of vox crackle. Vertain tuned his receiver and narrowed his eyes. In his headset, a whispering voice hissed the same three words in an endless monotone.

Count the Seven… Count the Seven… Count the Seven…

'I hear it.'

'That's what they heard at Kasr Partain,' Greer said. 'Back when home first burned.' Vertain nodded, feeling the words leave a bitter taste on his tongue. Kasr Partain had been one of the first fortress-cities to fall on Cadia, only a handful of months before. Home was still burning, damn it. And they should be back there fighting for it, not wandering like rats in this city of the dead, half a sector away.

'Sir?'

'I'm here,' Vertain swallowed back a bitter growl. 'I'm here.'

He set his Sentinel striding forward again, opening a channel to the whole squad. 'Vertain to Dead Man's Hand. Change of plans. Everyone form up on my position immediately. Stay in visual range of one another from now on. Search pattern: Unity.'

'Acknowledged,' the chorus came back.

'Farl, you head back to the captain. Cycle vox channels as you run, alerting high command as well as Captain Thade. This is not something the lord general will learn from orbital picts, and he needs to be told immediately.'

'What's the exact message, sir?' Farl asked.

Vertain told him what to say. The silence from the other pilots was deafening as they digested the revelation. After Farl had voxed an acknowledgement and broken away from the loose formation, Vertain sat in the creaking leather seat, his pounding heart the loudest sound in the cloistered confines of his cockpit.

The rest of C-Eighty-Eight Alpha closed around him, drawing alongside in an orchestra of rattles and clanks. Each walker had a playing card painted on the cheek, above the stencilled pilot's name. Dead Man's Hand, the elite Sentinel squadron of the Cadian 88th Mechanised Infantry.

'We need visual confirmation of this. Prime weapons, check your coolant feeds,' their leader said. 'And follow me.'

CAPTAIN PARMENION THADE hadn't been home in three months, except in his nightmares.

The reports from Cadia still listed over sixty per cent of the planet in the hands of the Archenemy, but the numbers were almost meaningless. The statistics were cold and uncomfortable, but nowhere near as raw and real as his memories. Those memories replayed behind his eyes each night. Over and over, he saw his world fall.

The Thirteenth Black Crusade. For the first time in ten thousand years of defeat, a Warmaster of Chaos walked the soil of Cadia. The Archenemy finally had its first real victory, and the Cadians their first real defeat.

The sky had burned for weeks. Literally, it burned. The fires of the fortress-cities choked the heavens from horizon to horizon. Amongst the flames of burning cities, defence cannons roared into the sky, defying the landing attempts of enemy troop ships. This was not some provincial world with a volunteer Planetary Defence Force. This was Cadia, warden-world of the only navigable path from the *Occularis Terribus* into the Imperium. The planet was second only to Holy Terra in its might and importance.

Cathedral-like vessels of Battlefleet Scarus ringed the world, filling the night sky with their anger as they fired upon the Chaos fleet pouring towards the planet. Every city on the surface was a bastion of gun emplacements and void shield generators. Every citizen had trained to fire a lasrifle from their pre-teen childhoods. The planet itself resisted the attack.

By the time Kasr Vallock was lost to the flames of invasion, the populace was already underground. Regiments of the Cadian Shock and the Interior Guard guided the fleeing citizens into the tunnels beneath the city, engaged in a fighting retreat as the legions of the Archenemy flooded into the tunnels in pursuit. It was these tunnels that Thade dreamed of.

Each night, he heard his men shouting his name again, over and over. They needed orders. They needed ammunition. They needed to get out of the tunnels before the enemy destroyed the power reactors in the city above. Already, the evacuation tunnels were shaking, raining dirt on the fleeing defenders. They were far from the evacuation carriers that would take them to another Kasr.

Thade had turned to hear the howling sounds of their pursuers. He still had both his hands then, two hands of flesh, blood and bone. As he barked orders – orders for bayonets and blades for anyone out of ammunition – those hands gunned his chainsword into life. He'd fired his bolt pistol's last round in the bloodbath that erupted when the traitors spilled through the Kasr's sundered walls two hours before.

The disruptions above had killed the lights in this section of the tunnel network. The only light now came from the narrow flashlights fixed to the sides of the soldiers' blast helmets. Two dozen of those beams cut across the passageway at various angles as the men looked this way and that, using the respite to identify comrades among the survivors.

The tunnel shook again, showering grit and pebbles of the concrete used to reinforce the passageways. A chunk of stone the size of a child's fist clacked off the captain's helmet. Similar debris rained on the others, clattering down several times a minute as they waited in the darkness.

'That isn't the reactors,' one soldier said. 'Too rhythmic. Too loud.'

'Titan,' another man whispered. 'There's a Titan up there.'

Thade nodded, setting his helmet torch cutting down and up in the blackness. His heart beat against his ribs in anticipation of the next tremor, which shook his bones when it finally came. On the surface above, a towering God-Machine strode unopposed through the burning city. Every soldier down in the darkness knew the odds were heavily against the Titan being one of the Imperium's own.

'They're coming, sir,' someone said in the near-darkness. Thade faced the way his men had come, hearing the enemy's cries getting closer.

'Men of Cadia!' Thade's chainsword roared in emphasis, the sound jagged and close enough to equal the earthshaking footsteps of the gigantic war machine above. 'The Great Eye has opened and hell itself is coming down that corridor. Stand. Fight. Every son and daughter of this world was born to slay the Emperor's foes! Our blood flows so humanity may draw breath! No blood more precious!'

'No blood more precious!' the soldiers shouted as one.

'Calm hearts and ice in your veins,' Thade spoke softly in the lesser rumblings of the Titan's wake. Rifles and blades were raised as wild, spasming shapes flashed into view, screaming down the tunnel.

'88th! Fire!'

A chorus of cracks sounded. The las-fire volley scythed down the first wave of shrieking heretics in front of Thade before they were even in full view. More were rounding the corner and running to where the tunnel widened, but blood of the Emperor, if it was just a handful of cultists down here, they might win this...

And then he saw it.

At the heart of the second wave, boots crunching corpses underfoot, came death itself. Like a huntsman leading a pack of dogs, the foe that would take Thade's right hand towered a metre and more above its lesser minions. Gibbering, howling cultists ran into the tunnel bearing bloody knives and solid-slug pistols. Between them, walking with a distance-eating stride all the more terrifying for its slowness, was an immense figure in ancient armour of filthy bronze and cobalt blue.

It moved like a dead thing, mindlessly treading forward, scanning left to right with methodical patience. Its helm, warped into the visage of an ancient Terran death mask from some long-dead civilization, emitted a chuckle. The laugh was a hollow, brittle sound that wheezed dust from the archaic helmet's speaker grille. In the figure's fists was a bolter of antiquated design, notched with a hundred centuries of wear and tear. The muzzle was coal-black from countless firings on countless battlefields.

Thade's men had been firing from the moment the enemy entered the tunnel, but while rag-clad cultists died in droves, their armoured overseer barely flinched at the hail of laser fire glancing from its carapace. It finished its scan of the room, sighting the mortal shouting orders. That was the one that had to die first.

The Traitor Astartes fired once as it advanced, barely pausing to aim, unleashing the shot that stole Thade's right arm from the elbow. The Cadian dropped his sword, clutched what remained of his arm, and hit the ground hard. Through the agony of his bolt-destroyed forearm, he could still hear his men crying out, calling his name...

* * *

'CAPTAIN THADE?'

He awoke with a jolt as the dream broke. His adjutant, Corrun, stood at the side of his cot. The other man's expression was serious. 'News from the Sentinels.'

Thade sat up. His uniform was crumpled from a restless sleep, and his body armour was neatly stacked on the ground by his bedroll. The 88th was camped for the night in an abandoned museum, sleeping fitfully amongst a thousand minor relics. Here, a golden figurine of a Raven Guard Astartes on a small marble pedestal – shaped by a minor acolyte of Kathur many thousands of years before. There, a cabinet of trinkets once worn by the first of Kathur's faithful.

The relics didn't impress Thade. A pilgrim trap, nothing more: something to keep the visiting devotees busy while they filled the planetary coffers.

His head still ached from the day-long planning meeting with the lord general earlier, and he let his thoughts clear while he sipped from the standard-issue canteen by his pillow. The museum's air tasted of dust.

The water didn't help much. The chemical compounds used to purify fluid rations left a coppery aftertaste on his tongue. Even knowing all the water was purified aboard the ships in orbit didn't help morale. The Guard were fighting on a tomb world. The last thing they needed was water that tasted like blood. It was as if the death on Kathur touched everything that came to the planet even after the plague had burned itself out.

'How long was I asleep?' Thade asked, looking around the half-full chamber where thirty soldiers still slept on.

'Two hours,' Corrun said, knowing it had been the only two hours Thade had slept in the last fifty.

'Felt like two minutes.'

'Life in the Guard, eh? Sleep when you're dead.'

'I hear that.' Thade stretched, not altogether thrilled at the clicks in his back as he arched it. Cadian stoicism was one thing, but… 'Has anyone shot the Munitorum officer responsible for giving out these bedrolls?'

Corrun chuckled at his captain's banter. 'Not that I'm aware of.'

'That's a crime. I may do it myself.' Thade was already lacing his boots. 'Brief me now. What has Dead Man's Hand found?'

'It's just Trooper Farl. Vertain's taken the others closer to the monastery. Vox is down.'

'Vox is down. Throne, I'm sick of that refrain.'

'Farl returned with a message.'

'They've sighted primary threats,' said Thade, not a doubt in his mind. Few other reasons would be severe enough to split the Sentinel squadron.

'They've intercepted vox traffic that suggests primary threats close to their position, yes.'

'Listen to you, dancing around the issue.'

Corrun grinned. It was a grin Thade was very familiar with, and usually preceded something cocky at best, rash at worst. 'Didn't want to get your hopes up, sir.'

'How decent of you. So what have they got? Please tell me it's more than intercepted vox.'

'Just the vox. But Farl's got a recording, and it... Well, come listen to it.'

The captain buckled his helmet, pulling the chin strap tight. Embedded on the front was his medal – the medal he was known for. An eagle-winged gateway marked by a central skull, glinting in the dim light of pre-dawn coming through the stained glass window. The Ward of Cadia, flashing silver on the black blast helmet.

'Ready to stare into the Eye itself, sir.' Corrun said.

Thade smiled as he fastened the last buckle on his flak armour jacket, and strapped on his weapon belt. A heavy calibre bolt pistol hung against his left hip. Against his right thigh rested an ornate chainsword, its iron finish polished to chrome brightness, with acid-etched runes in stylised High Gothic along the blade's sides. To say a blade like that was worth a fortune would be to underestimate by no small degree. Lord generals wielded blades of poorer quality.

'Is Rax ready?' the captain asked, hope evident in his voice.

'No, sir, not yet.'

'Ah, well. Let's go see what Dead Man's Hand has found.'

CHAPTER II
Shrine

Solthane, Monastic sector

'COUNT THE SEVEN,' the vox recording crackled. The words were broken by distortion, but clear enough to be sure. Captain Thade's squads of the Cadian 88th, a full three hundred men and thirty support vehicles, moved out ten minutes later. The potential sighting of primary threats necessitated nothing less than a full response.

Dawn wasn't far away, though even in the daylight Solthane remained grey. The funeral pyres of weeks before still blackened the sky with dark cloud cover that refused to dissipate, and the habitation spires were discoloured by the smoke that until so recently had choked the skies.

With hulls the colour of iron and charcoal – a drabness that matched their surroundings – Chimera troop transports rumbled four abreast down city avenues, treads grinding precious mosaics into shards beneath the weight of the tanks. When the erratic city layout required divergent routes, the troop carriers navigated narrow streets and alleys in single file.

Occasional sniper fire from PDF remnant forces was answered with squads deployed to sweep and cleanse buildings by the side of the road, and orders to catch up when they could. Vox contact was a joke, but Thade wasn't worried. He trusted his men to do their jobs and get back in line without a hitch. They were no strangers to urban warfare. No Cadian was.

The convoy rode on towards the burning monastery, towards Dead Man's Hand, and towards primary-class threats that might or might not actually exist. The atmosphere within each of the tanks was an unsmiling mix of professional readiness and a muted sense of grim anticipation. No one wanted to engage primary threats unless the odds were heavily stacked in the Cadians' favour, but duty was duty. The Shock knew it was better they handled this than any of the other regiments garrisoned in Solthane.

The Janus 6th was a green unit. If the intercepted vox traffic wasn't just twisted propaganda or vox-ghosts, then they were already dead. Their ambitious assignment to hold the monastery, the great Shrine of the Emperor's Unending Majesty, was over almost as soon as it had begun.

Thade focused, rolling his shoulders in his matt-black flak armour and checking his chainsword for the eighth or ninth time. It was almost an hour since he'd woken and the last vestiges of the memory dream were finally fading from his mind. He hated to remember Cadia. Remembering home led his thoughts into how he and his men should be back there even now, and to the Eye with this upstart bastard of a lord general that demanded Cadian units be withdrawn from the front line of the Despoiler's Crusade to help with his little shrineworld reclamation.

The familiar rattling of the armoured personnel carrier soothed his thoughts. His right hand, gloved in black, whirred with soft mechanical purrs as he closed his fingers into a fist. He felt the rough mechanics of his augmetic wrist and knuckle-joints rotating, hearing the low buzzing clicks between the infrequent metallic judders of the Chimera's interior.

'Captain?' the driver called.

Thade rose from his seat in the passenger compartment and moved to lean on the driver's seat from behind. Through the wide vision slit, the soot-blackened marble of Kathur's largest cathedral district was visible. This was the heart of Solthane, in all its fire-touched majesty.

'What a cesspit,' the driver said. It was Corrun, as always, driving Thade's command Chimera.

'You're quite the poet,' said the captain. 'Now talk to me.'

'Two minutes, sir. We… Wait, hang on, we've got a roadblock.' The compartment shuddered as if kicked by a Titan, generating a roar of complaints from the ten soldiers strapped into their seats in the back. Thade's mechanical hand snapped vice-tight on the hand rail, keeping his balance.

'Roadblock cleared,' the driver grinned.

'Go around the next one, Corrun,' Thade tried not to imagine what that roadblock had just been. 'You said two minutes?'

'Confirmed, sir. Just under two minutes until we come up on where Dead Man's Hand have withdrawn. These streets are a bitch. Not exactly made for tanks.'

'Pilgrim roads. I hear you.' Thade narrowed his violet eyes and stared out of the vision slit. The limited vista on display raced past in a blur of blackened buildings. 'I can't see a damn thing out there. Any third-class threats so far?'

'Constantly, sir.' Again with the trademark grin. 'What do you think that last roadblock was?'

'Delightful. You're ploughing down plague victims now. What happened to respecting the dead?'

'They're not exactly respecting us.'

This generated chuckles from the soldiers in the rear.

'Point,' Thade conceded, 'but you know where the orders came from. These people were Imperial citizens, Corrun. Pilgrims. Priests.'

'I heard the stories, Cap. They were faithless. "Only the faithless will fall to this plague", isn't that what we've been told a thousand times?'

Thade dropped it. He didn't want to dredge this up again because he found it hard to argue with his driver tonight. He believed as Corrun did. The faithless had fallen. They deserved this fate. To hell with a mandate for 'clean kills at all times' and 'preserving the plague-slain to be redeemed in consecrated incineration'.

But Kathur Reclamation protocol stressed respect for the victims of the Curse of Unbelief. The lord general was keen to foster political allies within the Ecclesiarchy by retaking this world as cleanly and carefully as possible. The emphasis on respecting the tainted dead was just one more petty protocol in a long list that Thade hated to think about since he'd made planetfall. Destroying the dead wasn't enough. They had to be put down with grace, gathered by Guardsmen with a hundred better things to do, and ritually burned in the reactivated funerary cremation facilities.

By the Emperor's grace, the 88th hadn't been selected for gathering duties yet. Killing those that refused to die was bad enough.

'Drive,' Thade said. 'And don't argue. Besides, if Enginseer Osiron finds out you're using my command Chimera to ram gangs of plague victims clogging the road, he'll have your head. It's an insult to the machine-spirit.'

Corrun, grinning like he'd won a month's wages, wrenched the steering wheel to the left. Another three souls in the ruined rags of Kathurite pilgrims met their final end under the churning tracks of the racing troop transport. There was a brief wrenching of gears as something – some part of one of the plague victims – got caught up in the APC's moving parts.

Thade closed his eyes for a moment. 'I never want to hear that again.'

'It was a purr!'

'You're good, Corrun. But you're not irreplaceable. It would grieve me to see you shot for disrespect. Play safe this time. By the book, and no hacking off the machine-spirit.'

'Not at all.' The driver licked his lips. 'The old girl likes it rough.'

'When I say "ramming speed", then you get to play your game.'

'Understood, sir.'

Thade's vox-bead pulsed in his ear. The captain tapped the earpiece, activating the fingernail-sized receiver strapped to his throat. As he spoke, it picked up the vibrations from his larynx and filtered out background noise.

'Captain Thade, Cadian 88th.'

'*Count the Seven,*' someone hissed. Even through the vox distortion, the voice was wet and burbling. '*Count the Seven.*'

Thade cut the link.

'New orders?' asked Corrun.

'Just vox-ghosts.' Thade turned to the ten soldiers in the back. Each one watched him – quiet, attentive, at the ready. 'Janden,' he nodded to his vox-operator. 'Change command frequency and share the new wavelength with the other squads. The current one is compromised.'

He saw the question in Janden's eyes but gave no answer. The vox-officer leaned down to where his bulky backpack was secured by his seat, and made the necessary adjustments to his communication gear.

'Done, sir.'

Thade gripped the handrail running the length of the ceiling, supporting himself against the shakes. 'Get me Dead Man's Hand. Patch Vertain through to my ear-piece.'

'You're live.'

'Vertain, this is the captain. Acknowledge.' Thade listened to the reply, and narrowed his eyes. 'Thirty seconds, Vertain. That's all.'

He switched to the command channel. '88th, at the ready! Disembark in thirty seconds! The plaza ahead is flooded with plague-slain and Dead Man's Hand needs extraction. We go in, we kill anything not wearing our colours, and we move on to the monastery. Corrun…'

'Sir?' He was already grinning again.

'Ramming speed.'

THE AUTOCANNON ROARED.

'Fall back!' Vertain cried, wrenching his control sticks. His walker reversed, the backwards-jointed legs protesting with a hiss of angry pistons. Solid rounds pinged and clanged from the pod's sloped armour, while the Sentinel's underslung cannon replied in a percussive burst of thunderclap after thunderclap.

The plaza had erupted in gunfire a few minutes before. An expanse of concrete inlaid with a mosaic of the saint formed a courtyard between several towering temples. The squadron had been scouting here when the first sniper shots rang out. Within a minute, plague-slain were shambling from the temples, led by cultists wearing ragged remains of Kathurite PDF uniforms. They came in a tide, immediately broken in places as the Sentinels opened up with their autocannons, drowning out the grunts and wails of the dead.

'We are not dying here,' Vertain spoke into his vox-link. 'Break formation and fall back.' He never heard an acknowledgement from the others. He could barely hear his own voice over the carnage unfolding around his walker.

The squadron wasn't going to win a straight-up fight, and they all knew it. They were scouts, and the Sentinels were armed for taking shots at armoured infantry and light tanks. The high-calibre rounds from the walkers' autocannons were tearing holes in the crowds of plague-slain, but they were next to useless against such a horde.

Greer's walker staggered, almost thrown from balance as its stabilisers strained to deal with striding over piles of moving corpses. In a move worthy of a medal, Vertain saw the other pilot condense his leg pistons, lowering his cockpit pod for a moment, then spring upwards to clear the mound of writhing dead he'd been standing atop. Greer landed with a thudding clank that shook the ground, turning as he walked backwards and opening fire on the plague-slain again. A swarm of corpses dressed as monks flew apart in a grey-red cloud as three auto-cannon rounds hit home.

'That was beautiful,' said Vertain through clenched teeth as he kept laying down fire.

'I look forward to my promotion,' crackled Greer.

Vertain joined his fire arc to Greer's, and felt his Sentinel's gait start to drag. He was limping now, limping badly.

'You've got three of them on your right leg, sir,' Greer crackled. 'Kick them free.'

Vertain tried. His Sentinel replied by lurching violently to the right with a screech of protesting stabilisers. Alarms flashed across his console as his leg pistons vented air pressure.

'They've ruined my stabilisers. I'm not kicking anything for a while.' As he spoke, Vertain's cockpit tilted again. His helmeted head smacked against the side of his pod, the pain painting his vision in a palette of greys.

The dead were climbing his walker now. He heard their fists beating on the armour plating on his cockpit. They might even drag him down if enough of them could scramble up.

His vox sparked live with a burst of static. 'Vertain, this is the captain.' Emperor's blood, Thade's voice was clear. He sounded close. 'Acknowledge.'

With sick on his breath and half-blind through a concussion, Vertain reported the situation, ending with the four words Captain Thade had been praying not to hear.

'Dead Man's Hand: Broken.'

'Thirty seconds, Vertain. That's all.'

It turned out to be just under twenty seconds.

The Chimeras tore into the plaza, a rolling thunderhead that slammed into the horde of wailing dead. Black as a panther, the command Chimera pounded into the first group, grinding them into bloody gobbets. It swerved to a halt, cutting down the plague-slain nearby with angry beams of light from its multilaser turret. The irritated whine of high-energy las-fire shrilled above the moans and crunches of combat.

The other Chimeras, their hulls a gun-metal grey, followed in the wake of destruction. Dozer blades bolted to the front of the troop transports – specifically banned from ungentle use in clearing roads of corpses – now hammered the plague-slain to the ground to be crushed under heavy treads.

The drivers spread out to form a protective ring around the embattled walkers, turret fire slicing through the bodies of anyone approaching the tanks. In a chorus of clangs, thirty rear ramps slammed down onto the mosaic ground, and the 88th spilled from their transports: guns up and firing red flashes. Thade was first out of his Chimera, chainsword raised and howling.

'Secure the walkers! For the Emperor!'

The captain's first foe wasn't dead. A PDF traitor ran at him, slowed by the disease ravaging his body. In his fist was a broken bayonet. Thade's chainsword sang in a savage backhand swing, and the traitor's head left his shoulders.

'First blood to Cadia!' someone shouted to his left.

The fight lasted less than two minutes. Lasguns cracked out head-shots in orderly volleys, scything down the enemy in waves. The Cadians stayed shoulder to shoulder in their squads, taking no casualties in the brief battle. When the last of the plague-slain was dragged from the leg of Vertain's walker and shot in the back of the head, Thade holstered his pistol. The sergeants from all fifteen squads ringed him, every man standing ankle-deep in the dead. The stench rising around was enough for several men to don their rebreather masks.

'88th: status.'

'Unbroken,' fifteen squad leaders chorused.

'Unbroken,' Vertain sat in his cockpit, the door opened so he could speak freely. He made the sign of the aquila. 'Close call, though.'

Thade nodded. 'We move to retake the Shrine of the Emperor's Unending Majesty. We're hearing nothing from the Janus 6th in there, and if they have any survivors left, they're almost certainly retreating deeper into the monastery.' Every eye turned to the building a kilometre away through the winding streets. Half of it still burned. 'We're going in – securing it where the Janusians failed – and waiting to be reinforced. If the resistance is beyond our capabilities, then we get comfortable and ask Reclamation command what they want us to do. Questions?'

'Primary threats?' asked one of the sergeants.

'Potentially. Nothing solid yet. If we find them, we take them down. If there are too many, we consolidate and await reinforcement. Vertain, report.'

The Sentinel pilot cleared his throat. 'We pulled back to this plaza when the fighting in the temple grounds abated. We were looking for a staging ground, sir. The last we saw at the monastery, the enemy's rearguard was following the forward elements in. The main doors were breached. Six, maybe seven hundred Remnant,' he said, referring to Kathurite PDF traitors. 'Double the number of plague-slain.'

'Seven hundred secondary-class threats, and fifteen hundred third-class,' the captain confirmed. 'Nothing changes. We split into three forces, each with specific objectives. I'll take one hundred men to the central chambers. Lieutenant Horlarn, you take a hundred to the undercroft and make sure there's no way into the shrine from underground. Lieutenant Darrick, you've got the bell towers. Questions?'

No one spoke.

'The Emperor protects,' said Thade. 'Now move.'

RESISTANCE WAS NOWHERE to be seen. Gaining access to the monastery proved to be uncomfortably easy.

The towering gates were broken, torn from their hinges, and there was little sign of enemy forces outside of a few shambling loners wandering around the expansive courtyard. These ended their pathetic existences under precision las-fire, as the Guardsmen filed from their Chimeras and moved in squads up the wide marble stairway to the front entrance. The air reeked of the dead and the burning sections of the monastery itself, a potent musk that again inspired a lot of rebreather use.

Minutes became hours. Deep within the labyrinthine monastery, the Shrine of the Emperor's Unending Majesty, almost three hundred soldiers of the Cadian 88th were on the hunt. Bodies of plague victims littered the stone floor, just as they did in each passage and chamber the Cadians had passed through in the last few hours. The Janusians hadn't just been besieged; they'd been infiltrated and annihilated. Bodies of the regiment, blood soaking their urban camouflage gear, were strewn everywhere in the monastery alongside the enemy dead.

Their last stand had been inglorious and, to Cadian eyes, rather unimpressive. The Janus 6th was scattered in a poor defensive spread across the monastery's series of awe-inspiring sermon chambers, their final resting places showing to the trained glances of the 88th just which soldiers had died fighting, and which ones had broken ranks to seek an escape.

No sign of primary threats so far. In fact, Thade and his officers had just about abandoned the notion of seeing any first-class targets. They had real problems now – enough tertiary threats to last a lifetime. The plague-slain were everywhere inside the monastery, and in far greater numbers than those seen by Dead Man's Hand outside.

Room by room, the Guardsmen cleansed the holy site, cutting down the shrieking dead as they staggered in feral mindlessness, nothing but shells of unfocused malice.

Poisonous blood showered Captain Thade as he impaled a howling woman with a thrust of his chainsword. A hundred whirring teeth sawed through fleshy resistance, and the woman cried blasphemies as she was disembowelled.

It was hard to tell the dead ones from those that still lived. Neither would lie down and die when you wanted them to, and they all made the same noises.

Thade yanked hard, freeing the blade from her torso in a light spray of near-black blood and fragments of flesh that smelled beyond foul. The rot taking hold of the enemy made such work all the easier. Decay softened the flesh, making it weak under Imperial las-fire and vulnerable to the howling bite of chainswords.

The corpse began to rise again, ponderously clambering to its feet despite being gutted and missing an arm.

Thade's blade silenced as he killed the power. He'd been fighting with the weapon for almost half an hour, and his muscles burned with effort. Exhausted to his core, he pulled his bolt pistol and pressed the muzzle against the woman's broken skull. The air within the monastery was cold, but he blinked stinging sweat from his eyes.

'In the name of the Emperor, just *die*.'

The bolt shell hammered into the corpse's head and exploded within the brain, wetting the Imperial Guard captain with more chunks of decaying matter. A flying shard of skull hit his breastplate with enough force to leave a scratch.

The sharp cracks of a las-fire chorus died down around him, and Thade's command squad dispersed around the barely-decorated contemplation chamber. Each of the nine fighters scattered, but stayed in eye contact with at least one other member of the squad. Every man wore dark grey fatigues and black chest armour made filthy from the day's fighting.

'I need vox,' Thade called out across the cavernous sermon chamber. Janden moved over to him, jogging around the dip in the floor where a mosaic of the Emperor had been defiled some weeks ago. The room reeked of urine and the vast amounts of animal blood used to deface the image.

Janden handed Thade the speech horn connected to the bulky vox-scanner on his back.

'You're live, captain.'

'Squad Venator to Alliance. Acknowledge signal and give me a situation report.'

The pause of several seconds put Thade's nerves on edge. There were a million ways this mission could go wrong. Even with the greatest trust in his men, he hated his squads scattered in this hive of the dead.

'Alliance here, captain. Situation: Unbroken. We're close to the chorus chambers atop the north-eastern bell tower. We need ten, fifteen more minutes to get in place.'

'Acknowledged,' Thade replied, and nodded to Janden. 'Squad Venator to Fortitude and Adamant. Report.'

The pause this time lasted longer. Janden shook his head at the captain's glance; it wasn't interference. For once.

'Adamant here, captain. Situation: Unbroken. We're entering the undercroft now.'

'This is Fortitude, Unbroken. Moving with Adamant to support. Heavy resistance in the cellars delayed us. We found where the Remnant were regrouping, and they're not regrouping anymore, sir. Forty minutes to mission objective.'

'Understood. Be careful,' Thade said.

And so it went. Squad Phalanx next, then Endurance and Defiance, on and on down the line. The captain listened to the brief situation reports from each of his fifteen squads. Casualties were light, despite the fighting being fierce.

Thade led his one hundred men in a loose scattering of squads, moving to take control of the primary altar chambers at the heart of the monastery. Another hundred followed First Lieutenant Horlarn to secure the undercroft and purge the subterranean tombs of the enemy. Second Lieutenant Darrick led the last hundred, securing the four bell towers thrusting up from the monastery's central domes. The holy building was the size of a small town – the 88th had spent the best part of three hours cutting right to the core of it.

One last vox-report to make. The most important one.

'This is Captain Thade. 88th reports progress as expected. Resistance medium-to-heavy. No sign of primary targets, repeat: zero sightings on primary threat. Resistance so far, secondary threats twenty per cent, tertiary threats eighty per cent.'

This simple message was all that was required. He doubted it even reached the lord general's base, but it still had to be done.

Janden took the speech horn when Thade handed it back. 'Only twenty per cent on the secondary threat? Felt like more.'

Thade smiled at the vox-officer with the bandaged arm. 'I'll bet it did.'

At his order, the squad moved out, heading deeper into the monastery. The chambers grew larger, expanding into halls, each one majestic in size and increasingly grand in ostentation, built by faithful hands many thousands of years ago. Arched walls and ceilings were supported by great spines of stone, thickly jutting from the skeletal architecture. Stylised pillars rose to the roof, each one bathed in the weak dusk light coming through the shattered stained glass windows.

The ten soldiers in Thade's squad fanned out, stalking through the near-darkness in a familiar ritual of stops and starts. Run to a pillar. Crouch, rifle up to scan ahead. Run to the next pillar...

Something cried out ahead. It was either inhuman, or hadn't been alive in weeks. Thade looked around the pillar he was kneeling behind, one hand on the faded red carpet for balance. He saw nothing, but heard the moan again.

A few dozen metres ahead of him, the sight blocked by the pillars, a lasgun fired with a single, sharp crack. 'Contact!' someone called out. 'Tertiary threat confirmed.'

The Cadians advanced, rifles up and no need to hide. A small group of plague victims, no more than twenty, spilled sluggishly from an arch behind a torn red curtain.

Thade squeezed off a shot with his pistol, detonating the head of the lead curse victim.

'Kill them!' he shouted, and nine lasguns lit the chamber with flickering red flashes of pinpoint laser fire. Not a single shot missed, but the disease-wracked corpses still took several direct hits to put down for good.

The soldiers stood around the bodies after the killing was done. It was Kathur Reclamation protocol to speak short prayers for each of the fallen when time allowed. Captain Thade ordered his men on without a word. Time was not on their side.

The squad moved through a series of smaller chambers, each one a mosaic-rich tribute to Saint

Kathur's deeds, paid for by hundreds of generations of pilgrims. Progress was fast until the squad's eleventh man, wheezing as he leaned upon an aquila-topped black staff, rasped the captain's name.

Thade halted. 'Make this good, Seth.'

'I hear someone calling. Crying out, as if from a great distance.' The sanctioned psyker wiped a fleck of foamy spittle from his lips with a trembling hand. His powers were erratic at the best of times, waxing and waning without his control. This campaign was a nightmare – Kathur was wreathed thick in warp disruption, and the psychic toll on the Imperial Guard's telepaths was immense. Five had died of embolisms in the weeks since planetfall, one of heart rupture, and a further two had fallen under possession by nameless horrors born of the warp.

'Calling out to us?' Thade asked.

'I… I cannot tell. There is something ahead.' Here Seth paused to suck air through his teeth. 'Something powerful. Something old.'

'Primary threat?' asked Janden. This was greeted by a short wave of chuckles from the gathered soldiers and Thade shaking his head. 'Not likely,' he said.

The captain resisted the urge to sneer at the wheezing, thin-limbed psyker. Their eyes met and the gaze held for several moments. The captain's eyes were the typical pale violet of the Cadian-born, while Seth's were a deep blue, bloodshot under the band of metal across his brow that sank cables into his brain to amplify his unreliable talents. 'Anything more specific?' Thade tried to keep the dislike out of his voice and his expression. He was almost successful.

'An agent of the Archenemy.'

'In the next chamber?'

'In one of the chambers ahead. I cannot be sure. The warp clouds everything.'

Thade nodded, inclining his head and leading the squad on. 'Janden, what chambers are ahead?'

The vox-officer consulted his data-slate, tapping a few buttons. 'A series of purification halls. Pilgrims used them to bathe before being allowed entrance to the inner temple.'

'A bath house? In a cathedral?' Zailen, the squad's weapons specialist, walked alongside Janden. The hum of his live plasma gun set the troopers' teeth on edge. Thade felt his scalp prickling, but fought down the sensation as he spoke.

It was Thade who answered. 'Saint Kathur, Emperor rest his bones, was famed for his purity. It makes sense those who came to see his remains would be required to ritually cleanse themselves.'

Zailen shrugged and looked away – a habit of his when he didn't have the words to answer.

Ahead of them, the great double doors leading into the purification chambers stood closed. Defiled engravings of female angels, carved of marble now stained with blood and body matter, stared down at the eleven men. Thade cleared his throat.

'Trooper Zailen?'

'Yes, sir?'

'Open the doors.'

'Yes, sir.'

Zailen raised his plasma gun and squeezed the first trigger. The baseline hum of the arcane weapon intensified in an angry whine of massing energy. He breathed a quiet 'Knock, knock…' and pressed the second trigger.

The plasma gun roared.

Chapter III
Count the Seven

The Shrine of the Emperor's
Unending Majesty

SECOND LIEUTENANT TAAN Darrick was having a bad day.

There were two reasons for this. The first and least important was more of a wearying ache than a real worry – the 88th were mechanised infantry, and by the Emperor did Darrick hate having to walk everywhere. This monastery assault took a lot of foot-slogging, and while his fitness wasn't an issue it still irritated him that the regiment had been selected for this operation. Reinforce the idiotic Janusians on their vainglorious thrust into enemy territory? The fools had paid for it now. Sit in a damn church and hold out for reinforcements? Ugh. It hardly screamed 'mechanised infantry' to Darrick.

The captain, as the captain always did, took the orders without a complaint and made the best of a bad deal. But Darrick? Darrick was a complainer and damn proud of it. He felt it gave him character in the stoic ranks of his fellows. It simply didn't occur to him that he was just being annoying.

The second reason for his bad day, and much more of a real problem, was the fact he was being shot at. Darrick's squad had met serious secondary resistance as they neared the top of the massive bell tower. On Kathur, 'secondary resistance' meant the enemy had guns, too.

Crouched behind a wooden podium once used by priests to lead choir singers, Darrick reloaded his lasgun, slapping a fresh power cell into the standard-issue weapon with a professional shove. A las-round scorched a black streak through the pulpit a hand's span from his left ear.

'Wouldn't it be wonderful to have a little heavy support?' he asked the soldier sharing his pathetic cover. The other Cadian grunted agreement as he fired around the podium. He was new to the squad, and found Darrick's endless banter distracting, not endearing. He was hardly alone in this opinion.

The enemy, ragged elements of the Kathur PDF picking through the bones of the monastery in dis-organised packs, had entered the ancient chorus room at the same time as Darrick's men. A series of these same chorus chambers nestled atop each of the four huge spires rising from the monastery. The towers were crucial, both as a likely haven for Janusian survivors, and as the only decent sites Imperial forces could effect a supply landing for any regiment bottled in here for longer than they should be.

'I'm good with a heavy bolter, you know,' Darrick was opining to his captive audience now, and his squad shared grim smiles. The lieutenant's declarations were punctuated by enemy fire cracking and pinging off the stone all around him. 'And I enjoy it. The kick of actually being able to shoot your damn enemies without all this messing around, being denied any toys in case we mess up the architecture.'

One of his men, Tomarin, grinned at Darrick's observations. 'It's a shame to be denied one's passions, sir.'

'That it is. That it is. Now, time to ruin some assholes' days.'

Darrick's rifle bucked in his hands with each shot, and each shot was a kill. You didn't train every day of your life from the age of six and miss too often. The second lieutenant had been firing the same rifle for thirty years, and while most junior officers withdrew more advanced arms from the officers' arsenal upon achieving promotion, Darrick liked to stick with what he knew best. His one guilty pleasure was his never-ending supply of various grenades – but they were in his storage bag back at the base. Along with heavy bolters and other support weapons of any significance, it was hard to justify taking grenades into a monastery when Kathur Reclamation objectives clearly stated the architecture of the shrineworld was to remain 'undamaged by reckless interference'.

Denied his favourite toys, Darrick scowled as he gunned down the unarmoured soldiers of the Planetary Defence Force. When the soldier next to him fell back with hole in his head, Darrick had to concede that some of the Chaos-tainted scum over there were truly wicked shots. He broke cover to crack off three more rounds, killing two PDF soldiers and taking another in the belly. That one would take a while to die, thrashing around on the marble floor and turning his blue uniform red.

Counts as a kill shot, he thought, smirking as he reloaded again.

Darrick tapped the little pearl-like vox-unit in his ear. There was a rat's chance in the Great Eye he'd be able to make a break for his vox-officer, Tellic, who was pinned down across the room with most of the others in Darrick's squad. Las-fire flashed through the chamber in lethal strobes.

Range on the micro-bead vox was awful at best, especially when the stone walls played all hell with the signals, but Darrick pressed the throat mic against his skin and trusted his luck.

'Alliance to Venator.'

Nothing. Not even static. Tremendous. Really, just delightful.

Darrick's luck was dry, and so was his patience. A quick kiss of the aquila necklace he wore, and the lieutenant broke into a crouching sprint away from the altar he'd been hiding behind. Las-fire slashed past close enough to warm his skin, but either the Emperor chose that second to bless him with fortune, or the Chaos-tainted scum who could actually hit anything were busy shooting elsewhere. Whichever was true, Darrick leapt behind the paltry cover of a row of pews, kissed his necklace again, and came up firing on full-auto.

The tower-top choir chamber with its high domed ceiling and rows of pews now played host to a tune far removed from Imperial litanies and hymns. Lasgun cracks formed an incessant chorus to the infrequent percussion of heavy bolters hammering out their high-calibre rage. Explosive shells from these smashed into the white marble walls and detonated, leaving head-sized chunks of stone blasted free. Rubble rained on the Cadians from behind their makeshift cover.

'How come *they* get to shoot the place up?' groaned one of the Guardsmen to his lieutenant, sharing the pathetic and disintegrating cover.

'Because,' Darrick faked a thoughtful expression, 'it's more fun this way.' Those words spoken, he rose, rifle in hand.

Darrick fired the last shot in his power cell right into the open mouth of a shouting PDF sergeant, and ducked back under cover. With a silent prayer to the Emperor as he tapped his micro-bead, he repeated the words he was getting bloody sick of repeating.

'Alliance to Venator.'

'VENATOR,' THADE SAID, 'acknowledged.'

As he spoke, he fired his bolt pistol into the face of a young plague victim, doubtless a pilgrim or an acolyte of the cathedral. Now faceless, the child collapsed. The captain stamped on its throat to make sure it wasn't getting back up, wincing as the spine gave way.

'Talk to me, Alliance.' He glanced around the pillared chamber, which was swarming with third-class threats staggering this way and that, uttering howls and piteous little whines. More were coming through the great double doors at the end of the hall. 'Faster, Darrick, faster.'

'…resistance in force. In full force. Secondary targets, no fewer… seventy, reinforced… auxiliary passages in the towers… heavy bolters at the… my grenades, do you hear me? Captain? Captain! The Remnant is…'

Thade held a hand to his own micro-bead as he fell back, trying to insulate it so he could hear Darrick over the bark of the bolt pistol. Weighty standard-issue boots found awkward purchase on the blood-slick marble floor.

According to the maps, this was the penultimate preparatory hall before the first of the primary altar chambers. For thousands of years, pilgrims had come here to be blessed by clergy before being allowed barefoot into the presence of the great altars raised in Saint Kathur's honour. Now it looked like an abattoir, smelled like a plague pit and sounded like the Emperor-damned invasion of Cadia itself: all gunfire and screams.

'I copy,' Thade said, holstering his bolt pistol and drawing his chainsword. He cleaved the head of the closest plague victim from its shoulders, and kicked the headless corpse back into two of its advancing fellows. 'Acknowledged. Remnant sighted in the bell towers by Alliance. Darrick, do you need *Cruor*?'

'…would be lovely, Captain.'

'Copy that.' Thade killed the link and gripped his chainsword two-handed. Las-fire flashed past him, scything down the walking corpses in waves, but there were too many. They streamed at the Cadians in a relentless tide, screaming, howling and sobbing.

'Bayonets and blades,' Thade called, 'for Cadia and the Emperor!'

At the mention of the God-Emperor, the dead wailed as if through one voice. The Cadians locked ranks and answered with silence, awaiting the foe to reach stabbing range.

Seth gripped his staff, wheezing wetly as he stood by the captain's shoulder. It was he who broke the quiet.

'The warp is within them all. They have turned from His light.'

Thade powered his chainsword to full throttle. 'Then we will illuminate them.'

The staggering tide met the dispersed, outnumbered Guard squad in a roar of noise, and the soldiers set about tearing the plague victims to pieces. Bayonets knifed out to punch into eye sockets and laspistols flared at point-blank range. In the centre of the preparation chamber, Thade hewed left and right, his chainsword rising and falling in skill-less rhythm, spraying blood in all directions as it ravaged flesh. Cold droplets flecked his face, joining the sweat stinging his eyes. He'd always fancied himself a fair swordsman, but aptitude played no part in this eye-to-eye slaughter. In a scene where there was no room to manoeuvre, against an enemy that never defended themselves, all the skill in the world meant nothing. Moments like this came down to defiance; sheer, gruelling endurance.

A year ago the room had been devoted to purification. As Thade moved from corpse to corpse, scything them down in a relentless repetition of motion, he could scarcely believe this place had ever been anything but a slaughterhouse.

He cut left, lopping the head off an obese plague victim, and unleashed three bolts into the wretches staggering behind it.

'I hate this planet,' he said for what may have been the fiftieth time that week. 'Janden, look alive! Behind you!'

Janden's heavy vox-caster backpack made him a slow target compared to the others in the command squad. Stumbling over a body on the floor, the vox-officer went down as he turned to face the plague victims reaching for him. A white shock of pain flared through his skull as his head hit the ground with a meaty smack. Hands mobbed him, grabbing and tearing, none of which he noticed.

Dazed and barely conscious, Janden didn't realise the dull throb in his leg was because one of the plague-dead had wrenched off his shin armour and was devouring his right calf. The others seemed intent on battering him to death with their rotting fists, though Janden was so out of it he didn't feel much of that either. A shadow fell across his numb, unseeing face. A dead man was leering at him, a sick visage of shrunken eyes and black gums.

The grinding blade of Thade's chainsword burst through the chest of the corpse. With precise strikes and a few ungentle kicks, the captain cleared the walking dead away from Janden.

Five more came on with their characteristic shamble, reaching out for him. Each wore the soiled once-bright robes of Kathurite clergy.

'Eighty-Eight!' Thade cried, and threw himself to the ground. A storm of covering las-fire flashed over his head.

When it was done, the five plague-slain were holed and twitching on the ground, going nowhere. Thade dragged the delirious, bleeding vox-officer behind a pillar and sat him up.

Janden's helmet slapped against the stone behind his head. Blood gushed from the bite wound in his leg, which Thade bound with a hasty tourniquet.

'Pressure, Janden. You hear me? Keep pressure on this.'

'Captain,' Janden's eyes rolled back. 'There's blood. Blood on your medal.'

Thade's hand went instinctively to the Ward of Cadia on the front of his helmet. His gloved fingertips streaked even more dark gore across its silver surface.

'Captain...' Janden nodded like a drunk, looking over Thade's shoulder. 'Behind...'

The chainsword was in Thade's hands, revving up as he rose and turned. The teeth, each sharpened to a monomolecular edge, met the shoulder of an elderly plague victim in the filthy robes of a senior monk. The sword's teeth chewed down into the corpse with noisy efficiency. The holy man, dead for five months, screamed as Thade sawed him in two. Old, cold blood hit both Cadians in an icy shower.

Even through the burning in his muscles, even through fear-heightened senses and the adrenaline fuelling his instincts, Thade was annoyed enough to curse at getting sprayed again.

More corpses ran towards him, only to be cut down by precise swings of his chainsword and pin-point fire from Janden's laspistol.

'I need a signal to base.' Thade's sword dripped blood as it idled once more, and the captain turned to the wounded soldier. Janden was pale, sweating and bleeding from a score of wounds, but he nodded to Thade while reloading his pistol.

'Contact, sir?'

'Direct message to Colonel Lockwood. Demand immediate deployment of Strike Team *Cruor*. Authorisation: Thade thirty sixty-two-A. *Cruor* are to assist Lieutenant Darrick in taking objectives three through six. The bell towers. Alliance is losing the bell towers. Make sure the colonel realises that.'

Janden left his laspistol on his knees as he punched in the code and voxed back to base. Thade was already moving away, running back to the heart of the chamber where his men were fighting their brutal melee. As he ran, he messaged Darrick to tell of *Cruor's* impending arrival.

ALLIANCE HAD LOST the bell towers.

Darrick never saw the wall explode, and never saw half of his squad blown out of the gaping hole. As the detonation went off and threw him aside, he was knocked momentarily unconscious.

He did, however, recover fast. Sharp senses and a thick skull meant he came to in a hurry and heard the cries as the soldiers still alive began their long fall. Even over ringing in his ears in the aftermath of the missile blast, he heard them falling to their deaths.

'Alliance, come in.' Thade's voice crackled over the micro-bead. Darrick dragged himself, bleeding and battered, from under a pile of wrecked and smouldering pews. He reached a trembling hand to tap the earpiece.

'Alliance,' Darrick hissed through gritted teeth. 'Broken.'

'Repeat,' Thade said. The signal was bad. Interference from the explosion that had raged through the choir chamber and destroyed a whole wall? Probably.

'I am having absolutely no fun today,' Darrick hissed, pulling out a chunk of shrapnel from his thigh. He looked up from where he lay. His men – those that still lived – were rousing. Too experienced to rise fully and face enemy fire, they crawled through the shredded furniture, finding cover wherever they could. Las-fire was already flashing at them from the Kathurite positions across the chamber.

'This is Alliance, captain.' Darrick reached out bleeding fingers to pull his fallen lasgun closer. He'd carried that weapon since he'd been a Whiteshield over twenty years ago. Not a chance in hell he'd leave it here, no matter how battered it was. His fingertips snagged the strap, and he dragged on it. The rifle bore a palette of fresh burns and new scratches, but otherwise looked fine. He guessed it would still fire. 'Alliance: Broken,' he repeated.

'Acknowledged. *Cruor* inbound. Hold in the name of the Emperor,' was Thade's curt reply before cutting the link.

Easier said than done, thought Darrick.

* * *

A GANG-RAMP SLAMMED closed. Thrusters fired. A machine came to life, taking its cargo into the sky on screaming engines.

The Valkyrie tore through the air over the city. Its downswept wings carried racks of air-to-surface missiles the pilots could never fire, and the twin autocannons on the gunship's cheeks remained silent even as the Valkyrie flew over tertiary threat targets already beginning to flood the streets cleared by the Guard earlier in the day. The cannons' silence was not to save ammunition or, as in the case of the rockets, to prevent damage to the planet's sacred architecture. At this speed, there was simply no way the pilots could expect to hit anything. Dead bodies wept at the sight of the troop transport as it shot overhead, en route to the Shrine of the Emperor's Unending Majesty. The Valkyrie, crow-black and dragon-loud, roared onward.

On one side of the cockpit, which arched down like a sneering vulture's face at the cityscape flashing below, were two words in Imperial Gothic lettering. The name of the gunship itself: *His Holy Blade*.

On the opposite side was a simple word in High Gothic. The name of the gunship's cargo: *Cruor*.

AS THE 88TH hunted within, Enginseer Osiron remained outside the monastery with the thirty Chimeras.

He was not alone, of course. The drivers, armed and ready, stood by their vehicles. A handful busied themselves with minor maintenance on engines or armour plating. Between the orderly rows of Chimeras, lobotomised tech-servitors moved here and there, using their augmetic hands and machine tool limbs to aid in the repairs. One of the servitors – formerly a deserter, now a half-machine slave without a mind – had its forearms replaced with industrial scrubbers. It crouched by the command Chimera, its whirring hands scrubbing and flushing out gore from the tank's treads. Another servitor with a hammer for a left hand panel-beat another tank's distorted front armour back into Standard Construct regulation shape.

Dead Man's Hand stalked around the parked troop transports, their steps making a rhythmic drumbeat of blessed iron on stone. Perimeter defence duty.

Wreathed in a cloak of blood red, the hood pulled over his head and hiding his features, Enginseer Osiron nodded silently to one of the patrolling Sentinels as it passed. Vertain replied to the techpriest's nod with an acknowledgement blip over the vox.

None of the 88th knew Osiron's age. He could have been thirty or two hundred and thirty. His face was forever concealed by the low-hanging crimson hood and a surgically attached rebreather mask covering his nose, mouth and chin. The only visible human features beyond the pale skin of his cheeks were his eyes of Cadian violet, glinting in the depths of the hood's shadow.

His body – what there was to see of it beneath the traditional robe of the Machine Cult of Mars – was an armoured form of tarnished plating, whirring gears and hissing pistons. Ostensibly he was human, at least at the most basic level: two arms, two legs, and so on.

But everything visible was replaced or augmented with the holy alterations of his cult. His internal organs ticked and clicked loud enough to hear. His joints hummed as gears simulated bones moving in harmony. His voice was a toneless murmur emitted from the vox-speakers on the front of his rebreather. This last aspect betrayed his curious inhumanity most of all, turning every breath into an audible rise and fall of static. *Krsssh*, in. *Krsssh*, out.

Osiron leaned on the haft of his massive two-handed axe. The weapon was too heavy for an unaugmented man to lift, and sported the split-skull image of the Adeptus Mechanicus on its black iron blade. From a bulky backpack that thrummed with power, a multi-jointed mechanical arm rose and extended out, its clawed hand opening and closing as if stretching. A cutting torch on the arm's wrist flared briefly as the power claw whirred closed. Drill bits and other tools folded back into the arm's body. It coiled behind the tech-priest's shoulder, reposed.

'*Count the Seven*,' Osiron's internal vox said directly into his left ear. It had been doing that for an hour now and, unlike the squads engaged in the retaking of the monastery, Osiron had disobeyed orders, remaining tapped into the compromised frequency. It fascinated him.

'Curious,' he said in a murmur of vox-speakers. The servitor next to him turned slowly, unsure if it had misheard an order. Osiron tapped a button on the signum attached to his belt, hanging down his thigh like a metal pouch decorated with a hundred keys to press. The servitor cancelled its attention cycle, going back to staring mutely ahead, as dead in its own way as the poor wretches still staggering across this planet.

'Osiron to Vertain.'

'Honoured enginseer?'

'Monitor auspex for signs of jamming.'

'Yes, sir.'

Sir. The title always made Osiron smile. He held some minor authority in the 88th by dint of expertise, his ruthlessly logical mind and his close friendship with the captain – not from any formal rank.

'I'm not seeing evidence of jamming,' Vertain voxed back. 'Confirmed by the rest of my team. Dead Man's Hand reports no instrument glitches.'

'That, scout-lieutenant, is exactly my point. When have our scanners been so clear?'

'Maybe we're just lucky.' Osiron was no expert at interpreting human emotion through tone of voice, but Vertain's doubts were obvious as he spoke. He didn't believe what he'd suggested. Neither did Osiron.

'Unlikely. Auspex has been clear for over an hour. I detect none of the interference we have come to associate as standard for Kathur Reclamation operations.'

'Acknowledged, honoured enginseer. I've already logged the clarity of auspex readings with High Command. Can you reach the captain?'

'A moment, please. Suspicions must be confirmed before the captain is alerted. Osiron to inbound Valkyrie *His Holy Blade*.'

The reply took several seconds. When it came, it hit in a mangled wave of savaged vox. Just noise.

'Enginseer Bylam Osiron to inbound Valkyrie *His Holy Blade*.' The tech-priest adjusted his internal vox by tweaking dials on his forearm.

'*His Holy Blade*. Two minutes until arrival,' the pilot said. 'Problems?'

'*Count the Seven*,' Osiron's vox whispered again. '*Count the Seven*.'

The enginseer frowned. 'Pilot, report auspex performance as you enter standard close-range scanning distance relative to our position.'

It was an unusual request. Osiron waited patiently for the pilot to check his instruments. 'Standard distortion at medium range, sir. Reaching close range in twenty seconds.'

Osiron timed the estimate against the ticking of his own heart-engine. Twenty-three seconds passed.

'Auspex is… clear. Minimal interference.'

Osiron killed the link and switched channels. 'Scout-lieutenant.'

'Yes, honoured enginseer?'

'Deploy available resources in defensive spread.'

'What? Why?'

'Because you are the ranking officer here, and we have walked into a trap.'

THE DOUBLE DOORS were steel-shod Kathurite oak and had stood for three thousand years; consistently blessed, reinforced, redecorated and restored over the centuries. They were built in the same style as most of Kathur's savagely overdone architecture, but practicality was in their construction, too. In the event of a fire, these doors would seal closed and allow those within the preparation chambers to survive up to nine hours protected from the flames.

The ornate doors exploded inwards under the force of the plasma blast. With twin crashes, they flew off their hinges and clattered to the red carpet blanketing the floor. Eleven men stood in the torn opening, rifles and pistols raised. It was the third set of such doors Zailen had opened with his plasma gun. White steam, hot enough to scald flesh, hissed from the weapon's focusing ring in an angry gush.

Another preparation chamber opened up before them. Another hall filled with the enraged dead. The corpses turned their attention to the living interlopers, their ruined faces peeling into expressions resembling something like joy, and something like pain. Several began to wail.

Thade's sword cut the air and his squad opened fire.

After the mayhem, the squad reformed in the centre of the room. Blood marked them as surely as if they'd been painted with it. Their bootsteps echoed throughout the chamber, bouncing off walls that sported stone angels leering down in cold dissatisfaction. The reliefs in this room depicted scenes of the Great Crusade. Winged Astartes warriors standing tall and proud – a testament to the Raven Guard Legion that had forced this world into compliance so many thousands of years ago.

Another set of double doors barred their way into the next chamber. Thade shook his head.

'We're being herded. Like cattle to the slaughter.'

The Cadians nodded. Zailen said, 'Room after room of piss-poor resistance. They're wearing us down piece by piece.' Several of the soldiers checked their digital ammo readouts and muttered agreement.

'Seth?' Thade fixed him with his violet glare. 'We're running out of preparation chambers. This is the heart of the monastery. Whatever you've sensed is nearby.'

The psyker was trembling. Dark blood leaked in a viscous trail from his right eye. Thade considered shooting him on the spot. Seth's unreliability today was a little much even for the captain's patience. He knew a commissar would almost certainly have executed the shivering man by now, for dereliction of duty as well as the risk of psychic contamination. But Thade needed every advantage he could grasp.

Everything about this mission was a mess, right back to the fools in the Janus 6th who'd tried to take the shrine in the first place. Could the monastery be held? Maybe. Could it be held without extreme losses? Not a chance. Could some amateur outfit like the Janus 6th – just thrown out into space by their founding world – have any chance to cut it here? Never.

Thade had hoped to secure the key points with his divided teams and seal themselves in, awaiting reinforcement. A good plan, but getting more unrealistic by the second. Everything fairly reeked of deception and an enemy's pre-planning.

'Seth. I'm going to count to three.' Thade rested his bolt pistol against the sanctioned psyker's cheek. 'One.'

'So old,' Seth whispered. 'So old. So diseased. How do they live?'

'Seth, focus. Two.'

'So old…'

Thade backhanded him with the weighty pistol, not hard enough to injure but not a light slap, either. 'Seth, focus! Cadian blood, ice in your veins. You have a job to do. We're counting on you. What. Is. Ahead?'

Seth closed his bleeding eyes. The trembling ceased, and every man present felt the invisible tremor of the psyker reaching out with his powers. Zailen stepped back, as if the unseen forces at work could destabilise his temperamental, humming plasma rifle.

'I'm still hearing the voice. It's trapped, barely reaching the surface…'

'Seth, focus now or I shoot you where you stand. Ignore the damn voice.' Thade asked again, 'What do you see?'

The psyker smiled. A Cadian smile, a morbid twist of the lips, grim and humourless.

'Traitors.'

ENGINSEER OSIRON'S WARNING flashed through the vox network, squad by squad. No one was surprised. Hopes had hardly been high of the mission being a success, and many of the 88th had questioned the initial orders to reinforce the Janus 6th in such a tactically unviable location. The green unit had pushed too far, too fast, and it was down to the Cadians to get in there and do their best to keep the fresh meat alive.

In theory.

Of course, there was only so much you could do when the regiment you were supposed to reinforce was already annihilated by the time you arrived.

Taan Darrick crouched behind a row of stone pews, clutching his battered lasrifle. Chunks of his cover broke away in flying pieces or were disintegrated outright by the bite of heavy bolter rounds. His glance kept flicking up to the stained glass dome thirty metres above his hiding place. Kathur Reclamation protocol was adamant about avoiding collateral damage, but any second now, Kathur Reclamation protocol was about to go to hell.

Deft fingers ejected his rifle's spent power pack. The sickle-shaped magazine fell into his free hand, and he stored it in his webbing.

'Machine-spirit, forgive my actions. Soon you shall be whole again.' The Litany of Unloading. Taan's voice was cool and unshaking. Cadian blood, ice in the veins. There was no way he'd let himself die here.

He slammed the fresh power cell in and pulled the recharge slide, now speaking the Litany of Loading.

'Machine-spirit, accept my gift. Swallow the light, and spit out death.' Simple words. Even silly, in other circumstances. A grunt's attempt at something poetic. Yet Darrick had been saying the same words since he'd loaded his first lasgun at age four. They made him grin now. Funny how certain things gain such significance.

The last time he'd raised his head above the row of seats, he'd counted close to seventy of the Remnant scattered in a loose line, their numbers punctuated by hastily erected heavy weapons emplacements. Seventy soldiers. There had been over a hundred a few minutes ago.

Seventy left.

Taan looked left and right, counting his own remaining men as they crouched in the makeshift trench, sheltered from the onslaught by the rapidly-eroding stone pews.

He counted twelve. Wonderful. That's just wonderful.

'Darrick to *His Holy Blade*. In the name of the Emperor, where are you?'

'On approach, Alliance. *Cruor* requests pict detail of deployment.'

'Do I sound like I have time to start a career as a taker of rare and beautiful picts? We're pinned. You hear that gunfire? That's not us shooting, you son of–'

Taan was Cadian, born in a barracks and bred under the violet sky. Even as he ranted, he focused the lens of the picter attached to the side of his helmet, and took a peek – no longer than a heartbeat – long enough to take a single pict of the wall of Remnant forces across the circular chorus chamber. All the while, he swore. Darrick ducked again just as a lasbolt burned the stone black an inch from his eye.

'…raised by dogs, you ungrateful…' he trailed off, clicking 'Send' on the helmet picter. 'Can you see that?'

'Quite a party in there. Patching it through to *Cruor* now.'

'No rush.' The pew shook as a massive chunk of its front detonated under the full force of a direct heavy bolter round only three metres away. 'Take as long as you need. I'm starting to get comfortable.'

Taan couldn't resist. He looked up, taking a pict of the stained glass dome. It was the only point of entry unless the Valkyrie was going to drop *Cruor* through the hole blown in the wall. That was unlikely. Darrick clicked 'Send' a second time, transmitting the pict of the pristine dome.

'See that second pict? I'm not seeing much deployment here.'

The pre-dawn light filtering through the dome darkened under an avian shadow. The Valkyrie hovered, its thrusters screaming as they burned. Several of the Remnant cried out as coloured melted glass rained on them in sticky, agonising drips.

'Now!' Taan called to his surviving men. They used the momentary distraction to break cover, twelve rifles firing. Twenty-two Remnant soldiers went down, hit in the first or second volley. Two shots went wide. Taan laughed as he ducked back into cover.

'I saw that, Kallo! Are you sure your mother had violet eyes?' He knew Kallo had been hit in the shoulder and it was ruining his aim, but still... 'Two misses! The captain will hear about this!'

Kallo offered no excuse. Taan called out the Litany of Forgiveness with a wicked grin. 'Sweet God-Emperor, forgive Your servant Kallo his sins. Remember he is just a man!'

Several of the soldiers sniggered in their cover.

The gunfire renewed, but in less force. Some of it was angled up towards the Valkyrie, but the greatest difference was the fact that a third of the force was no longer firing.

'Strike Team *Cruor* confirm receipt of tactical situation. Deploying.'

'Oh? Nice of them to finally drop by.'

'I heard that,' came a deeper voice that Taan recognised instantly. 'See you in a second, joker.'

Taan grinned as Strike Team *Cruor* made their entrance.

Ten men in night-black carapace armour fell through the melted ruin of the glass dome. Boots first, they dropped like knives, firing as they plummeted. The Valkyrie above stayed locked in hover while the squad rappelled down.

On maximum power, standard issue lasguns constructed on the Cadian armoury world of Kantrael fired a finger-thin red beam of superheated laser energy. The blasts roaring from the ten rifles in the falling men's gloved hands were headache-purple with a blinding white core. Several of the Remnant hit by the las-fire burst into flames as their clothes caught light. They dropped to the ground, already dead, their clothes aflame.

'Stormtroopers!' one of the Remnant cried, and the devastated remains of the enemy force turned to flee. One of the black-clad soldiers cut down two enemy either side of the shouting Remnant warrior, and disconnected his rappelling cable. He caught the running Remnant in three strides and bore him to the ground, punching down with a double-edged combat knife.

'Stay awhile,' the soldier said, burying his blade in the traitor's neck.

The rest of Taan's men joined *Cruor*, leaping the cover of the pews and cutting down the foe. For a handful of seconds, the chamber was illuminated in an insane display of strobing laser light: red from the lasguns, purple-white from *Cruor's* hellguns.

Except for the ringing in the Cadians' ears, the chamber was silent less than a minute after *Cruor* deployed. The last surviving Remnant soldier was put down with a las-round to the forehead while he pleaded for his life, on his knees, insisting he had no choice.

'Ain't that a shame.' His executioner, faceless in his dark rebreather and full visored helm, turned from the falling corpse, scanning the room. Master Sergeant Ban Jevrian sighted Taan through the green glare of his visor. He popped his helmet seals in a hiss of air pressure as he strode over to the lieutenant, removing it to reveal a shaved head and the suggestion of brown stubble around his thin mouth. Jevrian wasn't so much in athletic Cadian shape as he was a layer of slab-like muscle over thick bone, encased in black carapace armour. His hellpistol, connected to a humming backpack via thick cable feeds, purred as he lowered the setting and holstered it.

'Sir.' He offered Taan a salute, his deep voice resonating across the chamber as he made the sign of the aquila over his chestplate. 'Kasrkin squad Eight-Zero-Eight reports successful deployment.'

'Took your time,' Taan saluted back.

'That's funny. You're a real joker,' Jevrian said, unsmiling. He didn't smile much. Jokes that had most men in stitches might, if they were truly worthwhile, lift the corners of Ban Jevrian's lips for the ghost of an instant. 'Where's Yaune?'

'Dead,' Darrick said. 'Blown out of that hole in the wall.'

The Kasrkin shrugged. 'He owed me money.'

'You're all heart.'

'Whatever. Orders?'

Taan did a quick count of his remaining men, thinking of the names he'd be writing on death notices once they were clear of this hellhole.

'Thade's pulling us back. We're running.'

'We don't run.'

'We're running. Captain's orders. When you wear the same silver on your helmet that he does, I'll start giving a damn about what you think, master sergeant.'

'We never run,' Jevrian almost growled. Talking to the Kasrkin sergeant was like talking to a bear in an insect's black armour. But he was right. The Cadian Shock didn't run. It was a point of pride, and had been for ten thousand years. The Lists of Remembrance were filled with hundreds of regiments that had been destroyed rather than flee before the Archenemy.

'We never run,' Jevrian said again. His hulking form promised pain. He bristled with firepower.

'No? We ran two months ago,' Taan said softly. 'We ran on Cadia.'

Jevrian had no response to that. He turned back to his strike team and raised a hand, closing it into a fist – the signal for forming up.

'*Cruor*, weapons hot. Let's do what the hero says.'

* * *

'IMMEDIATE FALLBACK TO the Chimeras.'

Thade's words had spread through the squads with the speed and fervour Osiron's warning had only fifteen minutes before. The 88th was breaking orders and running. It stuck uncomfortably in many throats, but none of the officers argued with the captain's appraisal of the situation.

'If we stay here, we die. If we die, we fail to meet our objectives anyway. The Janus 6th is finished. Our orders were to reinforce them, or hold this monastery if the Janusians fell. Our numbers make that an impossibility now we've come face to face with the reality. Immediate fallback to the Chimeras.'

Every squad but one obeyed this order. Thade's own didn't. The captain wasn't leaving until he saw the truth of Seth's proclamation. 'Traitors' was a word that covered a multitude of potential sinners. He wanted to know for sure.

'Open those doors,' Thade pointed at the set of double doors with his deactivated chainsword, but shook his head when Zailen raised his plasma gun. 'No, Zailen. I want you ready to fire when the doors open. Seth, if you please.'

The psyker clutched his dark grey leather jacket tighter around his wasted frame. A hand gloved in the same grey leather reached out, fingers splayed, towards the great doors. The temperature dropped a few degrees. The Cadians' breath steamed from their lips.

The doors shook once. Twice. Dust rained from the surrounding archway, as if the stone angels were shedding powdered skin. On the third shake, one of the angels – a winged representation of Saint Kathur himself – toppled to shatter on the red carpet.

'Not a good omen,' remarked Janden. Thade's scowl silenced him.

'I have a grip,' Seth breathed through clenched teeth. His power over the doors was visible: an ice-blue sheen of psychic frost was forming where the psyker gripped the portal with his mind.

Ten guns raised in readiness. 'Do it,' said Thade.

Seth did it. The double doors roared from their hinges in a howl of psychic wind. The soldiers felt ice crystals tinkling on their armour as the gust blew back to them.

Thade's men were scattered, some behind pillars, others kneeling, two lying down on their fronts – but each one was ready to fire. Each one was watching what was through the door.

A hundred and fifty dead. Two hundred. The plague-slain stood in a staggered horde – a mass of corpses that had no right to be on their feet. Heads bowed, they stood in silence, facing a towering figure. In that first instant, the scene poured into Thade's mind, making him think of a blasphemous congregation, a church of the dead and the damned.

The dead turned as the doors fell inward. Hundreds of rotting faces, the faces of the faithless, stared at the eleven soldiers. The imposing figure on the other side of the horde, some hundred metres from the Cadians, raised a scab-encrusted bolter.

Thade's men were firing in a relentless barrage before the doors even crashed to rest, but the towering figure's voice was a wet burble rising horribly over the stuttering cracks of las-fire. A single bang from the creature's bolter ended Etan's life, as the round detonated within the trooper's chest.

The Cadians fell back, rifles streaming out death, the true death, for the plague-slain that shambled after them. Thade grinned despite everything, because he finally had it confirmed. Firing his bolt pistol with both hands, he yelled into his vox.

'Captain Thade, Cadian 88th! Contact, contact, contact! Primary threat sighted!'

The Traitor Astartes stalked through the shambling crowd, parting the dead before its massive bulk like a ship cutting the seas. Its bolter barked over and over, but its aim was thrown off by the Cadian lasbolts smacking into its ornate helm. The rounds glanced aside doing no real damage, but they interfered with the archaic targeting systems in the creature's helmet displays.

'Count the Seven…' it burbled. Green ooze sizzled from its speaker grille. It seemed to be laughing and choking up acid, all at once.

The Cadians fell back faster, lasguns flashing angry and hot. Thade listened for his enginseer's acknowledgement, then spoke back.

'The Death Guard, Osiron. The XIV Legion is here.'

CHAPTER IV
Revelations

Reclamation Headquarters, outside Solthane

IT WAS FIVE hours since the retreat, and Seth's head still pounded as if his skull was shrinking around his brain.

Seth's camp was pitched several dozen metres from the neat and ordered rows of the 88th's communal tents. His thoughts would not leave the memory of the monastery. He'd heard the voice, screaming in silence, even hours before entering the shrine itself – a distinct, yet distant presence within the cathedral district. Unknown, unseen, almost unheard.

He coughed again, violently enough to bring the coppery tang of blood to his tongue. Trying to focus was an exercise in torment, listening to the sounds of the camp all around, shutting out the after-echo of the voice that still ghosted through his senses. Each time he quested after it with his thoughts, it dispersed into nothingness. Seth was no longer sure if he was hearing the voice now, or merely hearing it echo through his memory. Reaching out for it psychically was as impossible as catching mist in his closed hands.

The thousand-strong Cadian regiment, of which Thade commanded a full third, was camped with the main bulk of Guard forces in the colossal plateau chosen for the initial landings. Making planetfall outside the capital city had been the only option. Most of Kathur was covered in the open ocean, and what little land mass existed was encrusted with towering stone cathedral-cities. But here the Guard had found grasslands expansive enough to accommodate the Reclamation forces tasked with retaking the northern hemisphere.

Tens of thousands of Guard soldiers had made the initial planetfall. Over half of them were still coming and going around the grounded troop landers that now served as Reclamation headquarters. A hundred thousand tents and hastily-erected communal buildings spread out from the clustered landers like a refugee city.

And this was just the spearhead. The forward force, sent to establish an Imperial presence. The main bulk of the Reclamation forces were still in warp transit.

The aerial view was breathtaking. Seth had seen it from a Valkyrie only a week before. The Janusians had been gone even by then, their animal hide tents dismantled as the regiment went deep into the city. The landers of the Vednikan 12th Rifles had made planetfall first, and they sat now in tidy formation, their massive hulls casting shadows on the grey tents below. Ash residue in the air had darkened the Vednikans' pristine white tents within hours of touching down. The serpent symbol of Vednika, proudly embroidered on each tent in black, was barely visible now.

To the east and west of the Vednikans were the 303rd Uriah and the 25th Kiridian Irregulars, respectively. The base camp of the former was a husk of the sprawl it had been on the days after planetfall, with only a handful of empty tents left while the regiment was engaged in retaking Solthane's power station district to the far north. The latter, in typical Kiridian militia style, resembled exactly what it was: a rushed camp set up almost at random as squads spilled from their landers and pitched their tents wherever they chose. Seth had smiled slightly upon seeing it. He was a student of other Imperial cultures – a personal passion – and knew something of the Kiridian military mentality. Their tradition was that every tent had to have a squad banner outside, and that each banner must face the regimental commander's pavilion.

Other than that one rule, their camp was as chaotic as can be imagined, as comrades sought to pitch tents near one another with no regard for order.

The Hadris Rift 40th Armoured showed no such disorganisation. Ordered rows of tents stood in ranks a little way from the tank garages. Orbital landers had brought down the structures almost whole, leaving enginseers and servitors to reinforce the buildings with armour plating against the ashy wind.

The camp of the 3rd Skarran Rangers was Guard standard. Billets and tents in an ordered spread around the few landers that remained, with regimental leaders stationed in the smaller staff tents away from the troops. Unlike the Kiridians, the Skarrans had left ample room for supply dropships in their formation, while the Irregulars were forced to land their supplies a kilometre from their camp and drive the crates in on cargo loaders and lifter Sentinels.

Seth's violet eyes drank in the scene, his gaze finally sweeping to the Cadian contingent. Tents in the black and grey of urban camouflage stood out stark against the dry grass of the plateau. A single lander punctuated the ordered ranks of tents – a behemoth of a craft with its swollen hold capable of holding over a hundred Chimeras. Patches of grass were quickly slabbed over with rockcrete for efficient supply drop landing sites. Each of the 88th's three divisions were separated by a short distance, with the soldiers' tents in rows near central communal mess buildings and officer barracks – the latter of which were landed from the troop ships in a matter similar to the garages of the Hadris Rift 40th. The Cadians used their great lander, *Unyielding Defiance*, as a fully-equipped garage for their vehicles.

Seth blinked, bringing his focus back to the present. The great bronze bell in the hangar bay of *Unyielding Defiance* rang out in the distance, signalling muster for Major Crayce's elements of the 88th. Wiping his lips with a bloodstained handkerchief, the psyker looked back at the tarot cards laid out on the small wooden table. A passing Chimera shook the tent and set the table rocking. Seth's powers earned him distance from the rank and file, but a military camp was never a noiseless place. It took all the psyker's meditative powers to focus sometimes. Blocking out the noise of rumbling tanks, clashing tools, marching boots, drilling men, live fire exercises… The very air tasted of iron and machine oil…

His focus had drifted again. Seth retrained his attention on the tarot cards spread before him, seeing each at first with his natural eyes. They were simple, plain white pieces of durable card, devoid of decoration on the back, bare of art on the front. The sensitive nerves behind Seth's eyes pulsed with the genesis of a migraine – a bad one, he could tell, it'd likely be one of the ones that left him almost blind for hours. Smiling skullishly, he whispered thanks to the Emperor. The pain was a message to pay heed to his duties, and it helped him focus on matters of the internal, not the chaos of the camp. A timely blessing.

He touched the first naked card with an ungloved fingertip.

A body, browned with age and blackened in death, sits locked within a great throne of gold, steel and brass. The corpse's mouth is open, projecting a silent scream that echoes through the unseen layers of the universe. Before the howling cadaver, a legion of angels kneels, crying violet tears.

The God-Emperor, Inversed

Seth was gone from his body now, deep within the tarot reading, but maintained a faint connection to his physical form. He sensed its muscles lock tight, a rictus forming across his own lips that he could neither feel nor control. A warm tickle on his chin – he was drooling already, and that was bad – threatened to violate his immersion and drag him back to the world of flesh, blood and bone. A second's refocusing; a twist of mental strength, like a contortionist escaping his bonds.

The temperature in his skull lowered again. Soothing. Very soothing. A mercy.

Unsurprisingly, the God-Emperor was an auspicious card in the Cadian Tarot. When drawn from the deck, it bespoke of warp travel, of discovery, of hope in the cold depths of space. Inversed, when drawn upside down, it foretold of the warp's malign touch infecting the servants of the Imperium. A hopeless war. Death from the far reaches of space.

Seth returned enough of his consciousness to touch the second card, unpleasantly racked by the fast-growing headache. He tasted blood. Was he bleeding from his nose? Already?

An eye. The Eye. A wound in reality, an open scar in space where the bruise-purple and blood-red eye of Chaos leered into the galaxy. The stars die around the Eye: some fading into cold blackness, others bursting in white hot torment. The Eye stares dully, as it always does, a malicious glare with little emotion beyond distant hate.

But the nebula flares, tendrils spreading across space.

The Eye has opened.

The Great Eye

Seth lifted trembling fingers from the card, sparing himself the vision. An uncomfortable constriction in his throat coupled with the flood of bitter saliva in his mouth threatened a violent purge of his stomach soon.

The Great Eye... The Archenemy's heart and the bastion of his strength. To draw this card was to foretell of war against Chaos, or an amplification of a current conflict. Specifically, it foretold that the conflict would be familiar to those born on Cadia, for the Great Eye was something they lived with each day of their lives.

Seth's queasiness arose from where the card had been drawn. Directly after the God-Emperor inversed? The second and fourth cards were drawn as signifiers, bringing clarity to the ones preceding them. Dark, dark portents.

Something will intensify this war. Something black and hateful from the warp.

Seth touched the third card, unaware of the bloody drool pinking his teeth.

The galaxy burns. A figure stands in ancient armour, wreathed in a billion screaming souls that encircle him like mist. In its right gauntlet, Holy Terra blackens and crumbles. A demigod's blood drips from the talons. In the dim reaches of the vision, almost an afterthought, a

*distant howling light fades into darkness
and silence. The figure smiles for the first
time in ten thousand years.*

The Despoiler, Inversed

The vision pained him, but Seth quenched the
agony with cold logic. *The card is inversed. The psychic resonance – the card's 'art' – is not the vital
factor here.* He caught his breath, removing the fingertips from its gentle rest against the blank card.

When drawn, the Despoiler card is the bane of
life, the truest indicator of coming loss and
unavoidable bloodshed for the Imperium of Man.
But inversed? The psyker breathed deeply, trying to
calm his aching heart as it pounded against his thin
ribs. He'd never seen the card drawn inversed
before. Indeed, he'd only drawn the Despoiler once
in his life before this moment, in the weeks before
the invasion of Cadia, three years before.

Inversed... A rival for the Despoiler? Someone
destined to stand against the Archenemy's machi-
nations? Seth's fingertips hovered above the card.
The clarity of the prophecy was clouded, ruined by
his own unfamiliarity with the card he'd drawn. So
tempting to touch it again and renew the fierce
vision. Just a few moments of pain. He could take
it.

No.

He couldn't.

A great portion of his training in the control of his wild, unreliable talent emphasised the limits of the mortal mind and the physical shell that carried it. To read the Emperor's Tarot was to open oneself to the warp, and caution was not a virtue to be discarded on a whim. This reading was already devastatingly potent, which lent credence to its import and accuracy. Seth's sight was blurred from the pulsing migraine and he smelled vomit, the scent thick and tangy, coupled with a lumpy warmth in his lap. Momentary blackouts. He'd not even felt the purging of his stomach.

One card remained untouched. The signifier. The card that would put a frame of reference on The Despoiler Inversed. His hand stayed raised above it for a second, a minute, an hour – Seth had no idea of external time with his thoughts so adamantly turned inward. He could feel his own life ticking away in time to his body's natural cycle, and felt the unnatural acceleration, the degeneration of his cells, from exerting his psychic strength day after day.

He sensed his own smile but did not feel it. To expend one's life in service to the Emperor was all he wished. He was Cadian Shock through and through, no matter if he was banned from marching and training alongside them.

His mother's eyes had been violet. She had died for the Imperium. He would die for the Imperium, too. The thought made his blood burn with pride. *A life spent bringing death to the Emperor's foes is a life lived in full.* Those words were etched in the stone above the doors of every building in Kasr Poitane, where Seth was born.

Now. Now was the time. What one soul would be the defiant fulcrum upon which the whole Reclamation spun? Who would be the bane of the Despoiler's plans?

Seth's fingertips landed, trembling but tense with purpose.

And he saw a face he had seen a thousand times before.

CAPTAIN THADE MADE the sign of the aquila over a chestplate still smeared with the blood of the plague-slain. He'd been back at the command base for fifteen minutes, and while Seth had retired to his tent, the captain had seen his men billeted and taken his inner circle to the lord general's tent.

He'd been handed a message from an engineering servitor saying that Rax was ready at last, but no matter how keen he was to deal with it, Rax had to wait. Before anything else, Thade had to deal with the lord general. He'd said to Darrick only the week before that he'd rather lose his arm again than report to Lord General Maggrig once more. Darrick hadn't laughed. He knew it wasn't a joke. Maggrig bled pettiness. He exuded a smirking, preening condescension. It ran from his pores the way a fat man sweats.

Lord General Maggrig was the wrong side of seventy, his long face characterised by age's lines rather than war's scars. While his rank and wage entitled him to partake of the youth-renewing juvenat drug process along with the accompanying surgery, Fineas Maggrig had chosen not to indulge. He believed in a man living out his natural span in service to the Emperor, and those who 'stole days' were wasting time in life when they could be beside the Emperor's throne in the afterlife. Unshakeable faith made him a preferential candidate to lead this theatre, and the Hadris Rift 40th Armoured soaked up the glory of their commander bearing the title Overseer of the Reclamation.

Thade had researched the lord general's history prior to planetfall. He needn't have bothered. Upon seeing Overseer Maggrig in the flesh he realised why using his clearance to study his new commanding officer's record had been a waste of time. The lord general had arrived a week after the rest of the Hadris Rift 40th, freshly promoted from pacifying some minor heresy near his homeworld and bearing three rows of medals upon his chest. Thade had tried not to smile as he'd recognised them all one by one. Long service, long service, long service. There, a Corwin's Cross for tactical genius. Another long service medal, then two more for tactical prowess in various theatres, and a Mechanicum Fellowship Skull for honourably defending a Forge World without the loss of any Adeptus Mechanicus hierarchs. Nice. Very nice.

But worrying.

Thade was smart enough not to judge the new lord general too harshly – he'd earned those medals for a reason, after all – but the captain was Cadian enough to secretly chafe at the thought of following the man's orders. The lord general had spent his entire career leading Guardsmen safely from the back.

It wasn't the Cadian way. With the Great Eye staring eternally down at their world, Cadian doctrine favoured the bold: those men and women who stood on the front lines, seeing the enemy with their own eyes and ordering their allies into battle with their own raised voices.

Thade's breast was hardly beribboned in honour's blazing colours, but the Ward of Cadia shone silver on his helmet. That counted. When he'd been awarded it only a handful of weeks before for his command in the Black Crusade, the captain had wanted to hide it away in his personal belongings. It had been Enginseer Osiron who'd advised him to affix it to the front of his combat helm.

'Others do not see it as you see it, Parmenion.' Osiron was one of the few members of the 88th to ever call Thade by his first name. 'To you it's something painful you fear you'll never live up to. To others, it's a symbol that even in defeat, their *first* defeat, heroism still thrives. It offers not just hope, but the hope for vengeance.'

Vengeance. That was an ideal every soldier in the Cadian Shock could cling to, as the Thirteenth Black Crusade raged. Thade nodded.

'I guess they had to hand one out to someone,' Thade had said, turning the silver skull-and-gate medal over in his newly-implanted bionic hand. The implant was so fresh it didn't even have synthetic skin grafted over it yet.

'You earned it,' Osiron breathed in his hissing way. 'We all saw you earn it.'

Thade said nothing to that. His gaze spoke volumes.

He lowered his hands at the Overseer's nod, dispersing his memories and returning all attention to the present. Lord General Maggrig's tent was erected in the shadow of the Hadris Rift bulk lander *Unity*. The tent itself was a cube of leather-reinforced cloth, useful for keeping the wind out and the sound of voices in. Expensive chairs of pale oak ringed a circular table made from the same wood. Maps were spread across the table, as were several data-slates and pict-viewers evidently left over from the last meeting. The lord general was alone. That fact surprised Thade, leaving him on edge. He couldn't think why Overseer Maggrig would need privacy to conduct a debriefing.

'At ease, warden-captain,' the lord general said in his usual clipped tones. Maggrig was the only man Thade had met who could make one of Cadia's highest military honour titles sound like he was swallowing something that tasted foul. *Warden-captain*, he said. To rhyme with *bastard*.

'Just "captain" is fine,' Thade said, and not for the first time. If he had to hear the title he hadn't gotten used to, he'd rather not hear it mangled. 'I've come to make my report, sir.'

'Then do it, soldier. But first, who are these men and why are they here?'

Thade gestured left, then right. 'Honoured Engin-seer Bylam Osiron. Scout-Lieutenant Adar Vertain. They stand with me to bear witness and make their own reports. I assumed the lord general would pre-fer first-hand accounts of what happened the night Reclamation forces sighted primary-class threats.'

'Of course. Proceed.' Maggrig offered a magnani-mous wave of a thin, vein-marked hand that sported three large rings. Thade caught himself wondering if those hands had held a lasgun once in the last forty years. What kind of soldier wore rings like that, anyway? Thade and Osiron shared a momentary glance, thinking the same thoughts. The rocks on the Overseer's knuckles could bring in enough coin to keep the 88th refuelled for a month.

Jewellery was another ostentation Cadians had little love for. When every scrap of metal on your home world went to the forge factories to be made into weaponry and almost all personal wealth was tied into military gear and property, displaying one's wealth in flamboyant displays seemed waste-ful and decadent. It was often said of the Cadians that they as a people had no eye for beauty.

Thade had no idea if that was true or not. He found beauty in many things: alien landscapes, the weather patterns in the heavens of other worlds,

slender women with dark hair… But self-awareness
was one of his strengths. He knew he had no capacity to understand what was supposed to be
attractive about wearing one's wealth in such a
pointless display.

'I'm waiting, captain.'

Throne, what a pompous ass. Thade drew breath
to reply.

'My Sentinel squadron first intercepted suspi-
cious vox-chatter as they scouted ahead to plot a
course to the monastery held by the Janus 6th.'

'You LOST OUR beachhead within the city.'

Once Thade had finished speaking, the lord general's appraisal was blunt and – at least technically
– correct.

'My orders were to reinforce the Janus 6th at
dawn and hold the monastery if we could. The
Janusians were annihilated before we arrived,
despite my men making for the monastery in the
middle of the night.' Thade narrowed his eyes, feeling his muscles tense. He didn't mention the idiotic
vainglory that sent the Janus 6th so far ahead of the
main force. The lord general's pursed lips twisted
into a thin frown.

'Your orders, warden-captain, were to hold the
Reclamation's most promising incursion point into
Solthane. You lost our forward base.'

'The Janus 6th lost it when they were slaughtered.'

'You were present after that event.'

Osiron shook his head slightly, setting his crimson hood rustling in a soft hiss of silken material. It wasn't a disagreement with the lord general; it was a warning to Thade not to lose his temper.

'With the greatest respect, Overseer,' Thade met the older man's gaze, 'I am Cadian Shock. We don't forget our orders. My men were to reinforce the monastery *if such a defence was viable.*'

'It was viable. You said so yourself.'

Thade detested this petty conversational thrusting and parrying. It wasn't in his blood to argue with an officer like this, but then again, he wasn't used to serving under such a pathetic excuse for a lord general.

No, that wasn't quite true. Maggrig wasn't pathetic. This was what Osiron was warning against. Don't disrespect the lord general purely for his variant approach to command. In arrogance, lay self-deception. Now focus.

Yet he wasn't going to allow his men to take a mark of cowardice on their records just because the lord general needed someone to blame for overextending his forces.

'Not at all, lord general. I said quite clearly the only way my available forces could have remained in the Shrine of the Emperor's Undying Majesty would be if they sealed themselves in the undercroft network and awaited reinforcement.'

'That would be holding, Thade.'

'Hardly, sir,' the captain laughed. It instantly set the lord general's glare aflame.

'Explain yourself.'

'It would be a few survivors languishing in the dark and voxing for rescue.'

'I had requested aid from Cadia in the belief its units were valorous. You disappoint me, warden-captain.'

The three Cadians fell silent. Vertain swallowed, clenching his teeth to prevent saying something he'd be executed for. Even Osiron's mechanical breathing slowed and quieted. Thade leaned on the table, knuckles down, and faced the ageing general.

'I will follow my orders to the best of my ability at all times. If the lord general of the Reclamation deems it necessary to send a fraction of my regiment into an engagement that the assigned campaign tacticians argued against, then so be it. If the lord general appoints a mechanised infantry company to lock itself within a siege situation, then I'll do all I can to make sure those orders are carried out. But I've been fighting the Archenemy since my recruitment into the Cadian Youth legion at fourteen years of age. Every single man in a Cadian uniform was raised to assemble and fire a standard-issue lasgun before he could read and write. If the 88th falls back, it's because in the considered opinion of every veteran officer among our number, we had to fall back.'

'I see,' the lord general said simply. It was almost a sneer.

'I confirmed the Janusians were dead – just as I'd said they would be when their initial assault was planned. My Sentinels have remapped over half of the eastern district, updating the data readouts with post-plague geographical analysis. I've confirmed the presence of the XIV Traitor Legion.'

At this point, Thade gestured with a bloodstained glove to the pict slate he'd placed on the table. Its surface display was still auto-cycling through images of the Death Guard Astartes confronted by Thade's squad. The final three picts showed the hulking creature dead, its armour blackened from las-fire and cracked open from bolt rounds. Maggots and black organic filth had spilled from the wounds.

'And my men killed several hundred Remnant as we fell back from the monastery,' Thade finished.

'They came for the vehicles,' Osiron's snake voice hissed mechanically. 'They struck in a horde of plague-slain as we readied to draw back.'

'We killed another three Death Guard as we fought off the Remnant and made ready to withdraw,' Vertain added. 'Confirmed kills, verified by the gun cameras of Dead Man's Hand.'

'By… what?' asked Maggrig.

'Sentinel Squadron C-Eighty-Eight Alpha,' Thade said. Vertain made an apologetic salute to the general. He'd not meant to fall into regimental slang.

Overseer Maggrig leaned back in his arch-backed wooden chair, gazing around the empty command tent with its unrolled maps hanging from the walls and his ornamental weapons on racks. His eyes fell upon Thade's chainsword. The captain had cleaned most of the filth from it on the drive back to base, but he was keen to tend to it properly. The weapon's spirit would balk at such disrespect soon.

'That is a beautiful sword, warden-captain.'

Thade inclined his head slightly in a look that could've said 'thank you' as easily as it said 'what in the hells are you talking about?' Ultimately, his voice went with the former.

'My thanks, lord general.'

'Where did you acquire it? You may have noticed I'm something of a collector.'

Thade had noticed. For all his faults, the lord general had a wonderful collection of blades and pistols. The captain doubted they'd been used even once by Maggrig personally, but what surprised him was the fact each piece of the displayed collection was an admirable and apparently fully-functional weapon. No one blade stood out as purely decorative. Not one pistol did Thade recognise as ornamental. They were tools of war, from the plainest sector standard Kantrael-forged bolt pistol similar to Thade's own, to the double-edged power sabre fit for a hive noble on Thracian Prime.

This one aspect of the lord general was the only facet Thade warmed to in his commander's personality. Of course, the Cadians had been joking for weeks the only way Maggrig could have acquired real weapons was to pilfer them from the corpses of men his orders had killed. But Thade doubted bringing up that little joke would crack a smile across the general's wizened features.

'I'd noticed, sir. Your collection is impressive.'

'And your blade, warden-captain?'

'It was a gift, lord general.'

'Of course, but from whom? Dispense with the modesty. It doesn't suit one with such silver on his helm.'

Was this the lord general's attempt at bonding with one of his men? Or just a deflection? Was this a friendly divergence from the conversation, knowing that Thade had been in the right? A clumsy attempt, if it was, but the captain was wrong-footed for a moment. The Overseer's voice remained pinched between a clipped reprimand and a sneer, but the captain had quickly grown used to that.

'It was a gift from Lord Castellan Creed.'

'Ah,' Maggrig smiled a honey-laden smirk. Apparently Thade's answer clarified something in his mind, though the captain couldn't guess what. 'In recognition for your brave efforts during the days before your world fell to the Archenemy.'

The Cadians stiffened for the second time. Vertain drew breath to speak but Thade cut him off with a brisk wave.

'Dismissed, lieutenant,' the captain said.

Chafing, almost shaking in anger, the Sentinel pilot made the sign of the aquila and stalked from the tent.

'Home has not *fallen*, lord general.' Thade's voice was measured and precise. 'We fight on, even now.'

Maggrig did so love to see the much-vaunted Cadian pride take a bruising. Superior bastards, every one of them.

'I've seen the reports, warden-captain. Months into this new crusade, and over half the planet still in the grip of the Despoiler's forces. A shame, truly. Rather an important world to lose like that.'

Thade's reply was long in coming. He took several breaths in silence, pointedly moved his hands away from his weapon belt, picked up the data-slate he'd brought in with him, and handed it to Osiron.

Cadian blood, he kept thinking. Ice in your veins.

'Am I dismissed, sir?' he asked after almost a minute had passed.

'No.'

Thade stood impassively. 'As you wish. Is there more you want to know?'

'No. But two points remain.'

'I'm listening,' said Thade. 'Sir.'

'Firstly, you're aware your questionable actions have earned my displeasure tonight.'

'I'm aware the lord general would have liked matters to have proceeded differently.'

'Exactly so. With that in mind… Tell me, the 88th makes use of a sanctioned psyker, does it not?'

'I fail to see what that has to do with the situation.'

'Answer me, warden-captain.'

'Seth Roscrain, ident number C-Eighty-Eight X-zero-one. Awarded the Blood Star at Jago III for wounds taken in an act of self-sacrifice.'

'Yes. Seth, that's the one. Am I to understand the 88th currently lacks commissarial support to deal with a sanctioned psyker?'

Thade smiled his crooked grin. He saw where this was going. 'I can recite the Cadian code of law that allows any officer above the rank of lieutenant to take additional training with regards to being qualified to deal with, and execute if necessary, a sanctioned psyker. I have that training, as does every lieutenant in my command.'

'All the same, this is my Reclamation and I will take no chances by relying on some Cadian loophole. You are to be appointed a commissar immediately.'

Thade watched the old man, his violet eyes narrowed. What game was he playing?

'The 88th hasn't had a commissar in over seventeen years.'

'I deem it necessary now.' The lord general thumped a wad of printed papers on the table. 'One day you charge into battle when it would be more prudent to fall back. Then the next you run when you have orders to hold. Thade, Thade, Thade… You're unreliable. It says as much in these reports. What are you trying to prove, boy? Trying to live up to that medal, eh? No, this is the right choice. It will put some steel in your spine.'

Thade could happily have lopped the old bastard's head clean from his shoulders at that moment. Instead, he forced himself to nod. The simple motion was one of the hardest things he'd ever had to do.

'Ha! I see that nod cost you. I see it in your eyes. "Cadian blood, no blood more precious." I know how you think, Thade. I know how all you Shock boys think. Let me tell you, warden-captain. We're all equal in my task force. So you'll take this commissarial appointment and you'll smile. Understood?'

Thade made the sign of the aquila again. 'And your second point, sir?'

The order to subject his regiment to a commissar's appointment had more than just surprised Thade: it had been the last thing he'd seen coming. That's why Lord General Maggrig's next matter rocked him to his core.

'Against my better judgement, your unit has been requested for a specific duty.'

Thade raised an eyebrow. 'Oh?'

'Yes, warden-captain. As of this moment, the 88th is seconded to His Imperial Majesty's Holy Inquisition.'

CHAPTER V
The Ordo Sepulturum

Aboard the Inquisitorial vessel,
The Night Star

INQUISITOR BASTIAN CAIUS was one hundred and nineteen years old. Behind his eyes simmered a thousand unspoken secrets. Sometimes he would muse upon his role: a life spent in devotion to finding truth in the darkness, learning of creatures and heresies that the overwhelming majority of the great and glorious Imperium would never see. Three quarters of his life had been spent seeing and hearing things that, to the overwhelming majority of mankind, didn't exist.

While Caius was over a hundred, he looked thirty. Juvenat processes were the privilege of the

Imperium's wealthiest and most valuable servants, and the inquisitor considered himself a member of both categories. He bore more than his fair share of scars, but that was to be expected given his interrogator years had been spent apprenticed to Inquisitor Shyva Kresskien. That old hag, may her bones rest in the Emperor's light, had always demanded the fiercest faith and fervour from her interrogator pupils. The list of her accomplishments was long indeed – one of the Ordo Xenos Scarus's lengthiest rolls of honour, as it happened – but so was the scroll listing interrogators and agents slain in her service. The few men and women that survived her demanding apprenticeships were rightly counted among the most capable inquisitors in the sector.

Caius himself had almost died in his former mistress's service on several occasions. His lips were split by a permanent scar near the right edge of his mouth, taken when a heretic had come too close with a knife. His left leg from the knee down was a bionic claw, his shin wreathed in thick metal and the foot itself a four-toed talon resembling a Sentinel walker's thudding limb.

The most obvious modification was his eye. Caius's left eye was an ugly augmetic, a blood-red lens fixed in a steel focusing ring surgically grafted to his face in a restructured eye socket of chrome. The implant had been costly (for the old crone always rewarded her worthy apprentices as befitted their dutiful service) but as with many bionics, the mechanical eye was all business and no artistry. The lens could detect the most subtle movement in its field of vision, even a man's breathing, and relay it instantly to Caius's shoulder-mounted psycannon, forming a fast and flawless targeting system. A further enhancement took the form of an attached aura-scrye scanner, forming a secondary red lens eye projecting from a bronze and steel implant attached to the inquisitor's temple. With his sight linked between these two false eyes and his natural vision, Caius could literally see psychic emissions, translated into his second lens as an angry heat-flare surrounding the psyker responsible.

Inquisitor Caius didn't care in the slightest that the left side of his face from temple to jaw line was a mess of expensive chrome and steel. He hadn't given any true regard to his appearance in decades. He'd seen too many others scarred in his former mistress's service to delude himself that his Inquisitorial duties would leave him attractive in any way. Caius was, in all things, something of a realist.

He was also one of the few who had known shrineworld Kathur would fall. That galled him even now, weeks later, not because his warnings had gone unheeded – indeed, they had been heeded well, the response to his warnings had been as impressive as they were ruthless – but because the pupils of Inquisitor Kresskien were simply not used to failure.

He waited now aboard his ship, *The Night Star*, sipping full-bodied vintage amasec and staring into the amber liquid's depths, enjoying this opportunity to swim in memory. As Caius waited for Captain Thade, he mused on the moment he'd learned Kathur's particular truth. The truth from the lips of a heretic. Such delicious irony. This had been months ago, in the weeks before the planet died.

The heretic had screamed, of course. They always did.

The traitor was incarcerated in the Kelmarl asteroid prison complex: a vermin-infested hole for some of Scarus Sector's more wretched criminals, all of whom were deemed unfit for immediate execution by Imperial authorities and sentenced to lives of slave labour. Petty thieves whose lawyers had allowed them to escape local mutilation laws were slammed into squalid communal cells alongside small-time embezzlers and underhive gangers who avoided death sentences by ratting out their friends. Life in the Kelmarl complex was an endless cycle of short sleep allowances and long shifts in pressure suits mining within the asteroid's tunnel network.

The heretic undergoing interrogation had been locked up for weapons smuggling, selling weaponry bound for Imperial Guard regiments to bidding mercenary outfits in the pay of local governors. It seemed a textbook case to Kelmarl's warden, and he had had the smuggler working his life away in the mines, breaking his back for the good of the Imperium. The Inquisition had arrived without warning, a single ship carrying a lone inquisitor and his small team, demanding to speak with an apparently minor criminal.

The heretic had been quite a screamer.

Caius swallowed a mouthful of the agonisingly expensive amsec, not enjoying the rich taste. The musing recollection turned sour. Even the memory of the moment annoyed him, as he'd faced the heretic at the end of days of torture.

That screaming…

…WAS RELENTLESS.

Inquisitor Caius ignored the sound, frowning at the blood on the floor. If this carried on much longer, he was going to have difficulty walking in the room. With a sigh and a brief wave of his gloved hand, the inquisitor stopped the torture. It was boring and unproductive, and Caius was not a patient man.

The solitary confinement cell was a box of a room with a red-streaked table as the only furniture. Pentagrammic sigils blazed on the grey floor, etched into the stone some hours before, each indented symbol filled with trickles of blessed water. The watery letters vibrated every time the heretic thrashed against the bonds that leashed him to the table.

'Enough,' said the inquisitor. His was a commanding voice, as one might expect from a man of his vocation, yet it carried with it an unnatural edge of roughness. The source of Caius's vocal harshness was as clear as a second smile: a jagged scar across his throat told of an old injury and semi-successful reconstructive surgery. This too was earned in his interrogator days under Kresskien.

The torturer stopped his work and stepped back from the surgery table, yet the man strapped there still screamed, his cries mixing with gasping breaths surging in and out of what was left of his face. Caius waited as the yells sank down into moans, then faded further into desperate, animalistic panting. He resisted the urge to look at his timepiece. The gold pocket watch rested comfortably in the pouch by his left holster. It had been a gift from his former mistress. A deathbed gift, in fact.

He had performed the rituals of purification and repentance only a few times alone, but had assisted many times at the side of the old woman that had trained him. Caius knew what he was doing.

'Jareth.' The inquisitor's voice was now that of a fine teacher or a gifted storyteller: engaging, considerate, emotional. It was almost impossible to tell his throat had been shredded by a xenos projectile weapon seventeen years before. 'Heretic, I grow bored of this. I am running out of patience, and you are running out of blood. We've come to the endgame. It's over now. Tell me what I want to know and I'll see you dead before your heart beats out another painful thump. Is that not what you desire? Fast passage away from this agony?'

Jareth's reply – after three mumbled attempts at speech – was a short insult in Cadian vernacular. Caius was too far away, so the heretic spat at the torturer. The effort resulted in nothing more than a gooey string of bloody saliva crawling down the heretic's own chin.

Now Caius checked his timepiece. He was getting hungry, and the prison warden's table had been surprisingly well-set with delicacies for the duration of the inquisitor's stay. Maybe another ten minutes.

Caius cleared his throat. The old damage to his neck made it sound like a dangerous purr, which reached the torturer's senses. The torturer in question was a servitor mono-tasked to serve in the role, and various small blades, bone saws, drill bits and flesh-peeling hooks deployed from its mechanical arms as it registered the inquisitor's displeased growl. Another gesture from Caius had the servitor backing down. He'd tried the scourging. Now it was time to offer mercy. No interrogation of lowlife detritus like Jareth, a mere cultist, should last this long. It was getting beyond the realm of being remotely amusing.

'Jareth, listen to me.' The inquisitor leaned close to the table now, gritting his teeth momentarily against the reek of disease lifting from the mutilated Chaos worshipper's open wounds. 'I know you sold those weapons to tainted men. You will die for that. But you suffer for no cause, enduring agony for no reason. In whoring your soul to the Ruinous Powers, you have ensured your death will be no release from pain. Unless you recant now. Unless you recant, pray for forgiveness, while there is breath left in your body.'

Freed of fresh torment for almost a minute, the heretic strained against the bonds securing his limbs to the bloodstained table. His only reply, if indeed it was supposed to be one, emerged as a slurred moan of effort.

'Jareth,' Caius narrowed his eyes. The cadence of his storyteller's voice altered, slowed, dropped a touch. He sounded like a spiteful parent telling a child that the monsters under his bed were all too real. 'Jareth, I am offering you salvation. I have stood in this room for three days, forcing myself to breathe in the stench of your lies and listening to you howl. Again and again you rave in the name of daemons. Those false gods are coming to eat your soul. I offer *hope.*'

As if on cue, the heretic launched into another shrieking tirade, calling upon unholy names that made the inquisitor's mind ache. Caius silenced the blasphemy with a nod to the torturer servitor. Drills whined as they came alive, made mushy sounds as they forcefully entered flesh, and protested noisily against the resistance of bone. Caius breathed easier. Even screaming was better than ranting to the gods of the warp.

When the noise subsided, Caius put away his pocket watch and tried again.

'Jareth, tell me what I wish to know and I will kill you now in the Emperor's grace. He will protect you. Or continue this performance, if you wish. I will seal you in this cell with my servitor, after programming it to skin you alive. When you finally die in several days' time, your soul will fall into the maws of the Chaos-things that await you.'

The heretic drew breath to speak, but convulsed in fevered thrashings, blood and spit spraying from his ruined lips. Several flecks spattered on the servitor's face, which it ignored completely.

'Every moment of pain is a prayer!' he cried.

'Is that so?' Caius kept his hand away from his holster. The effort it took was supreme.

'I am beloved of the Ruinous Powers!'

'You are a heretic strapped to a table, moments from death.'

'I suffer to prove myself worthy!'

'Then you learn now how it was all wasted effort.' Caius tilted his head slightly – a predator studying wounded prey. The psycannon mounted on his solid bronze shoulder pad whirred as it primed, building up power and auto-racking a bolt. As with the servitor, it responded to the inquisitor's darkening mood, and as with the servitor, Caius willed the weapon into calmness.

He watched Jareth with his dual sight: his natural eye seeing the bleeding, dying man, his red-washed false sight seeing the beginnings of a sickening blue corona dawning around the heretic's face.

Psychic energy. *Powerful* psychic energy.

In the weeks to come, when Bastian Caius looked back upon the events that transpired here, he would recognise this moment as the second when everything slipped out of his control. To his dying day, he felt sick just recalling what followed.

The heretic's head snapped round to stare Caius full in the face. Red tears ran in erratic trails down Jareth's lacerated cheeks.

Is he crying blood? Caius wondered, through the intensifying thunder of his own heart.

This was new.

And this was not good.

The inquisitor was about to speak when the dozens of pentagrammic wards acid-etched into the walls of the cell – which had taken an Ecclesiarchy priest over a week to complete in astonishing detail – flared with a dull light. Then they, too, started bleeding.

Yes. This was definitely not good.

For days, the room had reeked: a dank and obscenely biological smell. Now it soured further, the choking air turning thick with the taste of rancid copper. Caius rested a trembling hand on the aquila-shaped solid gold pommel of his sheathed and deactivated power sword.

'Inquisitor Caius.' The voice was a growl: an inhuman snarl from a human throat. Something ancient and deeply amused now spoke through Jareth's lips.

Oh, Throne of the God-Emperor. Possession…

As if hearing the inquisitor's thoughts, the entity wearing Jareth's body cried out a sound as primal and inhuman as a great tide roaring in. It drowned out the building whine of Caius's psycannon, and the hiss of the inquisitor's power sword as it was torn from its scabbard, yet not ignited.

Somewhere in the back of the wrath-driven howl, like an accompanying chorus, Caius heard Jareth – the real Jareth – sobbing. The sound made Caius's skin crawl, pressing into his mind like a cold slug slipping through his eardrum. The sense of something else within the room, something palpable but unseen, turned Caius's tongue thick in his mouth. His false eyes focused and refocused, trying to perceive the hateful blue miasma surrounding the heretic, burning brightest from his eyes, lighting his skull from within.

Caius's psychic strength saved him from a much worse fate. Unholiness battered against his skull, a wave of emotional malice projected with psychic force. The inquisitor sagged, but stood resolute. Unprotected from warp emanations, the torturer servitor shuddered as if shot in the head. Its left eye popped in a small welter of yellowing jelly and red juice.

Caius chanted creeds of admonition and exorcism, yet the words caught in his mind, snagging half-forgotten between his thoughts and lips. The massing hate, thick as fog in the air, spoke volumes. This was so much more than some mere warp-beast.

Daemon…

The ragged form which had once been Jareth Kurr, chief factory overseer of Kantrael's Gamma-19 Forge district, squirmed on the gurney, graceless yet perversely fluid in his motions. The petty heretic had pissed his soul away in sacrifice to a being far more powerful than Caius had predicted. The inquisitor's muscles seized at the heretic's laughter, spasming painfully. He couldn't raise his blade to strike the daemon down where it lay. He couldn't even take a step closer to the damn thing. The creature's howling merriment in Caius's mind fired his nerve synapses, rendering him unable to control his own body.

Detecting the inquisitor's panic through synapse-links, the psycannon mounted on his shoulder made a series of minor targeting adjustments. It pointed directly at the wash of blue energy invisible to mortal eyes, its ammunition feeds primed and the chime of readiness ringing in the inquisitor's mind like an alarm.

But it didn't fire. It *wouldn't* fire. His mind couldn't order it to – the daemon's psychic presence made sure of that.

'Kill it!' the inquisitor cried to the attendant servitor. The mono-tasked torturer moved forward, flesh drills and bone saws buzzing, oblivious to its ruined eye leaking a trail of dark fluid down its cheek.

Caius saw, with painful clarity, the paradox playing out before his unblinking eyes. Jareth was a frail, stick-thin factory boss in his fifties who had spent his adult life in offices tallying figures of weapon shipments for the Imperial Guard. The thought of such a man being able to overpower an augmented Inquisitorial servitor was too ludicrous to contemplate. But it was no longer Jareth. Caius sensed the heretic, like a ghost or a shadow, outside his own flesh. The daemon-thing's theft of the body was almost complete.

The servitor flashed backwards, hurled through the air and meeting the wall with a wrenching snap of vertebrae. Caius didn't spare it a glance, though he saw its dying twitches in the corner of his eye.

Finally, the daemon spoke again.

'My master is the death of worlds. He is the death of Scarus. His name is lost to you, lost to your pitiful brethren. Ten thousand suns have died since it was last spoken by the lips of men. Once it was known to many, in the era when your corpse-god reached out to reclaim the stars. My master was there then, and he laughed at your Emperor. He laughed as your corpse-god wept, finding nothing more than a galaxy that despised him.'

With each word, Jareth seemed to calm down more and more, falling into a state of trembling inactivity. The room resonated with the unearthly echo of the daemon's words forced through human vocal chords.

'I will end you,' Caius said through clenched teeth. It was all he could do to speak through the muscle-lock. 'In the name of He who sits upon the Throne of Holy Terra, I will end you.'

The daemon turned its head and laughed, a rattlesnake sound, and vomited a stream of black blood. The bile washed over the prone servitor slumped against the wall, and though the slave ignored the treatment, its skin began to darken and blister as if washed in boiling water. The tender flesh where the servitor's metal augments met nerve-dead human skin started to bleed. Its numbed brain registered damage, though not pain, and it started to emit monotone moans as the acidic gush ravaged its biological body parts. Its whines lacked both expression and emotion. It was, after all, capable of neither.

'Ignorance,' the daemon hissed. Hearing its voice was like standing in a room thick with flies. Caius felt each word like the unpleasant tickling of insect legs on his skin. 'Such ignorance...'

After throwing up the blackness, the daemon seemed to wither. Caius gasped as his muscles unlocked, immediately launching into a chant of the Fourteenth Creed of Admonition and Banishment. The words came to his mind now with ease, flashing behind his eyes like quicksilver, each hymnal sentence a brutal chastisement of all warp entities that defiled the perfection of human flesh by possession.

He didn't stop to wonder why the daemon's strength was eroding. For the moment, he didn't care. It didn't matter.

Jareth hissed through his teeth, letting out a terrible buzz as if someone had kicked a wasp nest into a snake pit. His flesh deflated, collapsing in on itself, and the air turned dense with the metallic scent of blood. 'This is nothing! It means nothing! On the saint's world it is fated! My master awakens! He will defile your holy world! Do you hear his cry echoing across the warp? He calls to many of us, across the stars… those with the senses to hear his cries… the diseased, the dying, the sickened… I will serve at his side! I will–'

'You will die.'

The buzzing ceased instantly as the shoulder-mounted psycannon barked once. The only sounds in the room were the echo of the gunshot and the final breath rasping from Jareth's exploded windpipe. The bolt shell, personally inscribed with litanies of purity by Caius himself, had taken the heretic in the chest and detonated in his lungs. Caius wiped flecks of blood from his cheek, noting with a grimace how the wetness stung his flesh. Toxicology tests would need to be done on Jareth's blood samples.

A final word rang in his ears as the aftermath of the gunshot faded. Caius would never know if it came from the air or Jareth's last breath.

'*Kathur.*'

He hefted his sword in hands that no longer shook, thumbing the activation rune on the hilt to wreathe the blade in crackling energy. Caius remained in the room only long enough to destroy the dying servitor with a precise beheading. Even if it could be saved, the thing was surely wretched with taint after such an assault.

After that was done, the inquisitor left without looking back at the mess that had once been Jareth. Outside the solitary confinement cell, the prison warden stood with a squad of guards. They had been waiting some time, and fairly reeked of fear. The grunts did, at least. The warden did not.

'Is all well, inquisitor?' the warden asked. He was an aged man, appointed from the Cadian Shock some years before. Where others in his position might be fearful of His Divine Majesty's Holy Inquisition, the warden was confident and strong-willed, taking an active hand in the running of his prison complex. It pleased him to serve the Emperor now, no matter how unpleasant the duty. No matter how unpleasant and cold the Inquisition's own men were to deal with. Caius had not made a warm impression on the prison warden.

'Burn the remains,' Caius said. 'Then seal the room. You will be contacted by the Ordo Scarus Inquisition when you are allowed to use the cell again. It may be several decades.' He took a deep breath and met the warden's eyes. 'It may be never.'

The warden nodded and gestured to one of his men carrying a flamer in readiness for this very order. 'Let me do it,' he said.

Caius walked away, leaving them to their work. There was research to be done, and a journey to prepare for.

The saint's world, the daemon had said. A shrineworld in Scarus Sector.

Caius sent warnings to the Ordo Scarus Inquisition, but on the shrineworld's surface, it had already begun. The warnings came too late; the psychic pleas for help reached out only hours after Caius's warnings reached his superiors' ears.

Caius was still in the empyrean, en route to Kathur, when the plague struck in full.

And that was how he failed. All because he reached that accursed heretic a week too late.

THE MINUTES TICKED by. Caius watched his pocket-watch, each tick of the second hand eroding his patience a little more. The captain's meeting with the lord general was evidently taking some time.

Caius looked to the other two men in the room, Colonel Lockwood and Major Crayce, both upright and at attention, both clad in the same winter grey fatigues and black body armour as every other soldier in the 88th. Their rank markings stood out in polished silver on their right shoulder pads and the front of their visorless helms.

Finally, the door into Caius's tactical chamber opened. This was the biggest room on his personal gunship – powered down not far from the Cadian tents – and the inquisitor used it for briefing his team and receiving visitors. Captain Thade walked in, making the sign of the aquila to his superior regimental officers, then repeating the gesture for Caius.

'You are late, captain,' said Caius, returning the Imperial salute.

'I am. I apologise, inquisitor.'

'No excuse?'

'No excuse. As I said, I apologise, and I am here now.'

Caius smiled. He liked that answer. 'I have spoken to Colonel Lockwood and Major Crayce, here.

And I have spoken to the lord general. I trust you have been informed of the results of those discussions?'

Thade nodded. 'My command, a full one-third of the regiment, is to be seconded to you, to use as you see fit in your duties to the Throne.'

'Quite so, quite so.' Caius returned his timepiece to his jacket pocket. His false eyes focused on Thade with muted whirring sounds. He dismissed the bio-scan readings that flashed up behind his retinas. Thade was healthy. Nothing else of interest.

Colonel Lockwood, pushing fifty now and still as tenacious and fit as a soldier in his prime, watched the proceedings in respectful silence. He had a lot of time for Thade – the boy was a hero in his eyes, and brought great honour to the regiment with the silver that shone on his helmet. He offered the young captain a subtle nod of encouragement.

Major Crayce, his thin face exaggerated by his drooping moustache, remained firmly at attention, violet eyes fixed on Caius. Specifically, he watched the inquisitor's psycannon, intrigued as the thought-controlled weapon turned and pivoted with Caius's movements, mirroring every motion of his head.

'May I ask why, inquisitor?' Thade finally asked.

'Why what?'

'Why you've chosen me and my men out of all the Reclamation's forces.' He knew the answer even before asking the question, but Thade had to be sure. Lockwood smiled. Crayce didn't break attention. Caius remained seated, and without a shadow of a smile he tapped the centre of his own forehead, touching his fingers to his skin in the place where Thade's silver shone on his own helm.

'I imagine it's easy to guess why. Now, gentlemen, the captain and I have much to discuss. I thank you for your time.'

Lockwood and Crayce saluted and left, the former with another nod to Thade, the latter with barely a glance. The door closed behind them, and Thade looked back at the inquisitor.

'Tell me, captain,' Caius said, 'what do you know of the Ordo Sepulturum?'

'WHAT IN THE Great Eye is the Ordo Sepulturum?'

Ban Jevrian lay back on his bedroll and looked up at the dark roof of the communal tent. The room smelled like what it was: a makeshift dorm for thirty dirty, sweating Guardsmen.

Taan Darrick sat on the cot next to him, which just like the others was an uncomfortable affair of squealing springs and thin blankets. The lieutenant murmured litanies of devotion and apology as he dismantled his beaten lasrifle for cleaning.

'Give me a moment,' he said between verses. All Cadians were meticulous about the maintenance of their weaponry, but Taan made cleaning into an art. It was all very ritualistic. Each dismantled piece rested on a small scrap of paper scrawled with prayers in the lieutenant's own messy handwriting.

There each metal fragment of the rifle sat until it was cleaned, whereupon it would be washed, polished and re-blessed with whispered prayers of accuracy imploring to the machine-spirit within. Finally Taan would reassemble the rifle while speaking the Cadian variant of the Litany of Completion.

'Spirit of the machine, know I honour you. In my hands you are complete, and all I ask is that you fire true.'

'Does your rifle ever talk back to you?' Jevrian asked. He was as diligent as any soldier in maintaining his overcharged weapons – even more so, due to the innate instability of hellgun-class armaments – but Darrick made one hell of a performance in his dutiful maintenance.

Taan finished his work and left the gun resting loaded by his bed.

'She sings every time I pull the trigger. Now what were you saying?'

'The captain is meeting with the Ordo Sepulturum.'

'So?'

'So what *is* the Ordo Sepulturum?'

'How should I know? Inquisition is Inquisition. A lot of locked doors and secrets I don't want to learn.'

Jevrian raised an eyebrow. Because of his stern, granite-hard face, it was like part of a mountain moving. 'Those who make war without knowledge invite defeat through ignorance.'

Taan laughed. 'That's officer material. A ranker like you should know better than to quote senior officer inspirational texts, master sergeant.'

'I like to read. Might make captain one day.' Jevrian was dead serious, but Taan still grinned.

'Read a little more, then. "Duty is trust. Our duty is not to question and seek answers to moments in life that escape our understanding. Our duty is the same as our mothers' and fathers' duties. To kill for the Emperor and die for His throne. We die in the trust that our sacrifice allows others to live on, doing that same duty. We're blind now. Blind and lost. But die doing your duty and trust our brothers and sisters as generations before us have trusted theirs". You recognise that one?'

'I was there, Darrick. I remember when the captain said that.'

'Actually, that's our very own Colonel Lockwood. He's got some footnotes in the latest edition of *The Valorous Path.*'

Jevrian raised his eyebrow for the second time in the same hour. This was about the most expressive he'd been since Cadia had been invaded, and even when the skies of Home had burned, all he'd said in reaction was to mutter 'Going to be a busy week…'

But then, learning one of your own regiment was in the Cadian officer-only version of the *Imperial Infantryman's Uplifting Primer* was definitely not small news.

'Just a few footnotes,' Taan said again. 'Lockwood transcribed Thade's speech at Kasr Vallock, citing the captain as the embodiment of the values of Cadian officerhood.'

Jevrian was silent. He remembered that speech, that moment, as the shells howled all around and Thade committed the 88th to the field in open battle to… well, Jevrian hated to think about it. But it was hard to forget. That damned Titan. Throne, that had taken some killing.

'I bet Thade is furious about that.' Jevrian knew Thade well, and besides, the captain's loathing of his men making a big deal out of his medal was well-established.

'Rax is functioning again. That'll cheer him up.'

'Sure, but he'd never give his permission to be quoted.'

'Lockwood's a colonel. He didn't need permission. And you know how much the old man loves Thade. He fought this commissar business tooth and nail.'

Jevrian's gaze met Taan's. Word spread around camp fast, but apparently it hadn't reached the Kasrkin squad yet. 'What commissar business?'

'Ah,' said Taan. 'That.'

CHAPTER VI
First Blood

Reclamation Headquarters, outside Solthane

COMMISSAR TIONENJI WAS waiting for Thade.

As the captain left the inquisitor's gunship, the commissar stood at the bottom of the gang-ramp leading from the vessel's small internal hangar, his hands loosely clasped behind his back, and his black leather stormcoat flapping in the breeze kicked up by a Valkyrie taking off a short distance away.

He made the sign of the aquila as Thade neared, which the captain returned in kind. Thade hid his expression of annoyance. He'd been hoping to check in on Rax, but that was going to have to wait… again.

This is what people see when they look at Commissar Adjatay Tionenji: a tall man, his dark skin showing his heritage stretching back to one of the Imperium's countless jungle worlds. He was broad-shouldered, but his frame was slender, sculpted and kept that way by the rigours of constant exercise. His hair was also dark, scraped back from his unkind features and scented with expensive pomade, all under a standard red-trimmed black commissar's cap. His ankle-length jacket was left unbuttoned, revealing his black uniform and a weapon belt with a holstered plasma pistol and a sheathed chainsword – this last forged into an unusually thin, curved shape.

Thade took all of this in before he even made the sign of the aquila, but none of these observations were the first things he noticed. The very first thought that crossed Thade's mind was the instinctive and natural reaction bred into him from birth and through decades of training.

He's not Cadian.

He grinned at the lord general's implied insult, appointing an off-worlder to the 88th. He lowered his hands as he finished the Imperial salute.

'Why do you smile, warden-captain?'

Thade wasn't much for lying. 'Because your eyes aren't violet.'

'Should they be?' Tionenji's voice was soft and measured, but Thade could already discern the edge of strength that would no doubt show in full when the commissar shouted in battle. It was a mellifluous voice, his tone gentle and honeyed with only a hint of accusation at the captain's words.

'It's a tradition from my home world,' Thade said, certain the commissar knew that anyway. 'Shock regiments regard it as a point of honour to have Cadian-born commissars appointed to them.'

'Your world is a world of war, and such planets breed many orphans.' Tionenji referred to the commissarial custom of selecting its recruits from children who'd lost both parents in battle. He was still as rigid as if he stood on the parade ground. 'I imagine Cadia provides many candidates for the Schola Progenium, yes?'

Thade nodded, trying to make up his mind on how to judge the man. 'Your accent is Rukhian.'

Finally Tionenji smiled – a toothy grin that flashed across his handsome features and vanished so fast Thade wasn't sure he'd even seen it. 'Not quite, captain. My birth world was Garadesh, and that shares a similar culture with Rukh. Good guess, though. Why did you say Rukhian?'

'The way you elongate your vowels. We fought with the Rukh 9th seven years ago.'

'The Battle of Tyresius,' Tionenji said immediately.

'You've done your research.' Thade wasn't remotely surprised.

'I am a commissar,' Tionenji replied simply. Thade seemed to muse on something for a moment, then offered his left hand – his human hand – for the commissar to shake. He hoped the

Garadeshi wouldn't miss the significance of the act.

'Welcome to the Cadian 88th.'

The commissar hesitated just as the captain had, but accepted the awkward left-handed shake.

'It will be a pleasure to serve the Emperor along-side you, warden-captain.' Thade forced a smile. Tionenji caught the expression. 'I am given to understand Cadians are grudging and untrusting with their welcomes, and you are not adept at hid-ing your discomfort. I am correct, yes?'

Thade chuckled despite himself. 'Commissar, may we just establish one thing at the beginning of our association?'

'Name it. I shall give your wishes all due consid-eration.'

'Don't call me "warden-captain".'

'Your own rank offends you?'

'Something like that.' Thade sought a quick change of subject. 'Have you been briefed regarding our... unusual assignment?'

'I have.' Again, Thade wasn't surprised at the honey-voiced answer.

'Have you served with this new ordo before?'

'I have not.' Tionenji and Thade talked as they walked back to the Cadian encampment, a small city of black and grey tents. 'The Inquisition's new divi-sion is something of a mystery to me. I am aware of their mandate to hunt and destroy the plague-slain, and seek the source of the Curse of Unbelief that has ravaged so much of our glorious sector in recent years.'

The two officers neared the Cadian base now, falling under the idle shadow of the massive bulk lander that formed the centrepiece of the camp. 'That's more or less my understanding,' Thade replied. 'Inquisitor Caius wants to make a sweep of the reliquaries in Solthane and seek the source of Kathur's outbreak.'

'Then so it shall be.' Tionenji nodded. That matched his briefings as well. Now he looked around the near-deserted camp, at the vista of silent tents and the occasional wandering servitor. 'By the Holy Throne, your camp is as silent as the city itself. Are all Shock outposts so quiet?'

Thade thought it was interesting that the commissar hadn't even served with Cadians before. Tionenji wasn't out of his twenties, and it was usually common for veteran commissars to be appointed to the Cadian Shock over younger officers. Again he found himself wondering at the lord general's reasoning behind the dark-skinned man's appointment.

'It's almost midnight, commissar.'

'The men sleep?'

Thade laughed, the sound unnaturally loud in the empty camp. As if on cue, the sounds of distant engines roared.

'No. They train.'

THE MASSED MIGHT of the Cadian 88th eclipsed Thade's mere three hundred men. Over a thousand soldiers were packed into a hundred and fifty

Chimeras and Sentinels, driving up a muddy storm as they manoeuvred across the grasslands the regiment had set aside for daily training. Thade's three hundred men joined Major Crayce's three hundred and Colonel Lockwood's four hundred for the midnight exercise.

Thade and Tionenji watched from a gentle rise that might generously be called a hill. Enginseer Osiron and Seth Roscrain were also present, both men's non-standard duties removing them from the need to train now. The *hfffff-hsssss* of Osiron's breathing was audible over the sound of the revving engines as dozens of Chimera transports powered alongside each other in a series of various formations, moving positions with ease and maintaining equal distance with each other at all times. The tech-priest listened to the roar of the engines, hearing only the voices of an angelic chorus. He was alert to every nuance in the symphony, every engine that whined too hard when its driver hesitated at a gear change, every cry of brakes that needed a touch more maintenance.

Seth leaned on his black staff, his eyes bloodshot and his lips cut where he'd bitten them during his earlier visions.

Osiron and Seth both made the sign of the aquila to the commissar and the captain as they approached. The commissar returned it earnestly, Thade did so with a nod of greeting. Seth's gaze lingered on the captain for a long moment, then flicked to Tionenji. He couldn't resist testing the new commissar. His unseen sense reached out, enveloping the dark-skinned man's invisible aura, probing the outer edges of Tionenji's thoughts.

Tionenji shuddered despite Seth's delicacy. *Ah, not just another blunt*, he thought, slipping into Guard slang for those without psychic talents. Seth withdrew his hidden sense, satisfied that the commissar would be extremely resistant to psychic manipulation.

Seth shuddered, his talents still open to the warp, and in that moment he could hear it again: the voice from the monastery. Something (*…beneath his feet… Something below…*) crying out from a great, unknowable distance. He heard it each time he used his powers now, and feared the onset of warp taint in his mind. With a glance at the commissar, Seth sealed his mind off from the world, relying on his five natural senses.

'Your drivers are skilled,' said Tionenji, watching the grasslands being chewed up into a morass of meaningless patterns. Hundreds of tank treads gouged across the muddy earth.

The commissar pointed to ten transports spread out in a V-formation, which promptly screeched to swerving halts in unison, forming a tight circle of armour with their fronts facing inward and rears out. Ten gangways slammed down into the ravaged mud and a hundred men ran from the vehicles, taking up positions with rifles raised.

'I know that formation,' Tionenji said.

Thade smiled at the perfect deployment, recognising Taan leading the hundred men there. He flicked a glance at the commissar. 'Is that so?'

'That is the Steel Star.' Tionenji's oak-brown eyes smiled even if his lips did not. 'Worthless in an urban battlefield, but extremely difficult to perform as precisely as I see it being done here. One might think you were showing off, captain.'

All three Cadians laughed, though only Thade's was a natural sound. Seth's laugh was a low, wet chuckle, Osiron's a mechanical wheeze. Thade shook his head.

'We call it Opening the Eye, but yes, it's the same manoeuvre. And in all honesty, commissar, we don't show off. Perfecting moves like this is one of the ways the 88th trains for formation deployment.' Thade inclined his head, gesturing across the field where ten Chimeras under Major Crayce's command repeated the move in an orchestra of grinding gears and roaring engines. Osiron closed his eyes, listening intently to the music only he could hear, making silent notes about which Chimeras to check over once the training was complete.

'Tonight is used for this deployment training, yes? No combat exercise?'

'Not tonight. The colonel deemed this necessary instead.'

'Ah, I see.' Tionenji nodded.

'You do?'

'I am not blind to your, forgive me, *our* regiment's expertise. The monastery fight must have tasted foul to many of the men, yes? There was little opportunity for the rapid deployment and tactical insertion the 88th excels at. And the colonel decided to allow the men to... relieve some stress. Am I correct?'

'You see clearly, commissar.'

Tionenji nodded, already looking back to the field. 'I try.'

Thade looked at the jungle-worlder for a moment. Tionenji was making an open effort to connect with him and show his willingness to bond with the regiment, which was not what the captain had been expecting in a commissar appointed by the lord general.

'I believe it's time you met the men,' Thade said. He was acutely aware of Seth's and Osiron's eyes on his back as he spoke to the commissar. Tionenji turned to the Cadian, regarding his violet eyes under the silver winged medal.

'I was going to wait until tomorrow morning for a formal presentation alongside the inquisitor's briefing. What did you have in mind, captain?'

Thade told him. Tionenji considered the ramifications for a moment, and eventually nodded.

'I agree to this contest. But tell me, why is it to first blood?'

'Cadian duels are always to first blood. If you strike true, first blood is all you need to make the kill. And if you don't strike true, you're not Cadian.'

'Your people are very arrogant,' Tionenji said without any real judgement. It was merely an observation.

'Cadian blood,' whispered Seth. 'The fuel of the Imperium.'

'We are the ones that die so all others might live,' said Osiron.

'That is a boast the men and women of many worlds can make, enginseer,' retorted Tionenji.

'Take one look where our home world is, commissar,' Thade said. 'Now take note that the Imperium still stands. We have every right to be arrogant.'

THE GRASSLAND PLAIN was silent but for the murmurs of men placing bets. Tionenji allowed them this, knowing it would be good for morale and seeing no need to begin his tenure with unnecessary confrontation. If the lord general was right in his assessment, the newly-appointed commissar would be making enemies aplenty soon enough. Once the executions began.

He liked Thade, he had to admit. The captain was honest, if not entirely open, and his record spoke of an accomplished officer, perhaps even a gifted one. Would he shoot Parmenion Thade dead without a second's hesitation if the need arose? Absolutely. Would he regret the deed afterwards? Maybe. It would certainly not sit well with the men of the 88th. Tionenji scanned the crowd now, already committing faces to memory. Pale skin, bright eyes of blue or violet... A fey breed, these Cadians.

Initially the gathering had been limited to Captain Thade's three hundred men, but as the news had sped across the vox – *'Thade's fighting the new commissar!'* – the entire regiment had parked up and formed into a wide ring around the captain and Tionenji. Men sat and kneeled on the ground, others stood behind, and still others stood atop their Chimeras, eager for a view of the action.

Seth had gripped Thade's wrist before the crowd had gathered.

'I need to speak with you, sir.'

'I won't let him shoot you, Seth.' Thade found it easy to relate to his brothers in the regiment, but something about Seth always unnerved any who spoke with him. His ragged appearance, the psy-feeds buried into the back of his skull, the way he looked as if he was drowning in his own too-large jacket, the sucking of air through his teeth to avoid drooling; it was all something of a wretched picture, but that wasn't the whole story. Seth's power set him apart. In a culture centred so closely around the tenets of unity and brotherhood, those who stood alone were doomed to be forever distrusted.

Seth had grinned at the captain's reassurance. The effect was ugly, revealing several shattered teeth, lost when his powers had raged out of control and almost snapped his neck some months before.

'I do not fear the new political officer, captain. I need to speak with you about the cards.'

'Tomorrow, Seth.'

'Parmenion.' Seth's frail grip tightened on the captain's bionic wrist. Thade quelled the rush of instinct that almost made him pull his bolt pistol.

The use of his name unnerved him along with the grip and the sincerity in the sanctioned psyker's voice.

'What is it?'

'Tomorrow is fine. But this *is* important. For you, certainly, but perhaps for the entire Reclamation. Please, speak with me tomorrow. The tarot cannot be ignored.'

Thade nodded and pulled away. 'Fine, Seth.' He hesitated before walking off. The tension between himself and the sanctioned psyker was something he was grudgingly hoping to wear down one day. He looked at Seth's retreating back, hunched over as the smaller man leaned on his staff for support.

The moment passed. Others came to steal Thade's attention.

Colonel Lockwood was next to speak with the captain. He rested a hand on Thade's armoured shoulder, his weathered fingers covering the twin eights marked in white.

'Don't try to talk me out of this, sir,' Thade said. 'We both know this is a good idea.'

Lockwood's scowl spoke volumes. His lined face was a route map of battles he'd been fighting for longer than Thade had been alive. Veterans, true veterans over fifty years of age, were rare in the Cadian Shock. Such was the fate of the Imperial Guard's most often-tested regiment. No matter how good you are, the odds will always get you in the end.

The colonel pulled him aside. 'I'll get him transferred. We'll have a Cadian appointed before we leave for the next campaign. You have my word on that, son.'

Thade glanced around to be sure none of the nearby soldiers could overhear. 'Last time I checked, sir, men with violet eyes were trained damn hard not to complain about orders. We do what we do because we can and we must.'

'It's an insult. We all know it.'

'It's an order. The implied insult is meaningless to me.'

'It's not meaningless to the men, Parmenion. Not to the regiment.' The conversation halted as a cluster of soldiers approached to salute the colonel and wish Thade luck. The two officers nodded and waited until the men had moved away.

'I know it's not meaningless to them. That's why I'm breaking him in like this. I'll turn the insult into a blessing.'

'How does he seem? From first impressions?'

'Sincere. Cold. Astute.' Thade grinned. 'Cadian.'

Lockwood saluted, too stoic to say much more in front of his men. He'd never allow his iron-hearted reputation to take a dent like that, though his admiration for Thade was an open secret. 'I'm not arguing against the idea. It will work. Prove he's a warrior, and may the Throne's light guide your blade.'

Minutes passed as more men came to speak to Thade before the bout. Tionenji stood silent, waiting, no hint of impatience across his features. Finally Thade stepped into the circle made by the watching men and their tanks. Dead Man's Hand and several other Sentinel squadrons towered above the crowd, their pilots watching through vision slits or open hatches.

Tionenji folded his greatcoat and set both it and his peaked cap in a neat pile by the edge of the circle. He stood in his black uniform, his oiled hair still perfectly arranged.

Thade was still in his body armour. Seeing that, Tionenji wondered if he had already failed some kind of test. On Garadesh, honour duels were fought unarmoured with curved blades, with any additional protection considered ignoble and base. Tionenji watched the captain now, suspecting that the opposite was true of the Cadians. They probably adhered to some code where only a fool would enter a fight without the best protection available. Or perhaps a short lecture on how a soldier should always train weighted down by full armour.

A serious bunch, these Cadians.

In Thade's hands was his weighty chainsword, long and straight, with a single cutting edge. In Tionenji's own hands was the blade he'd named as a *nimcha*, thin and curved like a crescent moon, also silent in deactivation. Two live chainswords meeting would risk shattering and tearing the teeth from one another. Powered down, they could be used to duel without risk of damage to the precious weapons.

Tionenji advanced aggressively, his footwork graceful, immediately revealing himself to be a skilled swordsman. Thade kept his own footwork light, slowly circling and making theatrical cuts in the air that had a few of the men laughing at the obvious display. Most of them expected a casual bout, perhaps with the captain showing this newcomer who was really in charge, and the lord general's orders be damned.

The first strike and parry happened so fast that everyone except the combatants missed it. Tionenji sprang back from the blocked blow and slashed again, the flat of his arcing blade clattering against the side of Thade's bulkier sword.

It was the moment the fight began in earnest.

Thade trained with his sword daily, as did Tionenji. The Cadian was a product of his home world's Youth Legion, as were all soldiers of the Shock regiments, and had been reared to fight since his pre-teens. The Garadeshi commissar had been taken in by the Schola Progenium in his own youth, and trained to the exacting standards of the Imperial commissariat. Thade fought with a blade gifted to him by Cadia's finest leader and the hero of Scarus Sector. Pride and reverence flooded him each time the sword cleared its sheath. Tionenji fought with his father's *nimcha*, a weapon of the tribes of Garadesh, and honoured his father's shade with each victory the blade brought for the Emperor.

The swords met again and again, reflecting slivers of moonlight each time they cracked snake-fast against each other.

Scout-lieutenant Vertain had parked his Sentinel close to Taan Darrick in the crowd. He leaned from his vehicle's side hatch, watching the fight with unblinking eyes. 'I can't tell who's winning,' he said.

'I think they're both winning.'

Vertain broke his gaze long enough to look for Ban Jevrian in the crowd. The Kasrkin sergeant was regarded as the regiment's finest swordsman, but if the Sentinel pilot had hoped to glean some insight into the duel by reading Jevrian's expression, the measured stare of the Kasrkin leader offered no answers. Vertain turned back to the fight.

The fighters ducked and weaved, their deactivated swords slashing through the air to meet with metallic clanks once, twice, thrice a second. Both men were panting less than a minute after the duel had begun, neither used to facing a swordsman of equal skill.

In one of the moments when their swords met, both men came close, pushing their weight against each other. Tionenji had smiled as he looked into Thade's eyes.

'You're… doing very well.' His teeth were clenched in effort, as were the captain's.

'I'm better when my blade is live,' Thade grinned. 'Aren't we all?'

They flew apart, neither gaining the advantage from the sword-lock. More blows were traded, each one ending in a parry or a block that locked the two weapons together. The next time they met face to face, Tionenji was grinning mirthlessly and breathing hard.

'You… look tired… my violet-eyed friend.'

'Not at all,' Thade smiled back, sweat stinging his eyes. Five minutes of this was as tiring as the whole night in the monastery. 'But if you want a rest… I'll be a gentleman and let you take a break.'

As with the opening strikes, the finishing blows came with such speed that those watching only realised what had happened several seconds after it was done.

Tionenji threw himself backwards at the last instant to avoid a throat slash of Thade's sword that he had no chance to block. The Cadian was over-balanced in the strike's wake, and a single stumble heralded the end of the fight. The slender crescent blade licked out to crack Thade's sword from his hand, sending it spinning away to hit the muddy ground.

All of this happened in a heartbeat's span.

Tionenji had meant to rest the tip of his sword on Thade's chest. He'd meant to ask in his delicious orator's voice, 'Do you yield?' and make a short speech on what an admirable opponent the captain had been.

Admittedly, these plans would have gone down well with the watching regiment. The men were already impressed by the commissar's skill, and Thade had been right – in showing Tionenji's battle prowess as their first impression of him, the com-missar was walking into a warmer welcome among a band of soldiers from a warrior culture than if he had simply presented himself at a mission briefing.

However, his plans of gracious mercy never came to fruition. Believing he'd won, his defences were instantly lowered. It took him a split second to realise Thade wasn't finished. He remembered the captain's words then.

To first blood.

By the time he was bringing his blade up to block the continuing threat, Thade's roundhouse kick connected with bone-jarring force. Tionenji's head snapped back and he staggered away, blinded by his watering eyes and the web of white-hot pain his cheek had become.

He spat a mouthful of thick, coppery saliva, knowing from the taste that he was spitting redness. A thousand men roared their approval. As the commissar's eyes cleared, he saw Thade offering his hand – again, it was his left hand. His real hand.

'First blood to Cadia,' the captain said, still catching his breath.

Tionenji took the hand, flashing his short-lived grin in a display of blood-pinked teeth. 'First blood to Cadia,' he repeated, sensing a tradition behind the words.

The men cheered again.

CHAPTER VII
War Council

Reclamation Headquarters,
outside Solthane

THEY MET IN the lord general's command bunker –
a prefab structure just a short walk from his tent.
Around the room's edges, servitors and adepts
worked the banks of vox-scanners and tactical cogitators necessary to plan the Reclamation and
remain in contact with the vessels in orbit. Several
officers of the Hadris Rift 40th flanked the Overseer, spreading around the central circular table and
its cluster of maps. Each one was attired as the lord
general himself: a dress uniform of jade green with
gold trimmings. Overseer Maggrig gleamed in the
reflected light from the console screens. He was

wearing his finest dress uniform (and the accompanying gold that made up Hadris Rifter rank markings) for this meeting with the inquisitor. He'd ordered his men to do the same.

Inquisitor Caius had arrived early. He stood apart, his hands resting on the table as he pored over the maps. Upon entering he'd saluted politely and immediately ignored the pomp before him. The only words he'd spoken in the last five minutes were to ask where Captain Thade was.

Colonel Lockwood was present as Thade's commanding officer. The senior officer of the Cadian 88th stood impassive in his battle gear, watching the regions of the map that drew the inquisitor's attention. He was here to learn where a sizeable portion of his regiment was being dispatched to, and to plan for actions undertaken while they were seconded to the Inquisition. His displeasure at the situation was invisible. The colonel's face was an emotionless mask.

Thade arrived exactly on time, coming into the room wearing his battle armour and bearing his weapons. He saluted to all present, taking a position opposite Colonel Lockwood. Several men filed in after him. On his right were four junior officers in the same battle uniform as the captain.

'Inquisitor,' Thade said. 'This is my command team: Scout-Lieutenant Adar Vertain. First Lieutenant Korim Horlarn. Second Lieutenant Taan Darrick. And this is Master Sergeant Ban Jevrian of the Kasrkin.'

Each officer made the sign of the aquila as his name was spoken. Jevrian's bulky carapace armour rattled as he saluted.

'And these,' Thade gestured to the figures at his left, 'are Tech-priest Enginseer Bylam Osiron, Sanctioned Psy-Advisor Seth Roscrain and Commissar Adjatay Tionenji.' Once more, Imperial salutes were offered, though not by Osiron. No one was surprised at that. Tech-priests were famously loyal to the Cult of their Machine-God, the Omnissiah, and worshipped the Emperor in their own secret, Byzantine ways.

Osiron bowed, at least. The motion caused a mechanical purr from his augmetic joints.

'Gentlemen, thank you all for coming.' Inquisitor Caius gestured at the main city map. 'Lord general, if you would be so kind as to provide a summary of the current tactical situation. How is the Reclamation proceeding throughout the capital Solthane?'

Maggrig stepped closer to the table. He held everyone's attention, though in a different way for each man there. His pompous self-importance bored Caius, whose attention was given grudgingly, while he was the figure of the perfect tactical genius to his own Hadris Rift officers. By and large, the Cadians considered him amusingly overdressed. Colonel Lockwood was especially unimpressed by the trimmings and wealth adorning Maggrig's dress uniform. He'd seen less gold on paintings of the God-Emperor's throne.

The Overseer took a moment to compose himself, ensuring he had the attention of all in the room. He cleared his throat and calmly met the inquisitor's eyes, hiding his inward smile at his own mastery of the situation. Bold, assured, calm, collected – he was the very representation of everything noble in the way the soldiers of the Hadris Rift went to war. He felt the gazes of his own men upon him. He could sense how he inspired them, and–

'The delay is boring me,' Caius said. 'Colonel Lockwood, please appraise me of the fighting within the city. Specifically, the main cathedral district.'

Lockwood was Cadian enough not to smile as he stepped forward. 'The purge of Archenemy elements within Solthane proceeds on schedule to date, all in accordance with Lord General Maggrig's designs.' Lockwood took up a pointer and started making gestures to certain southern sections of the city.

'Here, here and in this grand concourse here, resistance has been far heavier than expected.'

'Why?' The inquisitor looked up into the colonel's violet eyes. Lockwood had pointed to three sectors scattered across the cathedral district, which was the size of a city in itself.

'These are habitation areas of the monastic sector. Tens of thousands of citizens and pilgrims died in their homes there. Orbital picts suggested – and Reclamation tacticians anticipated – intense numbers of the plague-slain in these areas. No surprises there, but while building-by-building purges were planned for, we've discovered that the remains of the Kathurite Planetary Defence Force are entrenched in force there, too.'

'The so-called "Remnant".'

All of the officers nodded. All except Maggrig, who was struggling to contain his fury and shame at being treated so shabbily by the inquisitor.

'What's this section? Why is it so much more detailed?' Caius asked.

'My Sentinel squadron mapped several square kilometres of the city on our recent advance,' Thade said. 'That is the region leading up to the monastery lost by the Janus 6th.'

'Which brings us to the latest development,' Lockwood continued. 'Since we made planetfall, every vox-channel has remained scrambled and prone to extreme interference from an unknown, untraceable source. Additionally, no auspex or scrye scanner has given us a reliable reading. We're hunting half-blind.'

'Until last night,' Thade said.

'Until last night. The 88th's attempted extraction of the Janus 6th was the first time the interference was cleared for any significant period of time over a confirmed span of territory. It was also the first time any Reclamation units have come into contact with primary-class threats.'

'Traitor Astartes,' nodded Caius.

'Exactly, inquisitor. It stands to reason the presence of the Death Guard is linked to the clarity of the scanners. Thade?'

The captain spoke up again. 'Either the Traitor Legion cleared our scanners for a reason we're not aware of, or something they're doing in the Shrine of the Emperor's Unending Majesty disables their own jammers as a side effect.'

'Best guess?' asked Caius.

'We think they're scanning for something. And they can't jam us while they scan,' Thade said.

'I concur,' said Osiron. 'The tech-adepts of every regiment are working on methods to counter the interference based on the latest development.'

'As expected. But what is there to scan for?' Not a man failed to notice the edge to Caius's voice as he asked that question.

'We have tacticians, savants and teams of research servitors working on that, sir,' said the lord general. Caius waved the reply away.

'Does the Inquisition know?' asked Thade suddenly.

'What?' Caius was momentarily blindsided. The silence that followed was intensely awkward.

'The plague has ravaged Scarus Sector for months now, on worlds closer to the Warmaster's front lines. Now we know the Death Guard are present; the Legion historically responsible for the other outbreaks and the likeliest source of this most recent one.'

'That's guesswork,' said Maggrig.

'It matches the facts,' Thade replied. He was careful to keep the irritation from his voice.

'I respect your position, Captain Thade,' Caius began, 'but the Holy Ordos of the Throne will make you aware of what you need to know when the time comes for you to know it.'

'I'll take that as a "yes",' Thade smiled. Commissar Tionenji pointedly cleared his throat. Thade quieted down and worked hard to kill his smirk.

'The Ordo Sepulturum is here to sweep the reliquaries and places of greatest faith within the cathedral sector. I seek the source of the plague. Indeed, I seek any information at all that can help us better understand this grave threat.'

'Understood, sir,' Thade said. *How very rehearsed,* he thought. *And vague.* Thade had never worked with the Inquisition before. It was a record he'd been keen to keep. Following orders was one thing; he was used to it and it rarely rankled. But information was power, and going into a fight without the facts was not the way any soldier wanted to make war.

'We're not children,' Thade said. 'If you're keeping the truth from us to save our sanity, I tell you now that we'd rather know exactly what's going on.'

'Thade,' Lockwood warned.

'I mean no offence,' the captain said. 'But we're not some green unit on our first campaign. We'll fight and die or fight and win, no matter what the truth is.'

'Thade,' Lockwood warned again, frowning now.

'Your stubborn insistence is noted, captain.' Caius gestured to the Overseer. 'Lord General Maggrig, what are your current intentions?'

There were no hesitations from the lord general this time. 'I am ordering the remaining forces at this position into the city to take and hold several key locations along the western edge. We will establish a forward base within Solthane by the end of the week.'

Over the course of the following two hours, the lord general detailed his plans to retake Solthane, street by street, building by building.

The plans drew no criticism. The goals were ambitious but realistic, uninspired but tactically sound. A series of implacable advances preceded by Sentinels and sniper teams, to secure defensible structures within each notable district nearby. At one point, Lockwood and Maggrig debated the merits of dividing the Reclamation forces so thoroughly.

'I'm not disagreeing, lord general,' said Lockwood. 'But we're all aware that the forces we command here are just the Reclamation's spearhead. We have a mere month left before the main attack force arrives in support. The regiments en route should be made aware that they'll be landing in a hot zone with several outposts along an urban front line rather than the single stronghold they're expecting.'

'Duly noted,' said one of Maggrig's colonels – a handsome, unscarred man in his mid-thirties.

'Is there a final count of the arriving regiments?' Thade asked. The rumours circulating put the numbers at the wildest outcomes.

'An additional two hundred thousand men in total,' the same colonel said. 'They entered the warp earlier in the week, and are currently estimated between twenty-five and forty days distant.'

Thade nodded, while Lieutenant Darrick whistled low. 'Throne,' he said, 'now we know they're taking this seriously.'

'This is a shrineworld to the God-Emperor and one of His blessed saints,' said Maggrig. 'Nothing could be more serious.'

Thade wasn't done. He'd been waiting for this. 'Will the 88th be allowed to return to Cadia to fight there, once the main forces arrive?'

'I will make my decisions based on deployment data at the relevant time, captain,' Maggrig said.

The meeting proceeded, with the officers ignoring the hustle of the meeting room as they talked on. Adepts and junior officers leered into the eye-straining, flickering screens of wall cogitators, absorbing streams of jade green letters and numbers spilling across the black screens. Regiment positions, lists of the dead, city plans – data in all its relevant forms.

Only one new arrival broke the briefing's flow.

They heard his footsteps before they saw him: resounding clunks of heavy metal that thudded on the plasteel decking of the prefab command structure. When the newcomer came through the doorway (after needing to duck to do so), the head of every officer present was turned to see the man make his entrance.

In his armour, Brother-Captain Corvane Valar was just over two and a half metres tall. 'Massive' barely described him. He was broader than even Osiron, whose bulky body augmentations in many ways mimicked the suit of powered armour worn by the brother-captain. He was also almost half a metre taller than Ban Jevrian, the tallest officer present, and Jevrian was tall by anyone's reckoning.

Corvane's bulk was alien, threatening, and spoke of raw power no mortal man would ever achieve. While Osiron's augmetic joints clicked and whirred according to their own intricate, arcane workings, there was no over-complex devotion to the Machine-God in the armour of the Astartes warrior that now stood among the Guard officers. The thrum of his power armour's joints was an angry murmur – an agitated growl that buzzed with a waspish edge.

The armour itself was the un-colour of onyx or jet, somehow as dark as volcanic glass without obsidian's sheen. Every man's vision seemed to bore into it, as though trying to see deeper, the way the eyes stare hard into the worrying black of a lightless room, a depthless ocean or a moonless night, seeking any detail at all to cling to.

The Astartes's face was hidden behind his helm, a muzzle-mouthed bone-white relic reverently maintained down the millennia. Red eye lenses regarded each man in turn.

The Astartes made the sign of the aquila, his oversized gauntleted hands banging against the carved white stone of the Imperial eagle on his breastplate. A Hadris Rift captain flinched at the loud snarl of servos from the giant's armour joints.

'I am Brother-Captain Corvane Valar,' the giant said. His helmet speakers, mounted into the muzzle of his relic helm, rendered his voice distorted and harsh. 'Commander of the Fifth Battle Company of the Adeptus Astartes Raven Guard Chapter.'

Matters of rank and seniority between the Imperial Guard and the Astartes were far from straightforward. The Astartes Chapters were autonomous servants of the Imperium, and answered to no authority but their own. And yet technically, the lord general held rank here. It was a tension repeated countless times across millennia. The Adeptus Astartes operated under a mandate from the God-Emperor – their genhanced bodies marked them as his chosen sons, living on as shadows of his image. Yet the Imperial Guard answered to Segmentum Command and, in turn, the High Lords of Terra. Cooperation was common between the Guard and the Astartes, but conflict was hardly unheard of.

The Cadians, as if on cue, returned the sign of the aquila immediately. Tionenji was a moment behind them, as were the Hadris Rift officers. Overseer Maggrig bowed his head in a shallow nod, made the sign of the aquila himself, and smiled in what he hoped was a superior, yet warm, expression. He assumed it hid his nervousness to be before one of the Emperor's chosen. In that, he was wrong.

'Welcome to the war council, brother-captain.'

'Good to see you again,' said Colonel Lockwood. The giant in black nodded, taking several moments to stare before replying. Thade wondered if the Astartes was scanning the colonel.

'Cadia. The siege of Kasr Vallock. Colonel Josuan Lockwood, Cadian 88th.'

'Good memory, brother-captain,' smiled Lockwood. 'And I thank you again for your Chapter's assistance in the defence of my home world.'

'Dark days. I remember them well. But not fondly. Much of my Chapter's strength is still garrisoned there. My own force will be returning as soon as we are finished with our duties here.'

'That's good to know, captain.'

That seemed to be the end of the conversation. Maggrig continued discussing his plan. The Astartes was content to listen, standing still as a statue but for the occasional turn of his helmeted head to regard another part of the cityscape map.

'There.'

Several of the officers started at his sudden voice.

'Brother-captain?' Maggrig asked. He'd been pointing at a district towards the centre of Solthane, housing the great Cathedral of the Archpriest. It was there that the bones of Saint Kathur were laid to rest.

'There,' the Astartes repeated. 'That is where the Raven Guard will focus its efforts. I will dispatch scouts immediately to prepare the assault. The Fifth Battle Company will link its intelligence with yours, lord general.'

'We would be honoured,' Maggrig said. He was flushed with pleasure and pride to see an Astartes officer showing such respect to him before his own men. This would surely spread through the ranks…

'It is the disposition of your own forces that necessitates our deployment.' The giant pointed a brutish hand at two points in the cityscape. 'The Cadians and Vednikans are your principal source of veteran strength. They are here and here, respectively.'

Here, the Astartes turned to look at Captain Thade and his command team.

'The Raven Guard Fifth has served with the Vednikans and the Cadians before. We have judged their characters as a planetary people, and assessed their prowess as regiments in service to the Emperor.'

He turned to Maggrig, those blood-red eyes staring without mercy. 'They are the claws of your plan. They are the killing talons sharper than all others at your disposal. Therefore, we will unleash our fury and the anger of our weapons elsewhere, where they will most assuredly be more needed.'

Silence greeted this. Thade and several of the Cadians nodded in respectful thanks.

'Whatever you see fit,' Maggrig murmured.

'Then I am done here,' the giant said. Someone cleared their throat at that moment. Unseen servos growled in the joints of the Astartes's armour as he inclined his head to Seth.

'You. Sanctioned psyker. You would speak with me?'

'Yes, lord.' Seth's voice was a wet whisper.

'Brother-captain.'

'Yes, brother-captain.' A little more strength to his tone this time. Thade noticed Tionenji's hand inching towards his own holstered laspistol as Seth spoke. He read caution in the gesture, not aggression, and said nothing. But it still aggravated him.

'Speak. I have no wish to seem rude, but my time is limited.' The eyes of every man present fell on Seth now. What in the hell was he thinking?

'I am given to understand the Adeptus Astartes have… individuals… that share my talent.'

'It is so. We name them Codiciers and Epistolaries, depending on rank. Again, forgive the implied insult, but their powers eclipse those of an unenhanced human psyker by a great degree.' The Astartes paused here and Thade, for some reason, imagined him smiling behind the impassive muzzle.

'You delay the deployment of the Emperor's finest to question me on trivia?' asked the giant. His voice was different now: less stern, despite the vox-speakers distorting his tone. Maybe he had been smiling, after all.

'No, sir,' Seth said. 'I would ask if you have one of these men among your force here.'

'I do.'

'May I speak with him?'

The Guard officers stared in silence. Was this an affront? An insult? A breach of decorum, certainly. Thade tongued his teeth, trying to think of something to say should the Astartes take offence. Looking up at the towering black figure with its snarling joints and red-eyed mask, absolutely nothing came to mind. Not a Throne-forsaken thing. Tionenji's pistol had cleared its holster now.

'Tell me why,' the giant said, his tone still neutral.

'Matters of the Emperor's Tarot.'

The awkward silence returned, intermittently broken by a curious addition. A series of muted clicks came from within the Astartes's helm. Vox-clicks, Thade realised. He was using his suit's internal vox to speak with someone.

'It is done,' the Astartes said only a moment later. 'Brother-Codicier Zauren is aboard our strike cruiser, *The Second Shadow.* He will make planetfall in fifteen minutes to attend to your request.'

Seth bowed deeply. 'A thousand thanks, brother-captain.'

The Astartes made the sign of the aquila to all present. Once more, his oversized gauntlets banged on the stone eagle across his breastplate.

'I will leave you to your planning. We will meet again, should the Emperor will it.'

'Victory or Death,' said Lockwood. That made the giant pause.

'A very fine memory, Colonel Lockwood.'

The colonel smiled. Without another word, without even waiting for their replies or salutes, the giant in black stalked from the room, parting the clusters of busy headquarters staff before him like a curtain. They scattered from the doorway as he neared.

Seth leaned on his staff in the silence after the Astartes had departed. 'If you will excuse me, lord general?' He addressed the Overseer but his watery eyes were locked on Thade, almost bleeding significance with an intensity that would be comical if it were any other soldier in his unit. Thade gently inclined his head. *Message received. You still need to speak with me.*

It was obvious to all of them that Maggrig had no idea what to say. The Overseer just nodded, and Seth left to keep his curious appointment. Only then did Tionenji's laspistol find its home back in its brown leather holster.

'The psyker,' Lord General Maggrig said with narrowed eyes. 'He must be watched.'

'He is,' replied the commissar.

'He always was,' added Thade.

THE GUNSHIP WAS the same deep and glossless black as the armour worn by Brother-Captain Valar. It came in low, throwing up a storm of dust as its thrusters howled and belched fire. Landing claws extended in a smooth dance of well-oiled technology, biting into the grassy soil as the Thunderhawk gunship came to a rest. The roar of the great turbines and engines faded as they cycled down.

Seth's eyes fell upon the great white symbol painted along the gunship's flank, repeated in smaller relief on the wings. A stylised white raven, wings outstretched. Heavy bolters trained left and right from the Thunderhawk's cheeks and wingtips. Seth was put in mind of a great bird of prey, powerful beyond words but sitting uneasily, alert to the possibility of foes even within the sanctuary of its nest.

And this was not its nest, of course. That was back in the cold of orbit: an Astartes strike cruiser named *The Second Shadow*, Seth recalled. Poetic, he thought, and marvelled at the notion of such brutish, war-bred men being able to choose a name with such nuance. He admired (or at least respected) the Astartes for the living weapons they were, but pitied them their lack of culture and humanity. Of course, it did not escape his attention that most Imperial citizens thought the exact same of the Cadians. That thought made him smile.

It humbled Seth for a moment to look upon this huge, dark instrument of war. It was almost certainly thousands of years old, still flying, still fighting, still shedding blood in the name of the God-Emperor. So much of Cadia's technology was forever new. New soldiers bearing new rifles and driving new tanks – all to replace men, weapons and resources lost in the planet's endless wars against the raiders that spilled from the Great Eye like unholy tears.

The Thunderhawk's mouth opened, the gang-ramp several metres under the cockpit lowering on whining pistons. Seth's mouth was suddenly dry. He'd had no idea if the psykers of the Astartes read the Emperor's Tarot, but rather than feel reassured by the brother-captain's answer, he now found himself worried. What if this codicier's own readings were so strong, so accurate, that Seth's visions were disregarded entirely? He had never fully trusted his erratic talent, but it was one of his senses as surely as the capacity to see and touch. If the Astartes psyker banished Seth's faith in his own abilities, it would be like living half-deaf and never being able to trust what he heard.

The thought made his skin crawl. Maybe this was a mistake. Yes, hell yes, this was all a mistake, and it took all Seth's resolve to remain where he was.

The Astartes psyker, Brother-Codicier Zauren, walked down the sloped gang-ramp. His armour was as dark as Valar's had been, but instead of the off-white helm sported by the brother-captain, this Astartes warrior wore a helm of midnight blue with a mouth grille. Seth was no expert on the armaments of the noble Astartes Chapters, but he recognised the shape of the helm as a newer mark of armour, perhaps only several hundred years old.

The giant approached, his heavy armoured boots crunching soil and gravel underfoot. Sheathed across his back was a two-handed blade as long as Seth was tall. The Cadian doubted he could lift it unaided. He doubted even Ban Jevrian could fight for long with that beast in his hands.

'You are the sanctioned psyker attached to the Cadian 88th Mechanised Infantry, are you not?' The Astartes's voice came in the same toneless vox-speech as the brother-captain's had.

'I am.' Seth looked up at the giant's helm. The eye lenses staring back down at him were golden.

'Excellent,' the giant said. 'I am Brother-Codicier Zauren Kale. You may call me Zaur, if it is not uncomfortably familiar for you to do so.'

'I... I...'

'A moment, please,' the Astartes said, and reached up to do the very last thing Seth had been expecting.

He removed his helmet.

'WHERE ARE YOU going?' the commissar asked as they emerged into the dim daylight.

'Maintenance,' said Thade. He clenched and unclenched his bionic hand as he walked, and Tionenji wondered if the Cadian even knew he had that habit.

'Overseeing the honoured enginseer's work?'

'Osiron? He'd never put up with that. This is pleasure, not business.'

'Pleasure? In maintenance?' Tionenji fixed him with a bewildered look that perfectly matched the incredulity in his flowing Garadeshi accent. 'I am relatively well-informed, culturally speaking, on the Cadian people. I understand that you regard rifles as more precious than your wives, you'd rather kill someone than make love, and that you're only happy when bragging about the most recent time you remained awake for five days straight to win a war with your hands tied behind your backs.'

'You know us well.' Thade grinned, his violet eyes bright below the black widow's peak of his hair. 'But not that well. Seventy-five per cent of the planet's adults and children are under arms, and most Cadians don't marry. We have breeding programs to maintain the population.'

'Is that a joke?'

Thade kept grinning. He didn't answer.

'Even so, captain, never in my most uninspired dreams did I imagine your idea of leisure would be to watch tech-servitors repair your tanks.'

'You don't have to follow me,' said Thade, knowing that was a lie. Tionenji smiled.

'And miss entertainment of such magnitude? Never.'

'I knew you'd be game. And no, we're not going to watch them repaint the tanks and tune the engines. We're going because I've been getting word since last night that Rax was ready.'

'Who, or indeed what, is Rax?'

Thade smiled again as he neared the towering form of the Cadian bulk lander. Machine sounds of maintenance and repair echoed out from the open bay doors.

For a moment, he looked on the edge of boyish. No easy feat for a man who'd been fighting the

Archenemy since he was fourteen. Thade wasn't quite thirty. Tionenji felt the captain could all too easily pass as a man nearing forty.

'Rax,' Thade said, still smiling the rare, warm smile, 'is my dog.'

ZAUR WAS PALE, the pale of pristine marble. Not that Seth had been expecting much overt humanity in the oversized body and face of an Astartes warrior, but the ice-white skin tone was another layer of surprise. And his eyes were black. That unnerved Seth to no small degree. He'd never heard of such an... alteration.

Zaur's scalp was shaved bare – so bare that the Cadian was sure the Astartes had either shaved only hours before, or was genetically modified so that no hair would grow. A few sockets stood out on the white skin, polished chrome showing an edge of redness where they aggravated the surrounding skin: the implants for the codicier's psychic enhancing technology. Seth had no idea what equipment the Astartes psykers used and wasn't about to ask, no matter how fiercely his curiosity burned.

The amplifying band of psychoactive metal implanted across his forehead suddenly itched abominably. He kept his augmentations clean and disinfected them twice daily, but they were the fruits of crude surgeries. Sanctioned psykers deserved no better in the eyes of the Guard; the majority were destined for a messy death before they earned any long-service medals. The polished bionics punctuating the Astartes's skull were almost artistic in comparison to the cheap bronze plugs that bored into Seth's flesh and bone.

'You seem discomforted,' Zaur said. His real voice resonated, deep as distant thunder, but wasn't unkind.

'I have never seen an Astartes without his helm. Not once.'

'Ah,' Zaur smiled. That unnerved Seth even more. Even the Astartes's teeth were overlarge, though everything about Zaur was in proportion to the giant's physique. 'You wished my counsel?' the codicier reminded him.

'Yes. Yes, over matters of the Emperor's Tarot. Do you read the cards?'

'Are you asking if the Astartes as a whole practice the tradition, or are you asking if I do?'

'Both.'

'I suspect our methods are not dissimilar, Cadian. But come, this is not a matter to be discussed on a landing zone. Even in the shadow of my Thunderhawk, some ears are not to hear of what we speak.'

Zaur led Seth into the waiting maw of the gunship, clanking up the gang-ramp. Once inside the internal hangar, Seth scanned the rows of chained combat cycles and archaic thruster backpacks that waited in secure wall housings for use by the Astartes. Zaur thumped a black fist against the door lock panel, and the gang-ramp whined closed, ending with a metallic slam.

'Now,' said the codicier, his voice echoing eerily around the empty hangar. 'What are the cards saying to you, Cadian?'

Seth took a deep breath. 'The Archenemy is not done with Kathur.'

'And what if I told you I had seen the same?'

'I would be… reassured. Reassured that my talents were not flailing wildly. But if you are seeing the same, then perhaps we can–'

'Be at ease,' the Astartes said, cutting the air with his hand. 'I have seen dark portents, but the specifics matter above all. And I wonder if they align. Speak clearly.'

'A grave threat, as yet unmet,' Seth's eyes unfocused, losing their strained intensity, and his voice took on a dreamlike quality. 'The echoes of heresy ring out across the shrineworld's sky. Something is coming. Some resurgence of the Archenemy. Something familiar.'

'I have read the same fate in the tarot. And yet what is familiar to both the Cadians and my Chapter? I am not as gifted as many of my brethren among the Librarium of the Raven Guard, but I know to trust my talent. The evil that draws near is utterly familiar. The hatred that rushes to eclipse us is personal. I felt that surging from the cards, and it is in no doubt. The only answer that fits is, of course…'

'The Death Guard.'

'The Death Guard.' Zaur nodded. 'The traitorous XIV Legion. The scourge of Scarus, at the

Despoiler's right hand. They carve wounds that take decades to heal, if they will ever seal at all. The infection. The taint. How many worlds in this segmentum have been lost to the Curse of Unbelief in Abaddon's thirteenth war?'

The question was obviously rhetorical. Seth nodded slowly, his thoughts coalescing.

'The Cadian Shock are the guardians of Scarus. But forgive me, brother-codicier. I do not see the ties between my home world and your Chapter. What are the Death Guard to you? How grave are their sins, that no other evil can match them in your eyes?'

Zaur stood in silence for some time. When he finally moved, it was to place a gauntleted hand, cold as fresh snow, on Seth's head. When he finally spoke, it was in a buzzing voice contained within Seth's own mind.

+See, Cadian. *See* what they did to us…+

The vision began. A vision of a war – The War – that began ten thousand years before. In a distant solar system, one hundred centuries ago, Seth witnessed the betrayal that scourged the hearts of the Raven Guard against their Astartes brothers.

It was soon over. When the vision faded, Seth felt pale and weak. He bolstered his strength to speak his last question.

'Zaur…'

'Yes?'

'Since coming to Kathur… Do you hear the voice, too? Something has awoken on this world. It cries for aid.'

Zaur nodded once, very slowly. 'I hear it. I hear it even now.' The codicier looked down at the Cadian. 'Have you heard the reply?'

'No.'

'That is my true fear, and the reason I have taken such stern heed of the Tarot's warning. Because I not only hear the voice crying for aid, I also hear something out there answering.'

'This second voice, what does it say?'

'It is wordless, much like the plea for aid we both hear. A simple, powerful projection that conveys a single message.'

'What message?'

Zaur opened his mind once more, letting his sixth sense envelop Seth's surface thoughts. He could feel the rhythms of the mortal's body, beating and bubbling in their short lifespan. The Astartes knew, just for a moment, how frail and mortal it felt to be truly human. He feared nothing in his service to the Throne, yet he felt himself fearful of that incredible weakness.

'Listen,' said Zaur, letting the voices flowing through his psychic sense wash gently into Seth's lesser mind. It was a simple diversion of mental energies, the equivalent of a man damming one river to form another.

Come to me, the first voice said without words.

We come, was the equally-wordless reply.

We come.

Part II
The Herald

CHAPTER VIII
Echoes of Heresy

Within the warp

We come.

It pulsed this wordless reassurance in a relentless stream of subconscious telepathy. *We come. We come. We come.*

Sometimes it would forget its own name.

It knew this was because of the warp. Travelling in the domain of its master brought the creature close to its god's touch, and all that was still human within it would slip into unremembered darkness.

On these occasions, occasions which might last a mere hour and might last anything up to a decade or more, it would simply self-identify by the title its various minions used when addressing it.

The Herald, they called it. The Herald of the whispering god they all served.

The Herald had not moved from its throne in many months. Barnacle-like scabs, crusty blooms of dried blood and calcified pus, now bound it to the bone and corroded metal of its command seat. The Herald felt the encrusted gore connecting him to the throne, and by extension, to the ship all around it.

The Herald knew its strength, its incredible might. It knew it would take little effort to move and shatter the solidified filth, but it wanted to enjoy the serenity of its repose for a few more moments. It breathed deeply within the decayed shell of its armour, feeling the silent rumble of its vessel spearing through the warp. Daemon-things in the darkness beyond the ship's hull shrieked and clawed at the vessel, desperate to enter and prostrate themselves before the Herald. They left streaks of diseased flesh along the rancid hull as the great ship powered on, ignorant of the would-be supplicants.

The Herald chuckled.

Some of the creatures populating the bridge – the weakest ones, whose lives meant nothing – cowered and whimpered at the sound. It was the first time the Herald had made any noise in weeks.

One of the bridge crew, long deprived of its legs, crawled up the steps to the Herald's throne. Once, it had been a man. Now it left a viscous trail in its legless wake, and had too many mouths.

'We draw near, Herald,' several of the thing's mouths said.

Now the Herald stood. The crusted gore binding it to the throne shattered into powdery, infected shards, many still sticking to the Herald's armour like warty protrusions.

With the Herald's sudden, albeit slow, activity, the hollow bone spines jutting from its back began to emit a low buzz. The Herald was awake, and the hive within its body awakened as well. The first flies, bloated and sticky, skittered from the flared holes at the tops of the hollow spines.

The Herald turned its horned helmeted head, seeking something. It could barely see. Its eyes were gummy with bloody tears, having been closed for too long. Sight pained it.

'Weapon,' the Herald growled in a low, burbling voice. The bridge crew shrank back, some pressing against their consoles in fear, some because their own organic corruption bound them to their stations just as the Herald had been bound to its throne.

One of the figures flanking the great throne stepped forward. Its armour was that of an Astartes, but swollen, corroded and cracked through ten thousand years of plague and battle. It was the same gangrenous colour of the Herald's own armour.

'Herald.' Blood-caked respirator pipes thrust into the front of the Astartes's helm vibrated as the second figure spoke. 'I bear your blade.'

At these words, the corrupted Astartes held out a colossal scythe in his swollen fists. It was over three metres long, the pole as thick as a man's thigh, the curving crescent blade glinting in places under a patina of bloody rot.

The Herald took the scythe in its own gauntleted hands. A memory swam up through the warp-holy murk of its thoughts. A name.

Its own name?

No… *Manreaper*. The name of the weapon it now held. With a psychic nudge, the Herald activated the antiquated power weapon. Its scythe blade hissed as energy flooded the ancient metal. The organic decay taking root on the blade itself crackled and popped as it burned away. The stench was cancerous, but that was far from unusual in the Herald's presence. The entire ship itself reeked of the egg-like shit-smell of a terminal wasting disease. The air within the vessel was poison to all but the creatures that dwelled within.

The Herald took a deep breath within its enclosing armour, savouring the holy scent that reached its acute olfactory senses. Vision returned with increased clarity now, shapes resolving clearly to make out the scene of the bridge all around. A great screen faced the throne, showing the beautiful chaos of warp flight. It was like looking into the mind of a madman, seeing all his thoughts as colours.

'Near?' the Herald growled. 'Soon?'

Speech was also difficult. The Herald swallowed to clear its throat. Whatever had been lodged there wriggled as it went down.

'We are only hours from our destination, Herald,' the Traitor Astartes said.

'The Legion?' snarled the Herald.

'The Legion stands ready, great Traveller.'

Traveller. Another of its titles. And… tied to its name…

'My ship,' purred the Herald wetly. Its scabby gauntlets stroked the corroded throne. 'My ship. *Terminus Est.*'

'Yes, lord.' The Traitor Astartes was used to the warp-sickness affecting the Herald. He knew it would pass soon.

The Herald grinned behind its horned helm, facing the screen ahead and clutching its scythe in a greedy hand. The bulk of its Terminator plate would have been immense anyway, but the scabs, buboes and bone spines thrusting from the off-green armour swelled it to four times the size of a mortal man.

'Kathur,' it said. 'We draw near to Kathur.'

'Yes, lord.'

And then, like a bolt from the chaotic storm outside, the Herald recalled its name. Who it had been. What it had become. It smiled again, and began to give orders to its wretched crew.

In life, ten thousand years ago as the galaxy had descended into the war that would never end, he had been the First Captain of the Death Guard.

Now, the Scourge of Scarus, the Traveller, Host of the Destroyer Hive, Herald of the Grandfather of Decay, prepared to do battle once more.

'Kathur,' smiled Typhus through his black lips. 'Their... little... shrineworld.'

SETH MET WITH Thade as the captain was in his tent, performing the rites of maintenance on his chainsword. The smell of purified oils flavoured the air. Thade was on his bedroll, wearing his grey fatigues with the blade in his lap. It was the first time the psyker had seen Thade without his body armour on in weeks.

'Sir?' He stood at the tent's canvas entrance, looking in through the open door curtains. Thade was using a hand-pick to scrape dirt from the High Gothic runes etched into the blade's flat.

'Come in,' he called.

Seth stepped in and froze at the sudden growl. The sound was mechanical and very, very angry. Seth knew it well. He turned his head slowly to see Thade's cyber-mastiff, its bodywork of chrome and iron restored to its undamaged gunmetal grey. The size of a bloodhound, the shape of a wolf with particularly vicious jaws, the cyber-mastiff glared at him with black eye lenses.

It was still growling.

'Uh... Good dog,' Seth said, feeling foolish for letting it slip out.

'Down, boy,' the captain said. 'Sorry, Seth. One second. Rax, log target's bio-spoor. Record name: Seth. Record status: Null target.'

The robotic dog's eye lenses whispered as they turned – focusing, recording.

'Acknowledge,' said Thade.

The dog opened its beartrap jaws and its internal vox-speakers emitted a throaty machine sound. With some imagination, it was almost a bark.

'You're safe now,' Thade said, going back to scraping the last traces of gore from the etched lettering of his blade. 'When he was damaged last month, it wiped his cogitator's targeting and recollection file.'

'His... what?'

'His memory, apparently. Don't look at me like that; it was Osiron's explanation. Rax needs to re-record everyone's bio-spoors so he doesn't sight them as targets.'

'Am I a null target now?' Seth leaned on his staff, feeling his headache pound behind his eyes. Throne take that damned dog, he'd never liked it.

'You should be. Rax? Prime for battle.'

The cyber-mastiff inclined its head towards Thade, its jaws opening slightly. Seth noticed its steel teeth glinting in the dim sunlight coming into the tent. Each one polished like a prize dagger.

'No need to test it, I'll take your word for it,' Seth murmured. 'Great Eye, did Osiron polish its teeth?'

'He did. If you get up close, you can see the Litany of Protection etched into each fang.'

'I'm not getting up close.'

'Well, I thought it was a nice touch. Stay still – let me test this. Rax? Kill.'

Seth felt his entire body tense at the command. He didn't expect the dog to attack, but the possibility made his stomach twist and his eyes ache. The captain's humour, such as it was, did not match his own.

Rax closed his jaws with a slam of meeting metal. Its internal speakers droned an almost puppyish whine.

'You're safe,' said Thade. 'Rax, stand down.'

The cyber-mastiff powered down, closing its jaw and clamping its rows of shark-like teeth. It sat much the way a real dog would: haunches on the floor, but its head tracked left and right, slowly, like a security camera.

'A simple "yes" would have sufficed.'

'Stop whining, you're still alive. Now, you wanted to talk to me,' Thade said, 'but first you have a question of mine to answer.'

'Of course.'

'An hour ago, you were with the Astartes psyker.'

'I was.'

'Now tell me why.'

Seth chuckled, but it became a cough that tasted of blood. 'That's not a question.'

'Don't mess me around, Seth. In the monastery last night, I refrained from chastising you when a commissar would have shot you dead.'

'You hit me with the butt of your gun.'

'Oh, you noticed that? Seeing as I probably should've killed you for how you were acting, you're not in a position to inspire much guilt in me. Throne, we thought you were going to start speaking in tongues. What the hell is this planet doing to you?'

Seth had no answer.

'Listen, Seth. As much as Tionenji is turning out to be far from the arsehole we might have expected, he's Commissariat to the core. A bolt in the back of the head next time you even think about stepping out of line. No questions asked.'

'Understood, sir.'

'I'm just warning you. Time to start being the model soldier. So talk.'

'The Emperor's Tarot is aflame with portents. Dark omens. My own readings match those performed by Brother-Codicier Zauren.'

Thade looked up from his cleaning and set the sword aside.

'It's safe to say you have my attention.'

'I appreciate we are not close, captain, but I respect you. And I thank you for the faith you've shown in my abilities in the past.'

Thade nodded, forcing a smile and wondering where the psyker was going with this.

'You're good at… what you do,' he began hesitantly. 'I'm no liar, Seth. I can't say I'm comfortable with your talents. But you serve, and serve well. I trust you.'

'I am under no delusions. The Shock treats my kind with infinite grace compared to the way we are shackled and despised by many other regiments.'

'I know.'

'Then hear me now.' Seth knelt awkwardly, sliding down his staff to the ground. Thade winced as he heard the psyker's knees pop. 'The heretics of the

XIV Legion are here. That much we know. But we have seen only the edge of their efforts. They will rise against us in massive force, and they will do it soon. All signs point to this… this holocaust.'

'The main force of the Reclamation is only weeks away,' Thade said.

'The tarot doesn't deal in specifics of time. Only urgency.'

'And this was urgent, I take it.'

'The last time I had a reading of this intensity…' Seth trailed off, meeting the captain's eyes.

'Home burned,' Thade finished for him. Seth nodded. 'Throne in flames, Seth. I'm just a captain. I'll warn the lord general, but don't expect him to listen. I need more. What did the Astartes tell you?'

'That he shared the same visions of what was to come. That he warned the brother-captain, who in turn has his men ready for whatever darkness is coming. And he showed me why the Raven Guard loathe the Death Guard above all.'

'One Astartes Chapter is the same as another to me. Except,' he clenched his teeth, 'the Flesh Tearers. Do you remember Kasr Hein?'

'I am unlikely to ever forget that place, captain.'

'Ugh. May the Inquisition take those bastards. So, what's in this for the brother-captain and his giants in black?'

'Simply put?'

'That's the way I like it best.' Thade was on his feet now, buckling on his weapons and reaching for his helmet. 'And it looks like I need to meet with the lord general as fast as possible, so putting it simply is putting it briefly.'

'Vengeance,' said Seth. 'They want revenge.'

Thade smiled his crooked smile. 'Maybe we do have something in common, after all. Revenge for what?'

'The Horus Heresy. Ancient grudges. Principally, the actions of the XIV Legion flagship, *Terminus Est.*'

'I pray that accursed ship burns in holy fire,' Thade spat. The name of the Traveller's vessel was a curse word on Cadia, long-hated for the ravages it inflicted across Scarus Sector. 'What did that damned ship do to the Raven Guard? Poison their world the way it poisons all others?'

'No. Their hatred burns over other matters. *Terminus Est* was responsible for the destruction of the flagship of the Raven Guard fleet during the Horus Heresy. That ship was called *Shadow of the Emperor.*'

Thade paused. His eyes met Seth's.

'The Raven Guard ship in orbit is called *The Second Shadow.*'

'It is,' Seth said.

Thade breathed deeply. 'This is starting to have the ring of something rather fateful about it.'

'It is,' the psyker said again. 'I've… heard a voice, sir. On the night of the monastery battle. It was just a wordless scream for help.'

Thade's jaw tightened. This didn't bode well. Sanctioned psykers hearing voices tended to be sanctioned psykers that ended up shot in the head for their own good a short time later.

'Fear not,' Seth smiled his weak, unattractive smile. 'Brother-Codicier Zauren has heard the voice as well. He hears it still. We are hearing some kind of psychic plea from Kathur, and it is being answered by something off-world. Something is coming, of that we are certain.'

'Go to Colonel Lockwood and tell him everything we just spoke of. I'll meet you both at the lord general's briefing room in fifteen minutes.'

'Yes, sir.'

'Rax, come.' Thade was already moving to the curtained door, but stopped to look back. 'Seth?'

'Captain?'

'Bloody good work.' And with that, he left, the mechanical dog stalking at his heels.

THADE WAS HALFWAY to the lord general's prefab command centre when he altered his course. He called over the first 88th trooper he saw – one of Taan Darrick's men shining his boots outside a communal tent.

'Trooper Cerdock.'

'Sir!' Cerdock made the sign of the aquila. Thade ignored the man's eyes flicking to the silver on the captain's helmet.

'I need you to take a message to Colonel Lockwood.'

'Anything, sir.'

'Tell him that I will not be present for his meeting with Seth Roscrain and Lord General Maggrig, so they should proceed without me.'

'Yes, sir. What should I say if the colonel asks where you are?'

Thade turned in the direction of the sleek, dark ship resting not far from the Cadian tents. The stylised 'I' of the Inquisition stood out along the vessel's flanks.

'Tell him I'm taking the matter straight to the top.'

THE INQUISITOR SIPPED his amasec.

Thade had never acquired a taste for the rich spirit but he had to admit, as his own drink hit his tongue, Inquisitor Bastian Caius had superb taste – and naturally, no shortage of money to appease it.

'This is good,' Thade said with feeling, taking another sip. 'Actually, this is excellent.'

'You're welcome,' Caius said. While Thade had told his story, the inquisitor had reclined on the soft leather chair in this, his sanctum, which resembled something between a personal library and a well-equipped study. The room, with its wooden flooring, wine-red carpets and antique wooden desk, looked utterly out of place on the inquisitor's dangerous-looking gunship.

'My own psychic gifts are not inconsequential,' continued Caius. He looked at Thade, and the captain felt his blood run cold at the hard, inhuman glare from the inquisitor's real eye and the false ones alongside it. 'But I do not read the Emperor's Tarot. And I am surprised your sanctioned psyker does.'

'He's unique.'

'In what regard?'

'Firstly, Seth has survived longer than most sanctioned psy-advisors in the Imperial Guard. Secondly, I have no way of judging it myself, no comparisons to go by, but officially, his powers rank him in the top tier of psychically gifted individuals suitable for Guard service.'

'Ah. Not just a rank and file bolt magnet, hmm?'

Thade smiled at the inquisitor's use of Guard slang. 'Bolt magnet' was a nickname given to sanctioned psykers due to the likelihood they'd be put down by a commissar 'for their own good'.

'He's powerful, lord. And useful. He is tested every three months for traces of taint, and is always utterly clean. The results show his will is strong, even if his body is not.'

'A bolt magnet with a touch of something greater, it would seem. It's rare to see one of the Guard-assigned psykers do more than kill himself with his own psychokinetic energy discharges.'

Thade said nothing. That had almost happened to Seth on several occasions. The most recent time had only been the year before, fighting heretics on the hive world of Beshic V, when the sanctioned psyker had half-melted an enemy tank with psychic lightning from the aquila atop his staff. The crew were cooked alive in their armoured tomb. Seth remained unconscious for a week.

'Well,' said the inquisitor at length, 'I will speak with the lord general myself. And the good brother-captain.'

'Thank you, lord. He mentioned… hearing a voice, as well.'

Caius rose to his feet, fixing Thade with an unsettling gaze. 'Talk.'

'A cry for help, apparently being answered from deep space. He has consulted with the Astartes psyker and they agree on this. But they can provide no details beyond that.'

'I will speak with your sanctioned psy-advisor as well. Where did he first hear this voice?'

'The cathedral district. The night we moved into the Shrine of the Emperor's Unending Majesty.'

'In the shrine itself? Actually within the building?'

'You'll have to ask him. He seems unsure. His powers are erratic.'

'Very well. Are your men ready, captain? We move out at first light tomorrow.'

'We're all ready, lord.'

'Then I will see you at dawn, Thade. But before you go, where in the name of all that is holy did you get that cyber-mastiff?'

Thade looked down at Rax, who was sitting in silence, scanning left and right with mechanical slowness. Logging the inquisitor's bio-spoor as a null target was the very first thing Thade had done upon entering the room.

'We defended the forge world Beshic V last year. My enginseer found the dog in the rubble of one of the great factories and repaired it as a personal project. The tech-priests used them as factory guards before the war there. When we shipped out, the governor of the city gave him permission to keep it.'

'I suspect there were bribes involved.'

'Why, you might just be right,' Thade said.

The inquisitor nodded, all trace of good humour gone. 'Very well. I will meet with Seth shortly. Dismissed, captain. See you at dawn.'

CHAPTER IX
Terminus Est

THE FOLLOWING DAY, as the weak afternoon sun began to slide lower in the sky, the Imperium of Man lost the war for Kathur.

In the months after this chronicle's conclusion, the Imperium would retake the shrineworld with almost no resistance. By that stage, the key figures of this record were, in most cases, killed in action.

Imperial records would identify this date, this single day at the beginning of the Reclamation's second month, as the turning point in the campaign. The personal logs of the soldiers on the surface said much the same, though in different terms. The recovered vox-record of events kept by Inquisitor Bastian Caius (deceased) of the Ordo Sepulturum stated the following:

'Without the last-minute warnings given by Brother-Codicier Zauren of the Raven Guard, sanctioned psyker Seth Roscrain of the Cadian 88th and several of the Navigators aboard the Reclamation fleet, the orbital battle would have been lost before it even began. Their warnings, when taken as a whole, were enough to convince many of the flag-captains that there was at least the chance all was not as it seemed.

We had no idea, of course. No idea from whence the threat would come. In the brief meetings I conducted with the late lord general, the available regimental officers and the flag-captains, the consensus that the main threat would rise from the surface. After all, the XIV Legion was already on Kathur. The pieces fit.

On one level, it was true. The insurgence of Remnant and Death Guard forces within Solthane was on a level unseen before.

But I had heard the voice. I knew something was coming from the warp. And though I warned the orbiting fleet to stand ready for battle, there was a certain laxity in their preparations. I was not enraged by this, but I admit to being disappointed. Several of the Navy officers had little fear that any threat would reach us before the main Reclamation fleet arrived – and several more simply did not believe a Chaos fleet would engage us over a world like Kathur. The Archenemy, they insisted, had already had its fill of the shrineworld. The corruption was complete, the blasphemy done, and the true threat was gone.

So imagine our surprise when we learned the truth.

Lord General Maggrig's urgency to retake Solthane and land an initial spearhead force was admirable, but flawed. He paid the price for his eagerness. The fleet above us was far too small to repel an assault of that magnitude.

And yet the defiance of the flag-captains whose vessels ringed the shrineworld was, for the ground forces, valuable beyond measure.

The fury of their defence gave those of us on the planet's surface the most precious gift possible, given the circumstances. The fleet captains could not buy us victory. All they could offer was time.

The time to choose how we would fight back.'

The recovered regimental journal of Colonel Jhek Antor (also deceased), Vednikan 12th Rifles, said much the same:

'We've lost contact with the ships in orbit. Order has broken down. Under Lord General Maggrig's orders, the remaining regiments have scattered into the city, dividing to minimise losses in case of orbital bombardment.

What may have been a sound tactic in other theatres of war is a messy dissolution of strength here. The vox-network is savagely unreliable on Kathur – it has been right from the moment we made planetfall. Now we're separated in a hateful, huge city filled with the dead, and we're coming to realise just how much the vessels in orbit were boosting the vox signal with their onboard instruments.

Vox quality has degenerated until it is all but useless. We fancy we can guess when one of our ships above has been destroyed, by the vox quality dropping another pitch.

There was talk of something happening, something big coming to wipe us all out. The talk was right. The Emperor-damned heretic cult has risen up in anger against us. I curse the Remnant,

> curse the plague-slain, and curse the
> Death Guard that leads them both.
>   Damn all that mess in orbit. Like we
> don't have enough problems today.'

The personal journal of Lieutenant Taan Darrick
of the Cadian 88th Mechanised Infantry offered a
much briefer summation:

> *'I hate this planet.'*

As THE EARLY afternoon sun beat down on the capital of Solthane, three hundred men of the Cadian
88th were footslogging slowly through the expansive garden grounds of a reliquary spire that
supposedly contained the fingerbones of Saint
Kathur himself. They'd been in the field for over
nine hours, having set out into the city at dawn.

Inquisitor Bastian Caius was with them, his
shoulder-mounted psycannon panning in mirror to
the movements of his head.

Colonel Lockwood and Major Crayce were just
rolling out of the main encampment, kilometres
away, thundering to their own objectives with a
force of seven hundred men in rumbling Chimeras.

Lord General Maggrig was within the main
encampment itself, inside his command tent rather
than the more formal prefab structure he used for
briefings, poring over maps of Solthane and direct-
ing junior officers to move icons on the table charts
to represent the positions of his forces.

Brother-Captain Corvane Valar was deep in his daily meditations, kneeling in a simple robe of black marked with his white Chapter symbol on the breast. He was in his private quarters within the belly of the Astartes strike cruiser, *The Second Shadow.*

Brother-Codicier Zauren was on the *Shadow*'s bridge, in full war plate. As space exploded before him and disgorged the Archenemy host, he shook his head with a rueful smile and whispered two words, too quiet for his helmet vox to amplify.

'We're dead.'

The exemplar of the orbital defence was not (as might be expected from an Astartes strike cruiser) *The Second Shadow.* That honour fell to the Imperial Navy vessel *Depth of Fury,* commanded by Captain Lantyre Straden.

Straden had been one of the captains to take heed of Inquisitor Caius's warning and to firmly believe the threat would come from the warp, not from Kathur's surface. So when the sirens started wailing and several of the limbless servitors connected to the navigation consoles began to babble and moan in alarm, Straden was not in the least bit surprised.

'Well, well, well,' he said at the blossoming warp vortex, bearing witness to the Archenemy ships spilling from the wound in space. Steepling his fingers, he lounged in his command throne, watching the view-portal for several beats of his calm heart.

'Sir?' asked a naval rating. Straden smoothed his greying moustache with his fingertips and nodded to the bridge officer. A grim grin creased his thin lips.

'All power to the nova cannon.'

TERMINUS EST TORE a hole in the stillness of space, ripping back into reality with hull-shaking force. The ship screamed forward through realspace, trailing warp-tendrils of psychic fog the colour of madness.

It was beyond big. The Herald's flagship was bloated and vast, built to be a battleship beyond reckoning and swollen by Chaos in the ten millennia since it first drifted from the orbital docks of the forge world that birthed it. Its ridged surface bristled with a thousand disease-caked cannons, each ready to fire. Its gangrene and grey hull was cooking as the last vestiges of the warp's psychic touch fizzled away, burning the organic filth coating the ship's metal skin. It took several seconds for the coldness of space to reassert material physics over the ship once again. The flames of corruption slowly flickered out, extinguished by reality.

Like flies around a corpse, lesser ships orbited *Terminus Est*, still clinging close to the flagship but already beginning to form into attack groups. In the wake of the great vessel and its interceptor parasites, bulky cruisers emerged from the agonisingly bright slit in the universe.

Three. Ten. Nineteen. And still they came, vomited forth from the empyrean and streaming trails of psychic fog as reality gripped them once more.

On the reeking bridge of *Terminus Est*, the creatures bonded to their stations hissed and shrieked. Typhus rose from his throne and leaned on the guard rail surrounding his podium.

'Surround them. Allow none to enter the warp.'

It was an unnecessary order. The Chaos fleet had broken from the immaterium a considerable distance away, but the severity of their emergence warp-wound would play hell with the Imperials' navigation systems. Interceptor fighters were already being scrambled. No Imperial vessel was going to be able to flee what was coming.

'Report,' Typhus burbled. The answer came from a mutated thing half-fused to its scanner console. Its voice was utterly human, though punctuated by hacking coughs.

'A cluster of twelve troop barges... Six Sword-class frigates in orbital spread... Two Dauntless-class light cruisers in a defensive ring... Five Cobra-class destroyers... One Dominator-class cruiser in high orbit...'

'They are nothing to us. But that,' pointed Typhus, aiming his Manreaper scythe at the cavernous viewscreen. 'What is *that?*'

'Astartes strike cruiser, great Herald...' the once-human creature choked out. 'Identified as *The Second Shadow*, Raven Guard allegiance–'

The rest of the creature's report was drowned out by the Herald's laughter.

* * *

THE IMPERIAL FLEET above Kathur was modest in size, to say the least. What orbited the planet was a battle group balanced for exactly what it was: the forward element of the Reclamation forces. The sluggish troop transports were next to unarmed and had nothing like the manoeuvrability necessary to survive a dedicated engagement. The destroyers and light cruisers flanking the wallowing troopships were jagged, bladelike and deadly, crewed by veterans of Battlefleet Scarus and each bearing its fair share of scars and memories from clashes with the Archenemy over centuries of war and refit.

Of the smaller ships, the Raven Guard strike cruiser was the unsubtle jewel in the fleet's crown. As the daggerish light frigates and their destroyer escorts banked to face the new threat, *The Second Shadow* powered up its ancient engines and primed a vicious weapon array designed to break any blockade and still have the firepower left to fall into a low orbit to hammer a city into dust.

Yet it remained in orbit, while the Imperial fleet tore away to meet the attack.

The *Depth of Fury* was the single Imperial Navy ship of true cruiser size present. The Dominator-class was rarely seen in Battlefleet Scarus, and was considered by many captains to be something of the Navy's bastard son. The more reliable Lunar-, Gothic- and Dictator-class cruisers held pride of place among Naval ranks and populated the majority of battle groups.

The Dominator's undesirability was centred on its main weapon mounting. Thrusting from the armoured prow like a bared lance and reaching almost half a kilometre in length, a nova cannon took a horrendous amount of preparation in order to fire even once. It was also inefficient in orbit-to-surface warfare, rendering it less versatile than standard lance batteries, which in turn rendered it even less desirable.

Lastly, it was not viable to mount a nova cannon on any ship smaller than a cruiser-class vessel, purely because the recoil of firing the weapon would, at best, throw navigation all to hell and take precious minutes to recover. At worst – and much more likely – firing the weapon would collapse a smaller vessel's superstructure and destroy the ship.

So this difficult, awkward weapon found its home on the prow of the often disregarded Dominator-class cruisers.

Captain Straden was all too used to being ordered into lesser duties – duties that he considered far below the honour worthy of an Imperial cruiser. He sat in his command throne now, feeling the heavy thrum in his bones as his beloved, underestimated ship came about to a new heading. The engines shook the entire ship, and well they might, for five thousand slaves and servitors laboured in the endless layers of the *Fury's* aft decks. The enginarium was a hothouse of banging machinery, burning furnaces, sweating slaves and bellowing petty officers armed with pistols and whips.

'I count twenty-six hostiles, captain,' called out a junior officer from his place in front of a bank of crackling scanner monitors. 'Sacred Throne!'

'Report,' Straden ordered, his voice still calm.

'The flagship reads as the… the *Terminus Est*.'

Lantyre Straden had captained *Depth of Fury* for eleven years. He'd captained a Cobra-class destroyer for six years before that, and served as a lieutenant aboard a Lunar-class cruiser before even that. A long career in the Holy Fleet. Honourable if not exquisitely distinguished, and with a record of victories that entitled him to sit where he was now: in the spacious, antique throne of one of the Emperor's own blessed battle cruisers. At his command was the power to obliterate incredible amounts of life, of entire cities, of whole worlds. He had done so many times before – simply by speaking a single word, he had annihilated thousands of lives. It was his duty, and his duty was his passion. Such was the power of *Depth of Fury*, ill-favoured main armament or not.

This was the first time Straden could ever remember thinking that the metres-thick adamantium armour of an Imperial ship, coupled with the invisible, crackling protection of void shields, would simply not be enough. Upon hearing those words, the name of that accursed ship that had been Segmentum Obscurus legend for thousands of years, he knew with cold certainty that he would die here.

He steepled his fingers as his elbows rested on the arms of the command throne. Death... The thought was oddly liberating.

'Bring us about until *Terminus Est* is in our forward fire arc. Status on the nova cannon?'

A weapons rating looked up from his console, one hand raised to his earpiece. 'Prow fire control reports all systems ready,' he said.

'Warn the enginarium to make final preparations.'

There was the chatter of dozens of voices around the bridge speaking into vox mics, alerting fellow officers across the ship that the main armament was readying to fire.

Straden requested ship-wide vox, and a rating patched it through to the systems within his enclosing command throne.

'This is the captain,' he began, and his mouth grew dry even as his calm took greater hold on his heart. 'All crew to battle stations. Brace to fire the nova cannon in thirty seconds. Station commanders to sound off when ready.'

The vox blared into life as returning signals crackled through.

'Navigation, ready,' boomed a voice across the bridge, emanating from the speakers.

'Port laser batteries locked down and ready,' came a second voice.

And on it went. As the districts of the colossal ship chimed back their readiness, Straden watched the rotted hulks of the Archenemy ships tearing closer. The ship began to shake anew, taking the first impacts from the light cruisers thrusting ahead of the behemoth, *Terminus Est*.

Fighters spilled from the larger Chaos ships, but while the smaller vessels of the Imperial fleet took a hammering from their interceptor weapons, *Depth of Fury* ignored them utterly. It speared away from the planet, launching towards its target like a shrike diving at its prey.

'Signal the captains of the *Precious Loyalty* and *The Lord Castellan* to power up and flank us for the first five thousand kilometres of our run. Then they are to break away when we fire the nova cannon, lest they catch the first wave from our broadsides.'

'Compliance,' murmured a vox-servitor, and relayed the orders to the commanders of the smaller frigates. *Depth of Fury* shuddered harder, taking serious impacts on its void shields and shaking through the stress of the plasma drives propelling the ship far in advance of standard thrust.

'Come on,' Straden whispered. 'Come on. Please, come on.'

'Enginarium…' the voice began, and the captain was already out of his seat before it finished, '…ready.'

Straden stared at the viewscreen, at the bloated shape of *Terminus Est* powering closer through the void. He drew his formal sabre, and aimed it at the image before him.

'Kill. That. Ship.'

* * *

THE PRINCIPLES OF nova cannon technology are relatively simple.

Generators mounted in *Depth of Fury*'s prow and the cannon itself charged up, creating a series of powerful magnetic fields. Teams of slaves in the prow work with great loading machinery to feed a specially prepared projectile – an implosive charge the size of a small building – into a great hallway known as the release chamber.

Bulkheads slam down as the nova cannon readies to fire. The firing mechanisms must be isolated from the rest of the ship, and it is rare that all slaves escape in time. As *Depth of Fury* thundered towards, *Terminus Est*, battered by the anger of a dozen lesser vessels, Straden demanded haste above all else. Hundreds of slaves and servitors were killed in the preparation even before the ship's destruction several minutes later.

Upon the order to fire, the magnetic fields accelerate the payload and hurl it from the fixed cannon at something close to the speed of light. Then the time-consuming and dangerous reloading process takes place, and the cycle repeats.

The payload hurtles through space faster than the human eye (and indeed, most instruments of human design) can track. It is programmed not to implode within safe distance of the firing vessel; a nova cannon's destructive force is immense.

This failsafe can, of course, be overridden. In only a handful of minutes, it would be.

The projectile lanced across the distance between the two converging ships faster than the blink of an eye. Once it struck, it was programmed to implode, collapsing in on itself and achieving a density so intense all nearby matter would be sucked inside it and compressed to practically nothingness.

This is how stars die.

And this is what hit the oncoming prow of *Terminus Est*.

A SIZEABLE CHUNK of the diseased ship simply ceased to exist, wrenched out of physicality and into nothingness. Consoles chattered and servitors grunted as *Depth of Fury's* bridge instruments registered the damage.

'Direct hit,' said the lieutenant by the main weapons console.

Now the gangrenous ship was wounded. Detritus, mutated crew and shards of armoured hull span away into space, drifting from the gaping hole ripped into the prow of the advancing Chaos warship. The blood Straden could see was a flood of dark droplets – some hideous fluid leaking from the wounded sections of hull, turning into glittering crimson crystals as they froze in space.

It began to rotate – a fat whale rolling to avert its face.

'She's hiding her bridge,' Straden cursed.

'Sixteen per cent hull damage, captain. They're venting air pressure and... and thousands of kilolitres of some kind of dark, organic fluid. *Terminus Est* is still coming, captain.'

Straden looked at the man as though he were the lowest form of idiot.

'Then by the God-Emperor,' he said, 'you will *fire again*.'

THE UNFOLDING DRAMA above Kathur became a smooth orbital ballet as the ships slid past each other in graceful slowness. Formations broke and reformed. Lesser ships danced around the greater ones, and the heavier cruisers unleashed silent beams that lanced across space to burn out as fountains of high energy sparks spraying away from crackling void shields.

When a ship's shields finally buckled, the lances of light cut directly into the hulls, scarring them deeply, cutting ships into pieces one shard at a time.

The Second Shadow did not follow *Depth of Fury*. The rest of the Imperial fleet did.

These lighter cruisers and destroyer frigates powered at the Archenemy flagship, plasma drives leaving streams of energy-charged mist in their wake. While the slaves and servitors in the bowels of these vessels laboured on, unknowing of their fates, no bridge officer in the fleet was under any illusions. There was no hope to survive this. All that remained was to sell their lives as dearly as possible.

Had *The Second Shadow* joined this assault, Imperial forces would have inflicted a great deal more damage on their foes. But the strike cruiser remained in orbit – the very embodiment of Astartes autonomy. Frantic calls for aid clashed in the vox as the Navy vessels demanded (and in several cases, pleaded) for aid. Yet the black cruiser sat in seeming silence, its outward calm concealing the activity within.

The frigate *Precious Loyalty* was captained by Lieutenant Terris Vyn, born to a wealthy family on the planet Gudrun. In the final moments of its life, two thoughts span around his mind, casting all others aside. Firstly, that these were the worst circumstances one could make the rank of captain, and secondly, that he had no idea where his right arm was. The torpedo had struck, and after a moment's blackness, he found himself crawling to his feet a great deal less whole than he had been a moment ago. Choking smoke flooded the bridge as blood poured from the stump of his severed bicep.

Every other officer of higher rank was dead, buried under the wreckage of what had been a fully-functioning bridge only scant minutes before. Half the servitors and ratings were similarly incapacitated: dead, dying, or doomed to spend their last seconds of life trapped under twisted metal rubble.

Terris Vyn ordered the enginarium to give him maximum thrust, little realising only a quarter of the one thousand slaves were still alive down there. The same torpedo barrage that devastated the bridge had inflicted equally horrendous damage across the rest of the vessel. By all design logic, it was a miracle the ship was still holding together.

He then ordered the helm to stabilise course and make straight for the *Terminus Est*. In this, his orders were more successful. The Dauntless-class vessel veered sharply, and plunged back on course.

Another Chaos cruiser, the dark-hulled *Daughter of Agony*, drifted between Terris Vyn and his target. The cruiser was busy opening up with its broadsides, unleashing hell on the flaming form of *Depth of Fury*.

'Forward batteries!' he cried through the smoke. 'Forward batteries fire!'

Half of the batteries fired. Due to the excessive damage already sustained, the other half no longer existed. They were reduced to deep, ruined scars in the *Loyalty*'s prow.

The diminished cutting beams sliced out, making harmless lightning patterns as the *Daughter of Agony*'s void shields repelled the incoming fire.

'Go around!' Terris Vyn screamed. 'Ram the *Terminus Est*!'

A noble plan. Had it succeeded, it would have been delicious vindication for the slain Imperial crews.

Instead, *Daughter of Agony* began to twist. Lance fire licked from the turrets across the vessel's back, turrets so numerous they were like scales on a reptile's skin.

'Lieutenant...' a helm officer began a sentence he would never finish.

Precious Loyalty exploded in a bright star of plasmic energy, sending debris slashing through space in a thousand directions.

It was a scene being repeated across the Imperial fleet.

DEPTH OF FURY powered on, shieldless and streaming jagged metal from its wounds. Like a plague of locusts, Chaos fighters flitted around the cruiser, a cloud of annoyance harassing all four kilometres of the great vessel. *Depth of Fury* shuddered under the withering hail of fire, geysers of pressurised air and quickly-killed flames gushing from the holes blasted in its ridged hull. The cathedral-like structures adorning its long back were in ruins, resembling the bones of some long-dead civilisation. The ship's destruction was inevitable. The damage was already nearly total.

The reports reaching *Fury's* captain flashed through his mind and were discarded by all but the core parts of his consciousness. The hull was literally collapsing on too many decks to keep track of. The void shield generators had been ejected into space to prevent a critical internal detonation. Half the plasma drives had ceased functioning. Navigation was fighting to keep the ship under control, and what control the officers had was unreliable in the extreme.

The cruiser passed between two Chaos vessels, and a final chorus of broadsides fired. The banks of cannons roared into the silence of space, tearing great scars along the edges of the grey-green ships as *Fury* sliced between them like a crumbling dagger.

Still, somehow, the prow was aimed at *Terminus Est*, following the larger ship as it rolled.

We'll only get one more shot, Straden knew. *By the throne, I pray we make this count.*

'Main weapon primed!' yelled a rating.

'Fire! In His glorious name! *Fire!*'

No preparations this time. The nova cannon charged its magnetic fields and spat its implosive gift at the Archenemy flagship.

Two things happened in the wake of that release. Close to the speed of light, the projectile hammered into *Terminus Est*, unleashing the physics of a collapsing sun into the ship's underbelly. Several decks simply ceased to exist as the implosion gouged a wicked, bleeding hole in the Traveller's vessel. More wreckage, more crew and more diseased fluids drifted into space from the grievous puncture.

The second thing was that *Depth of Fury* lost all pretence of stability. The kickback from firing the nova cannon was colossal, effectively killing the cruiser's forward motion and sending it veering to starboard, out of control.

The predator sensed its prey was crippled: *Terminus Est* loomed in the viewscreen, drifting closer.

'We're dead in space,' said one the younger bridge ratings. His face was white with fear. 'Do we abandon ship, sir?'

The side of the young man's head exploded outward in a dark mess. The corpse toppled over in the same direction a moment after. The ship's commissar, hook-nosed and thin-faced, lowered his pistol.

'How dare he shame this vessel's final moments with a coward's talk?'

Straden ignored the man. He was already on the ship-wide vox, speaking his last order.

'Stand to your final duties, men of the Imperium. Be ready to greet the Emperor with pride.'

THE SECOND SHADOW was also taking a beating. Encircled by lesser destroyers, frigates and fighter wings, the black strike cruiser still sat in orbit, returning fire with its formidable weapons array.

But going nowhere.

Boarding ports opened like widening eyes along the hull, and assault pods shot from the *Shadow*'s launch bays, engines burning with fiery contrails. Almost as small as the fighters swarming the strike cruiser, they fired across space in a formation blur, passing practically unnoticed. The few Chaos ships that did notice the pods failed to target-lock the fast-moving objects as they hurtled through the void, directly towards the distant shape of *Terminus Est*.

A Space Marine strike cruiser was a Chapter commodity so precious that its value to the Raven Guard could not be described. The lives of fifty of its Astartes were similarly priceless.

With no escape from this colossal tragedy taking hold, the Raven Guard had decided how best to sell their lives. The ship-to-ship assault pods streamed on, ever closer to the Archenemy flagship.

A textbook boarding operation.

PETTY OFFICER OVOR Werland laboured shirtless in the prow armament chambers of *Depth of Fury*. He was forty-three years old, and would never see forty-four. In his right hand was a laspistol, its ammunition expended. In his left hand was a whip, the leather cord slick with blood.

He'd lashed them, he'd shot some of them, but he'd done it. His team of slaves, now down to barely a hundred men, had reloaded the nova cannon in just under seven minutes. The mouth of the great turret had been fed with the huge warhead it would unleash.

Werland sprinted across the wreckage-strewn deck, leaping at the last moment over the still-twitching body of a man he'd shot himself. He dropped his weapons, keyed the wall vox-speaker active and shouted over the wailing sirens that the captain could fire the main armament.

His last duty done, Werland turned from the wall.

And froze.

The remaining hundred men of his slave team ringed him in an impenetrable semicircle. As the ship shuddered and came apart, the men stood there, pieces of wreckage held as weapons.

Petty Officer Ovor Werland paid the price many slavemasters have paid since time out of mind.

With nothing left to lose, his property rebelled and took their vengeance.

Depth of Fury was doomed. Although it would end its honourable but understated career in less than a minute, Ovor Werland was quite dead by then.

'THEIR CANNON AMASSES power once more, great Herald.'

Typhus nodded his horned helm once.

'End them. Now.'

'MAIN ARMAMENT READY!' crackled the voice over the vox. Ovor Werland's last words.

Straden's mouth fell open for a moment. For one insane second he wanted to get back on the vox and ask that officer's name, in order to recommend him for special citation.

'Fire my damn gun!' he roared at the surviving weapons officers.

They tried. *Depth of Fury* twisted slowly, exploding as it turned, bringing its cannon to bear with agonising slowness.

Their bridge. Straden breathed fast, unable to believe what he saw. The Archenemy flagship was filling the viewscreen now. And he saw…

Their bridge!

'It's too close to fire, sir,' spoke one of the ratings. 'We'll be caught in the implosion.' Straden couldn't believe what he'd heard.

'Do I look like I give a shit? We're dead already! Fire! Fire, fire, *fire!*'

The magnetic fields powered up. Straden could feel them. He didn't care that it was impossible. He could feel the magnetic fields charging, heating his blood, vibrating his bones. He ignored the bridge detonating around him.

'Kill them!' he cried out with a savage brightness lighting his eyes. 'For the Emperor! Kill them!'

DEPTH OF FURY's plasma drives finally exploded under the last sustained lance volley from *Terminus Est* and its support cruisers. The explosion sent shockwaves that rocked the nearby Chaos vessels, creating a great cloud of plasma residue and debris, hanging in space like a bruise-coloured nebula.

Terminus Est parted the dust cloud like a shark cutting through water.

'That was close, Lord Typhus,' said one of the Death Guard flanking the Herald's throne. 'If they had fired…'

Typhus ignored him. 'Make for *The Second Shadow*. That dies next.'

CHAPTER X
Survival

Solthane, Yarith Spire Graveyard,
Monastic sector

THADE CROUCHED WITH his back against the ruined wall. Las-fire made little hissing sounds as it chipped the other side of the stone.

'I hate this planet,' he said, reloading his bolt pistol without looking. Crouching in the mud of a sprawling garden estate, using waist-high marble walls and huge trees for cover, several squads of the 88th were engaged with the Remnant, and engaged hard. Thade was used to his fair share of battles that began when the enemy came from nowhere. This time, the bastards came from *everywhere*.

They spilled from the tower at the centre of the ten-kilometre-square estate, then flooded in from the edges, running from every direction. The 88th had been surrounded in a heartbeat, pinned between the enemy coming from behind them and from their objective.

Yarith Spire. The saint's fingerbones were supposed to be here. The tower itself rose up like a spear splitting the sky. It was black – some hideously rare and expensive black stone, Thade guessed – and as overly ornate as the rest of this tomb city. Rings of gargoyles and angels leered down in all directions. It looked like a particularly unfriendly nightmare.

Nine hours deep into the city, and enemy resistance was supposed to be light. Not medium, not heavy and not medium-to-heavy thank-you. Light. The Vednikan 12th Rifles had swept this area clean only a few days before.

'There shouldn't be a soul here,' Corrun said as he reloaded his rifle next to the captain. 'Nothing ever goes right on this planet, eh?'

Thade wiped a bleeding slice along his cheek – a gift from shrapnel when the last wall he'd been behind had exploded. This resistance was neither light nor medium. In fact, it even left 'heavy' some way back in the dust.

His dirty glove smeared the dark facial blood across his cheek, and it kept coming from the cut. *That'll leave a scar,* he thought. *An ugly one.*

The squads had scattered at Thade's order, taking shelter in the modest domed chapels and graveyards dotted around the huge garden estate. The horde of Remnant came on, the rear elements slowed by the heavy weapons they carried.

A stalemate now. At best, temporary. At worst, already breaking. The Cadians were holed up in detached pockets, many soldiers using gravestones for cover, holding off Remnant forces with far superior numbers. A solid slug clanged off Rax's chrome flank, and the beast growled low. Its photoreceptor eyes sought the shooter, calculating his location from the angle of the incoming fire.

'Take cover, idiot,' Thade said. The dog retreated further behind the wall.

Taan Darrick hurled himself into Thade and Corrun's cover, crawling on his belly until he was next to the captain.

'Join the Shock, they told me.' Taan was reloading his battered lasrifle. 'Serve the Emperor. Meet overwhelming numbers of arseholes…' the lieutenant kissed his rifle once it was rearmed, '…and shoot them in the face.'

'Considering the number of heretics howling for our blood,' Thade said, 'you're in good spirits.'

'I heard there's a pay rise if I get made into morale officer.'

'Shut up, Taan.'

'Shutting up, sir.'

'Captain?' Thade's vox-bead crackled. The sound was distorted. As reliable as always, then.

'Thade here. Identify.'

'Squad Vigilant: Unbroken.' Commissar Tionenji's voice, his accent adding an exotic twist to the regimental words. 'Thade, I need Sentinels. I have armour incoming.'

Throne in flames. 'Confirm that you have *armour* incoming.'

'Confirmed. Armour incoming. They look like Repressors and Chimeras. Riot-control... Troop transports... Fitted with additional weapons. Captain? Captain?'

'I'm here. Dead Man's Hand will be routed to you.'

'Acknowledged.' The link went dead.

'Who was that?' Taan asked as he kneeled up, firing around the edge of the wrecked wall.

'Vigilant sighted armour. Tionenji's unit.'

'Still...'

'Still what?'

'It's good the new boy is getting his hands dirty on his first day.'

'Shut up, Taan.'

'Shutting up, sir. What do you say about a brisk run back to the Chimeras?'

The transports had been abandoned at the edge of the graveyard several hours before. They were several kilometres distant from the Chimeras.

'I'm fairly certain I said you should shut up.'

'You say a lot of things.'

Thade raised an eyebrow. Taan grinned. 'Shutting up, sir.' Any other time, Thade would have laughed.

'We're being ringed. Take Alliance further down into that graveyard to the west. If the Remnant takes that ground, they'll split us up from Loyalty and

Adamant.' The inquisitor was with Adamant. It wouldn't do to be split up from him, of all people.

'Sir.' Taan took out his viewfinders, holding them up to his eyes and panning across the western graveyard. Dozens of Remnant, dressed in their filthy PDF uniforms, were already running across the dead grass. 'You always give me the fun jobs,' he said with a grin. Then he was running, voxing his squad to follow.

Thade keyed his vox again. 'Vertain, acknowledge.' Static. 'Dead Man's Hand, acknowledge.'

More static.

This is tremendous. 'Janden!' Thade called.

Thade's vox officer was kneeling behind a gravestone some thirty metres away. Las-fire flashed over his head as Janden hunkered down, gripping his laspistol. His bulky vox-caster backpack was on the ground, kept safely behind cover.

'Sir?' Janden called.

'Signal to Dead Man's Hand. Reinforce Vigilant in the north, immediately.'

Janden nodded and started punching keys. The strength and range on the vox-casters far exceeded the personal micro-beads carried by individual soldiers, especially with the interference on Kathur so eternally harsh.

'Sir, I'm getting scrambled signals.'

'That's not news to me, Janden.' Thade kneeled up, firing his bolt pistol two-handed. It bucked as it banged in his hands, round after round, again and again. Remnant soldiers died each time the gun sang.

Thade nailed seven of them in quick succession, picking them off as they broke cover to run forward.

The Remnant was using the low walls and gravestones as shields, too. Except they had the numbers to take horrendous casualties and still run right up to the Cadians' faces in a swarm.

'Sir, it's the fleet!'

Thade crouched to reload again. Throne, he was running out of clips.

'I'm listening, Janden,' he called. 'Get over here. Eighty-Eight, covering fire!'

The hunkered-down soldiers from Thade's nearby squads rose as one, letting rip with rifles on full-auto. Short bursts: just enough for each man to kill a target or two and get the rest of the wretches ducking. For a moment, the Remnant's advance across the mass graveyard halted.

Janden made a break for it. He sprinted the distance between his cover and the captain's wall. When he was within arm's reach of Thade's cover, a las-round tore across his chest, shattering his body armour. He hurled himself next to the captain, the way Taan had only minutes before. His chestplate was a smoking mess.

'Close,' he grinned.

'Close,' Thade agreed. 'You've had worse. The fleet?'

Janden offered Thade the speech horn, and the captain listened.

A storm of voices. Panicked, angry and pleading – all to a background of vicious static. Thade covered his other ear to keep out the sharp cracks of lasrifles.

'...hull breach at...'

'...engaging unsupported...'

'...seconds left... Dead in...'

'...the Emperor... Laser batteries f...'

'...too many!'

'...abandon... Reactor critical...'

'...*Fury* is gone! She...'

'...ing destroyed! The *Fury* is...'

'No,' Thade said breathlessly, and then in a stunned whisper, 'Throne of Terra, no.'

An explosion nearby jolted him back from the horror of what he was hearing on the vox. Now the Remnant was using frag grenades.

'Zailen?' Thade spoke calmly into his vox. Another detonation nearby elicited fresh screams.

Zailen was flat on his front some fifty metres away, his temperamental plasma gun hidden behind a gravestone in favour of his standard-issue lasrifle. Thade saw him roll back into cover, hidden from view, and heard his voice come over the vox.

'Captain?' Zailen was from Kasr Novgrad, on the other side of the world from Kasr Vallock, where Thade was born. His accent turned the word into *Keptane.*

'Zailen, you need to kill the ones with grenade launchers. All our heavy weapons are with the squads in the north and east. You're it, Zailen. Copy?'

'Yes, captain. It will be done.' *Yiz, keptane. It vill be done.*

'Good hunting.' Thade was looking around the edge of the wall, bolt pistol in hand. 'You see the domed chapel to our north? Look in the tower. They're up there.'

'Consider them dead, sir.' *Conzider zem dead, suh.*

Thade ignored the sun-bright spears of plasma burning from Zailen's gun a moment later. He was already focused on his vox-officer. 'Janden. Janden, eyes on me.'

'Sir?' Janden's pockmarked face, acne-scarring ruining his good looks, was set in a worried scowl.

'Get me Maggrig if you can. If not, get me Colonel Lockwood.'

'Sir.' Janden started working, hitting keys and turning dials to reach some semblance of clarity on his vox-caster. Headphones on, mic extended, he repeated the same call, hoping for an answer with each new frequency he tried.

Thade resorted to his vox-bead for squad-to-squad contact.

'Venator to Adamant, Thade to Horlarn, respond.'

'ADAMANT: BROKEN.'

First Lieutenant Horlarn had to shout above the gunfire. His platoon was still taking position in the graveyard, the men setting up around small mausoleums and the unluckier ones using gravestones for cover. The Remnant came on in a horde, thankfully without heavy weaponry. The few heretics that sought safety used similar cover to the Cadians. The rest just ran on, closing fast.

Amongst the men, fighting with a borrowed lasrifle, was Inquisitor Bastian Caius. Evidently he had no desire to use his psycannon on these wretches.

Streams of angry red las-fire flashed across the distance between the two forces, scything down Remnant as they ran. The return fire hammered into the Cadian position. Not ten metres from Horlarn, Trooper Ceale flipped onto his back, spasming on the dry grass. A solid round had taken him in the right eye.

'Horlarn?' came Thade's voice again.

'I'm a man with a problem, sir,' Horlarn racked his rifle's slide to single-shot. Killing these scum was chewing through his ammo reserves. He risked a glance over the gravestone he was kneeling behind. Remnant everywhere. Just ahead, several of his men were getting into some serious bayonet work, duelling with Remnant soldiers over gravestones and low walls.

'We all are. The fleet is gone.'

'Say again, captain.'

'The fleet is *gone*, Horlarn.' Thade's voice muted and the throaty whine of a chainsword took over. After a moment, the captain returned. 'Get me the inquisitor now. We might be getting a dose of orbital bombardment in short order.'

Horlarn yelled for the inquisitor, who disengaged from his half-hearted combat with an expression somewhere close to amusement. He acted (even

smirked) like this bloodshed was somehow below
him. Moving from wall to wall, Caius hunched and
ran to Horlarn. His bionic eye whirred to bring the
lieutenant into focus, adjusting from range-finding
moving enemies.

'Lord Inquisitor, Captain Thade has urgent news.'

'Give me your vox-bead,' the inquisitor said without preamble. Horlarn complied. Caius attached
the input mic to his throat and put the output bead
in his ear.

'Thade?'

JANDEN WAS GETTING contact now. The other unit
commanders of the Reclamation ground forces
were touching base, and every story was the same.
The fleet was being annihilated and screaming distress calls across every frequency. The soldiers on
the surface were encountering an uprising of Remnant that came from everywhere at once. Across the
city, the Archenemy's forces were massing to repel
the Imperial Guard.

Janden logged reports from the Kiridians that
primary threats were being sighted as the Guard
assaulted the hab-blocks in the city's residential
district. The Uriah 303rd was doing nothing but
yelling for immediate reinforcement to the south-
east. They'd encountered intense resistance as they
advanced down Solthane's main avenue. The
Imperial Boulevard, flanked by chapels, false
reliquaries and rentable pilgrim habs, had
disgorged floods of plague-slain. The Vednikan

12th Rifles were reporting armour contacts –
Remnant riot pacification tanks and troop
transports corroded by poor maintenance,
converted to bear heavy weapons.

There was no word from the 3rd Skarran Rangers.
Nothing but silence from Overseer Maggrig.

'Inquisitor?' Thade kneeled in the shadow of the
mausoleum, his chainsword purring in his hands.
Next to him, Janden spoke rapidly into his vox-
caster's speech horn, repeating himself as Kathur's
interference stole the sense from his words. The
vox-officer was still trying to establish contact with
the rest of the 88th.

'Inquisitor Caius?' Thade asked again, leaving
Janden to his work.

'What ails you, captain?' crackled the inquisitor.

'Lord, get to Lieutenant Horlarn's vox-officer
immediately. The fleet is under attack. The Guard
on the ground is being hammered city-wide by this
resurgence of the Remnant. We need to consolidate
our forces immediately. I recommend regrouping
and abandoning the spire objective. I'll be in contact soon.'

At that moment, Janden turned to Thade and
mouthed the word 'Lockwood'. Thade cut the link,
snatching the offered speech horn. Such was his
haste, he almost crushed it in his augmetic hand
without realising.

'Colonel Lockwood?'

'He's dead,' said the other voice. 'Who is this?'

Thade didn't answer. 'Where is Major Crayce?'

'Also dead. Who is this? Confirm status of Captain Thade.'

Thade swallowed. 'Confirmed alive. This is Thade.'

'Sir!' the voice on the other end of the link was muffled by violent distortion. '...Lieutenant Reval... We're being overrun, capt...'

Thade could feel how pale he'd become. His cheeks were as cold as ice. If Lockwood and Crayce were dead...

'Reval, can you hear me? Confirm status of Colonel Lockwood and Major Crayce.'

'...firmed. Primary threats sighted. Lockwood's Chimera was... No survivors... I saw Crayce die myself. Frag grenade. Barely anyth... left of him, sir.'

'Transmit exact coordinates immediately. Damn it, where are you all? Reval?'

'...opy that, captain. Transmitting. Sir, the casualties are...'

'Are what? Reval? The casualties are what?'

'Lost the link,' said Janden. 'I've got the coordinates, though. Only six kilometres to the direct north. We can meet them on the way back to headquarters.'

'We've got to link up with them. Or they've got to link up with us.' Neither option seemed likely. Six kilometres wasn't far, but it became a nightmare trek when it was through enemy-held territory. It may as well have been a continent away.

'You think we can convince the inquisitor that we need to link up with the colonel?'

'I'm not sure I care what the inquisitor thinks at this stage.'

'But the inquisitor's mission–'

'Will have to wait,' snapped Thade. 'The Reclamation is over.'

All around him now, Thade could see his men being forced into hand-to-hand fighting. The Remnant was on them, vaulting the low walls and running among the gravestones. Thade geared his chainsword up and rejoined the fight. Blood of the Emperor, if he was going to die today, he was going to slaughter a hundred of these bloody heretics first. Rax ran at his heels, its Litany-etched jaws opening in readiness.

Chainsword growling, Thade carved through a Remnant soldier from behind. The man howled as Thade's sword hammered into his lower back and churned his guts to soup in a whirr of grinding teeth. The captain tore the blade free and ran at the next closest heretic – a filthy, skinny bastard with a blood-spotted lasrifle in his grimy hands. Thade sprinted at him, leaped from a tumbled gravestone, and snapped the heretic's neck with a flying kick that pounded into the traitor's throat. His bolter sang as he landed, banging out a thunderous refrain and slaying three more Remnant in showers of gore.

Rax leaped at a nearby Remnant soldier, jaws snapping shut on the traitor's throat in a vicious clamp like a bear-trap closing. The cyber-mastiff landed before the decapitated corpse even hit the ground, its polished jaws smeared with blood.

Zailen, hefting his steaming plasma gun, joined the captain. So did several other soldiers, rallying to Thade and lending their las-fire to his fury.

Thade's vox-bead chimed. The signal was poor, but there was no chance to head back to Janden to use the vox-caster now. They were surrounded. Pistol in one hand, blade in the other, the captain moved from wall to wall, killing the Remnant that came within reach. The voice in his ear was muffled beyond comprehension. His pounding heartbeat added to the maelstrom of noise all around.

'Thade,' he breathed, tearing his chainsword free from the chest of a Remnant soldier. 'Speak to me.'

'...link up...'

Thade's bolt pistol roared, cutting the voice off again. The soldier that had been running at him, bayonet lowered like a spear, collapsed without a head.

'Repeat.'

'This... quisitor Caius. We're being overwhelmed. Plague-slain and Remnant forces. We must retreat, Thade.'

Thade laughed. He actually laughed. As the inquisitor demanded he abandon this doomed mission and his chainsword stripped the face from a howling heretic, Captain Thade laughed. He'd never expected to die like this, and now the time came, he found it inexplicably funny.

'We're Cadian, lord. It's not called retreat, it's called consolidation. I already gave the order: fall back to regroup. Otherwise, we die here.' The trooper next to him took a hit in the belly and dropped like a sack. Thade and his shattered squad took a moment's refuge behind a row of tombstones.

'Captain Thade. Give me a full tactical assessment of–' Caius started.

'Not now!' the captain barked. He looked back at the downed trooper. It was Zailen. 'Cover me, gentlemen,' he said to the three soldiers crouched with him. And then he started running. 'Rax. The gun!'

It was only fifteen metres, but he felt shots whickering past his body as he covered the short distance. Thade's gloved bionic hand gripped Zailen's collar, knuckle-servos closing with silent, inhuman strength. Bolter up and firing, Thade dragged the bleeding man behind the insignificant cover of a large gravestone. Rax was at his heels, jaws clamped on the grip of Zailen's priceless plasma gun, moving backwards as he dragged the weapon.

'Sir,' said Zailen, unsuccessfully holding in a gush of bright blood from his stomach. Even if he survived the gut-shot, which was unlikely if he remained in the field, the chances of infection in Kathur were almost one hundred per cent. All Reclamation troops were issued with anti-infection gel to fight the increased risk of wounds turning foul on this fallen world.

'I'm here, I'm here.' Thade gunned down another Remnant soldier that was too close for comfort, and turned back to Zailen. 'Still with me, Zailen?'

'You have no idea how much this hurts.' Bright blood oozed between his fingers, soaking his uniform. 'Wasn't this sector supposed to be almost clear? The Vednikans cleared it, they said.'

'Shut up and stop dying,' Thade said. He pulled his blood-wet gloves off, taking his anti-ague gel pack from his hip webbing. He was out of bandages. 'Tasoll, get over here!'

A nearby trooper made a break for Thade's limited cover, throwing himself prone to clear the last few metres. Tasoll was clutching a laspistol in each hand, which he holstered as he knelt up next to the captain. He also removed his dirty gloves, reaching for the medical narthecium pack at his hip. Syringes and bandages were packed neatly within.

'You got shot, Zailen?' Tasoll said. He had a gentle voice, totally at odds with his hulking form.

Zailen hissed through clenched teeth. 'Looks like it. The Vednikan 12th said they'd cleared this place. What is this, then? I've – ow, that hurt, watch your fingers – I've been shot in the bloody stomach.'

'Yeah, yeah, life in the Guard. They don't give medals for getting shot, boy.'

'Boy? I'm twenty-five.'

'And I'm forty, so shut your mouth, boy. On three, move your hands. Understood?'

Zailen made a teeth-gritted noise approximating an affirmative. Thade tapped the anti-ague gel and tossed it on the ground next to Tasoll. The medic acknowledged it with a curt nod and started counting.

Then the feeling hit Thade. A skin-crawling feeling, like a wave of insects under his armour, a million legs tickling his sweating flesh. The yells started from just ahead. Something was coming.

'Thade?' A voice in his ear. The inquisitor again.

'Copy,' Thade was already moving, his eyes flickering through the flashing las-fire and duelling groups of men, seeking the source of unease.

'We're falling back to you. Is that understood, captain?'

The source of Thade's unease was almost three metres tall, clad in ancient armour, and swollen with disease. An oversized bolter chattered in its greenish fists. And it was not alone. From the spire ahead, more Death Guard marched slowly, bolters held at the hip. He had no idea if they walked because their ruined bodies made them unable to run, or if it was just another intimidation tactic, but they fired and Cadians started to die. Soldiers were hammered to the ground all around him. The Death Guard's volley scythed down Imperials and heretics alike. The Traitor Astartes cared nothing for butchering their own minions.

'Understood, inquisitor. The faster, the better,' Thade said, throttling his chainsword. 'Primary threats sighted. '

'The XIV Legion?'

'In the flesh. And lord, we absolutely don't have the men to win this.' Thade ducked back into cover, firing his pistol at nearby Remnant soldiers before they could run into close combat with his men. The

Death Guard were still a distant threat, out of the range of his bolt pistol even as they cut down his soldiers.

'General order, Cadian 88th. Consolidate all force on Venator's vox-caster coordinates. Vox back acknowledgement.'

Miraculously, every platoon leader voxed back.

Caught in the jaws of the Archenemy, the 88th abandoned its objectives and now fought just to survive. The squads fell back, metre by metre, in an organised retreat. Like a flower closing its petals, the scattered elements of Thade's forces came together in unity. They were bloodied, beaten, and suffered losses each step they took.

Above the ash-grey clouds, the Imperial fleet burned. Vox-casters on the surface picked up stray screams from the men aboard those dying ships.

CHAPTER XI
Consolidation

Solthane, Yarith Spire Graveyard,
Monastic sector

TECH-PRIEST ENGINSEER OSIRON swept his metal fist in a gentle panning motion, from east to west. The signum in his hand pulsed its electronic signal to his attendant servitors, and the half-living drones followed the path of their master's hand, unleashing a withering hail of fire. Heavy bolters surgically attached to the servitors in place of their left arms chattered and blasted. The graveyard vista before Osiron cleared as the few Remnant left alive after the volley sought shelter.

'Ammunition depleted,' said one of the servitors in its dead voice. The heavy bolter that formed part of its body clanked as the auto-loaders linked to the slave's backpack cycled through empty chambers.

Away from the other officers, Osiron couldn't have cared less about Kathur Reclamation protocol regarding the sanctity of the architecture. His servitors were armed with heavy weaponry. He was going to use it.

In the wake of the assault, the moans of wounded Remnant reached Osiron's ears. Although it would have been a pleasant vindication to remain and finish the heretics off once and for all, the tech-priest was obeying Thade's fall back order.

Without a word, he turned from the scene of carnage he'd wrought, and his servitors followed in similar silence. The 88th squad with Osiron's unorthodox squad was a group of Whiteshields, under the command of Squad Leader Farren Kel.

Kel was a Whiteshield himself, just turned fourteen years of age. His black helmet was marked with the central white stripe denoting his membership in the Cadian Youth Legion, though a badge of minor rank was evident on his shoulder pad. Bylam Osiron, the Honoured Enginseer, made him nervous. And it wasn't the slaughter the machine-man was capable of. Seeing the tech-priest's servitors gun down over a hundred Remnant was nothing. The Cadian boy was almost fifteen; he'd already killed that many men himself.

'Lord tech-priest?' Kel asked, as the Whiteshields – all under sixteen years old – fell back in smooth formation, each squad providing covering fire for the others. The Remnant was already retrying its rush at the Cadians.

'An unnecessary honorific,' Osiron murmured.

'Sir, the captain's orders are to proceed to his position.' Kel tightened his helmet strap, his blue-violet eyes fixed on the black depths of Osiron's hood.

'I heard them,' Osiron said. Kel just nodded to Osiron's words. No sense asking how the Mechanicus holy man had news the squad had only just picked up on their vox-caster.

'Forward for Cadia,' Kel called out, pointing his own newly-issued chainsword towards the distant figures of the embattled Vigilant platoon. He still felt faintly ridiculous shouting out battle cries like that. He felt like he was doing a bad imitation of Captain Thade, but his troopers followed his every word without any laughter.

They made good time, moving swiftly through the graveyard. Osiron and the servitors were forced into an awkward forward-tilted walk to keep up. Kel heard the tech-priest's breathing coming in harsh metallic rasps, and not for the first time he wondered just how old Osiron was. Was this laboured breathing natural for one of the Machine Cult?

Commissar Tionenji met them on a small rise. A dozen of his men were still alive, the rest lay strewn around the hill. Flanked by Dead Man's Hand, the survivors were enjoying a momentary respite as they readied to fall back to Thade. The tanks that had been assaulting their position were burning husks some distance away, shattered and wrecked by the fury of the five Sentinels' autocannons. Kel stared at Tionenji for several moments.

'Squad Leader Kel,' Tionenji flicked gore from his chainsabre. 'Never seen a commissar before?'

'No, sir. Never, sir.' This was a lie. Kel had seen plenty, but this was his first time off-world. He was staring because he'd never seen a man with black skin before. 'Courage: Broken, sir,' Kel added.

'Ah.' Tionenji noted the Whiteshields had only a few casualties. Their success was the tech-priest's doing, no doubt. Or perhaps the children had simply been sent to a section with less intense fighting. But why had the boy said 'Broken'? He smiled as he gestured to the men preparing around him. 'Vigilant,' he said, 'in bad shape, but Unbroken.'

Kel forced a smile. It must have looked awkward, because the commissar straightened his cap and frowned. 'Something wrong, squad leader?'

'It… doesn't mean that, sir.'

'Hm?' Tionenji turned as one of Dead Man's Hand opened fire once again, the heavy bang-bang-bang of its autocannon echoing across the graveyard as it pounded a distant group of what looked like plague-slain. 'What doesn't mean what?'

'Unbroken, sir. It's just slang. Code for "able to complete mission objectives".'

'Then we're all Broken, eh?'

'Yes, sir.'

'How very uninspiring that thought is.' Tionenji signalled the move-out with a short blast of the whistle around his neck. 'Thank you for the tip, young man.' He made to move, then turned back to Kel. 'Tell me something else, if you would.'

'Anything, sir.'

'The Sentinel squadron. Why are they called "Dead Man's Hand"?'

Kel grinned. It made him look even younger. 'Named after the captain, sir.'

'Named after his lost hand?' asked Tionenji. A trifle grim, even for Cadian humour.

'Ha! No, sir. Have you ever played Black Five? It's a card game. We play it back home. If you get dealt all five black cards in your first turn, it's impossible to win. We call it a dead man's hand.'

'And the captain...'

'...is the worst card player you've ever seen, sir. Adar – that is, Scout-Lieutenant Vertain, sir – he named the squadron after he won three months' wages from the captain. They're the captain's elite scouts, there're five of them, and the name stuck.'

The two platoons fell back together, closing on Thade's position. Tionenji made a promise to himself then: if he survived this, he was going to do his damnedest to make some money off Thade at a card game.

THE SECOND SHADOW stood alone. The Chaos fleet closed in, and only now did the strike cruiser turn to face its oncoming attackers. The wreckage of enemy fighters drifted around the black ship like a corona.

The half-human creature at the *Terminus Est*'s void shield console writhed in the Herald's direction. It tried to speak for the first time in months, but the taint within was so rich, the creature could barely recall human speech. Instead it psychically projected its message in a burst of panic.

Typhus, still standing, turned his colossal armoured bulk to the nearest Death Guard warrior.

'We have been boarded. Assault pods have breached...' the Herald paused, reaching out with his powerful sixth sense, sending his consciousness throughout the halls of the diseased ship. He felt the intrusion as wounds in the flesh of his beloved vessel.

'...decks nineteen, thirteen and six. Starboard. Sections twenty to twenty-four.' *Strange*, he thought. *No sense of intruding life.* 'The Raven Guard have not left the pods, yet. Slaughter them as they emerge. Slaughter them all. Bring me their skulls so the lowliest of my slaves will have new pots to piss in.'

THE DESTROYER HIVE stirred with the Herald's anger. The hollow, bony protrusions jutting from the archaic Terminator armour began to expel flies from their openings. Fat, blood-wet insects thrummed around the bridge, released from the Herald's innards. His god's greatest blessing, contained within a once-mortal shell.

Terminus Est had been boarded. This was not amusing. This was an affront.

* * *

Seth.

Seth.

Seth.

Seth screamed. Psychic lightning raged from his outstretched fingertips, enveloping the Death Guard warrior in tendrils of coruscating energy. Its armour blackened and cracked under the psychic onslaught, and the reek of burning flesh was made far worse by the foul stench of cancerous diseases cooking within the superheated power armour.

The sanctioned psyker broke off his attack, suffering a savage cough that brought blood to his lips. As the destroyed Traitor Astartes collapsed in a heap of ruined armour and burned flesh, Seth cried out at the headache heating the insides of his skull. His brain was boiling. He was sure of it, his brain was boiling. He'd pushed himself too far.

Ban Jevrian pistol-whipped him. It was an ungentle blow that made a loud crack as it connected with the psyker's skull. Seth cried out again, but forced the sound to burst quieter from his lips this time.

'Keep it down, warp-touched freak.'

Seth nodded dumbly, blood streaming from his tear ducts, ears and nostrils.

Jevrian's Kasrkin unit, like the rest of the 88th, was falling back to Captain Thade's position. They were under the graveyard, deep within an underground mausoleum, with Seth seconded to them for support. They'd been exploring until a squad of Death Guard had emerged from the shadowed corridors adjoining a large burial chamber, opening fire. The Kasrkin had taken the two Traitor Marines down with a blistering volley of hellgun fire aimed at the Astartes's armour joints, thirty grenades, and Seth's psychic fury.

Jevrian knelt by the still form of a black-armoured Cadian. He'd lost three of his men to the Traitors' bolters. Three. Three Kasrkin, the elite, the best of the best. He could scarcely fathom the loss. And now he had the warp-touched mutant dribbling and weeping. To hell with Thade's pet wizard; Jevrian was tempted to shoot the bastard now and have done with it.

'Move out,' growled the Kasrkin sergeant. 'Get to the surface, double time.' The Cadians walked the corridors, leaving their dead down in the dark.

Seth.

The voice again. Familiar, but distant. Almost strained. It had been calling for several minutes now. He feared it was the voice from the night of the monastery, calling him by name.

Seth.

Seth took a shuddering breath, steeling himself by imagining his psychic inner walls back into place. With concentration, he could silence the whispering voices that stroked his mind. Daemons, warp-things, hellish creatures from the empyrean reaching into his mind and seeking a way into the world of flesh and blood. He was all too used to resisting their corruptive touch.

Seth! SETH!

No, wait. He knew that voice, sensing it through familiarity rather than any true vocal recognition. Instead of girding his mind in hatred, he opened up to the one calling his name. At the last moment, he feared he'd made a terrible mistake. The denizens of the warp would flood within his mind and steal his body, swallowing his soul.

That didn't happen. He'd made the right gamble.

+Seth.+ The voice was crystal clear now he wasn't fighting it or overexerting himself through use of his powers.

+Brother-Codicier Zaur.+

+Listen to me, Cadian, and listen well. We cannot reach the ground forces. Communications are impossible with the interference caused by the Archenemy fleet. You are my Chapter's only link to the Guard.+

'Keep up, freak,' snarled Jevrian. Seth picked up the pace.

+Is the fleet truly lost?+

+It burns and dies as we speak. *The Second Shadow* remains alone in orbit. We are the final defence before the Death Guard and their slaves land in full force. We have launched our ship-to-ship assault pods against *Terminus Est*.+

+A noble end, brother-codicier. To die taking the fight into the enemy's heart.+

+The fleet is lost, and with it, our precious *Shadow*. But it is not our time to die, Cadian. We need coordinates. We cannot escape this if we remain blind.+

+Coordinates?+ Seth's psychic voice asked, but he already knew why.

+Yes. Coordinates of the remaining Guard units. The assault pods are just a distraction. The *Shadow* was lost the moment the Archenemy fleet arrived, and boarding *Terminus Est* would be death through a thousand poisons. The pods are empty. We are making planetfall.+

+Understood. The only surviving senior officer in the regiment is Captain Thade. He is the only one that will know the exact disposition of Guard units.+

+Then find him! The vox interference is savage and we are deaf to the planet below. We cannot throw our drop-pods blindly at the surface, Seth. The *Shadow* is dying. We need coordinates quickly.+

+It will be done.+

'Master Sergeant?' Seth's voice was an unhealthy rasp, but full of cold threat. It made Jevrian's skin crawl.

'What?'

'On the authority of Brother-Codicier Zaur of the Raven Guard Astartes Chapter, get me to the captain immediately.'

'What in the hell are you–'

'Silence, blunt.'

The stone walls of the undercroft sparkled with the faint kiss of psychic frost. The Kasrkin, those that survived the Death Guard assault, saw their breath steam before their faces. Seth felt the tele-pathic withdrawal of the Astartes psyker with a pang of bitterness. Zaur's power was intoxicatingly strong. It left Seth feeling weak and wretched in its wake.

He reached out again with his ghost-voice, not to Zaur, but to someone much closer.

+Captain Thade.+

THE DEATH GUARD Marine had, in a life almost forgotten now, been Battle-Brother Ammon. He'd turned from the light of the False Emperor at the behest of his Legion commander, the mighty First Captain Typhon. His weapon, the bolter still in his fists today, had roared at the Siege of Terra in the fiery pinnacle of the Horus Heresy ten millennia ago. He'd existed, but not quite lived, each day since the Traitor Legions' defeat, hating everything uncorrupted and untainted in the galaxy.

In this attitude, he was hardly unique in the Death Guard.

Ammon had survived ten thousand years of war, existing as the host of a daemonic disease. He was immortal unless slain, ageless, deathless. The perfection of corruption. His plague-bloated body maintained its own twisted form of life, the way a cancer will feed on healthy cells and fuel itself off a victim's own body.

Ammon's fondest memories were of the great betrayal. The purification of the Legions, the virus bombs falling on their foolish brethren who refused to turn against the Emperor and, of course, the Dropsite Massacre. Astartes fought Astartes and a hundred thousand bolters roared. He still remembered the sound. It rang in his memory's ear like a daemon's screaming rage.

He had killed Iron Hands that day. He had killed Salamanders. And he had killed Raven Guard.

Ammon stalked down the corridor, mucus leaking from the snarling joints of his antique power armour. This area of the Herald's flagship was largely unpopulated except for the blooming diseases growing from the semi-organic metal walls. A sacred place. Holy to the Herald and the pestilence god. A breeding ground for the plagues that trailed *Terminus Est* and ravaged planets in the vessel's wake.

Ammon saw the defilement, black as coal and as large as a troop transport. A Raven Guard assault pod – the hull around its impact twisted and burned. A mag-locked bulkhead stared at Ammon, closed, silent. He knew it contained the loyalist fools within, and voxed for his brethren to come forward, ready to open fire.

'Great Herald,' he voxed. The fluids in his throat made him sound like a man speaking underwater. 'We have located the first pod.'

ON BOARD THE *Second Shadow*, standing by the command throne of a shuddering, burning bridge, Brother-Captain Corvane Valar made a cutting gesture with his black-armoured hand.

At the order, a servitor entered a five-digit code into its console.

Ammon, his brethren squad, the various mutated things with him, and a significant portion of three decks of the *Terminus Est*, were vaporised as the first of the assault pods detonated.

Explosions of similar size tore through the starboard side of *Terminus Est* as the other pods – each rigged with warheads and munitions from *The Second Shadow*'s weapon bays – detonated on cue.

The flagship listed, rolling off course, its insides flooded with alarms, screams and flame. In the course of a single battle with a grossly-outnumbered Imperial fleet, the Herald's vessel had sustained more damage than it had since the Siege of Terra. Bleeding and streaming ghostly, unnatural fire from its wounds, the huge ship broke off its attack run.

A great cheer sounded on the *Shadow's* bridge, cried by Astartes and Chapter serfs alike. Corvane let the cheer subside, feeling satisfaction course through him.

'Servants of the Chapter, you have served us well. Today you may die knowing your duty is done, and each of your names will be etched in the Chapter's records.'

Then he turned to his brother giants in their black armour. 'Raven Guard to the drop-pods. Make ready for planetfall.'

SETH'S WARNING WAS weak – the psyker had long sensed the captain was resistant to psychic contact, even for a blunt, but the message got through. With most of his surviving units reunited, Thade commanded over two hundred men defending a cluster of mausoleums in the graveyard grounds of Yarith Spire.

Squads were stationed in a ring around a central building – an ornate tomb raised in honour of a pilgrim of great worth who'd died some six thousand years before. The cover was better here; the Cadians moved between the mausoleums, firing out at the advancing Remnant horde. Thade's few weapons teams set up their heavy bolters in the shadows of these gargoyle-encrusted buildings, adding their furious rate of fire to the onslaught of lasrifles on full-auto. Dead Man's Hand stalked the edges of the Cadian defensive line, autocannons pounding into the disorganised ranks of the Archenemy.

Vertain swore as another group of Remnant cowered behind a small shrine building. A single round from his cannon would annihilate the marble structure and expose the enemy troops. Instead of firing, Vertain turned his Sentinel aside with a curse, opening fire at another group out in the open.

'This would be much easier if we could fire at the damn scenery,' he muttered.

'Copy that,' Greer voxed back.

'We're dead, either way.' Vertain switched vox-channels. 'Captain?'

Thade was in the centre of the Cadian defence, speaking with several officers, including Commissar

Tionenji, Seth and Inquisitor Caius. He turned his head and clicked his micro-bead.

'Thade, go.'

'Sir, requesting permission to ignore Reclamation protocol and open fire on blessed structures in order to prosecute the enemy to maximum effect.'

Thade laughed. 'Delicately phrased. Does the Emperor like gold? Fire at will. Inform the other squads.'

Tionenji narrowed his eyes. 'What was that order?'

'The order to abandon Reclamation Protocol Zero-Nine.' Thade met Tionenji's eyes. 'A problem, commissar?'

'The protocols are the underpinning of this entire venture. The destruction of holy structures is counted as blasphemy against the God-Emperor.'

'The protocol is a waste of life and a sure way of ensuring we lose this war. It's a rule set down by Lord General Maggrig, who – if reports are correct – is dead.'

'Confirmed,' Janden said. 'The landing site was overrun twenty-seven minutes ago. Lord General Maggrig's death was confirmed by Vednikan scouts. He was crucified by the Remnant.'

'I heard the damn reports!' Tionenji fumed.

'We'll minimise collateral damage as much as can realistically be allowed for, but by the Golden Throne, I will not die here so some Ecclesiarchy bastard can smile in a few years about how we helped save on reconstruction costs in one paltry square kilometre of a city the size of a continent. Winning the war is more important than saving a handful of credits.'

'You are committing heresy. I am within my rights to execute you.'

'I'm fighting a war. Which is the greater sin: losing the world to Chaos, or losing a few shrines in the world's defence?'

'Semantics, captain. Semantics that fail to justify blasphemy.'

'We're fighting a war almost entirely without our heavy weaponry, which was left neatly packed in crates aboard ships that are now nothing but wreckage in orbit. My men are as pious as any in the Imperium, Commissar Tionenji. They will use moderation.'

Tionenji did what Thade had been expecting since the moment he met him. He went for his side arm.

Tionenji was a fine example of the Commissariat's standards of training. He drew fast, his hand a blur, and had the pistol aimed at Thade's face before his heart had beat a second time.

'If you will not do your duty–' Tionenji began.

Then he swallowed, listening to the threatening buzz of live weapons. Thade stood unmoving, his violet eyes glaring into the commissar's own. Next to him, Ban Jevrian was holding his hellpistol in both hands, aiming at Tionenji's eye. At Thade's other shoulder, Lieutenant Horlan had his laspistol raised and similarly aimed. Tionenji flicked his glance left and right. Every Cadian officer had his weapon aimed at the commissar, even the fourteen-year-old boy.

'Drop it,' hissed Jevrian.

'Commissar or not,' Lieutenant Horlan said, 'you die if that gun stays out of its holster.'

Tionenji smiled. 'Gentlemen, you have just signed this regiment's death warrant.'

Jevrian's hellpistol whined as it reached full charge. 'I said drop it.'

'I'll see you all dead for this.'

'We're all dead anyway,' young Kel grinned without humour.

'Stop pointing that pretty pistol at a warden-captain of Cadia,' Horlan said. 'Right now.'

'Right now,' Jevrian growled as he repeated Horlan's words, 'or I kill you where you stand, you off-world son of a bitch.'

Tionenji holstered his laspistol, a patently false smile creasing his lips. 'Very well.'

The Cadians slowly lowered their weapons, each man still on edge. Thade cleared his throat, taking a breath before speaking. He almost looked shaken. It was clear he'd not expected his men to behave as they did.

'That was... unpleasant. Now, if we may focus on the matter at hand?'

'By what authority–' Tionenji started again, but Thade interrupted.

'By the authority that I am the highest-ranking officer in the Imperial Guard left alive on this world. That makes me Overseer of the Kathur Reclamation until a higher Imperial authority says otherwise.'

Inquisitor Bastian Caius coughed politely.

Thade and Tionenji turned to inquisitor. They'd both forgotten he was there.

'Are you quite done, gentlemen?'

Tionenji saluted. Thade nodded. Caius fixed Thade with his unnerving gaze, false eyes whirring as they focused. 'Captain, I am the highest echelon of Imperial authority here.'

'Lord–' Thade began. Throne of Terra, the inquisitor had just seen that standoff…

'Enough! Your cancellation of the deceased lord general's orders is acceptable. As for your confrontation with your commissar, I couldn't care less. It will be dealt with by the proper authorities when the time comes. Focus, you fools. We have a duty to do.'

Thade and Tionenji glared at each other until the captain broke the stare.

'Janden, are the coordinates ready to send to *The Second Shadow*?'

The vox-officer nodded. Through intense vox-tuning, he'd compiled a list of the remaining regiments and their locations within Solthane. It was a short list, and no officer above the rank of lieutenant still lived. The coordinates he'd gathered were precise landing points – no danger of hitting friendly troops or crashing into buildings on the way down.

'Good work,' said Thade. 'Seth, how long has it been since you received the Astartes's message?'

The sanctioned psyker checked his wrist chronometer. 'Just under six minutes.'

'Is vox clear enough to send the coordinates up there?'

'It's a fifty-fifty chance at best.' Janden looked ashamed. 'My set was winged in the last fight. I can barely get it working shortwave.' He tapped a nasty looking bullet hole that had sheared off a chunk of the vox-caster's casing.

'I can't send it,' Seth shook his head. 'I know what you're thinking. I can't link minds over that distance. Sorry, sir.'

'Noted. Thade to 88th. Any vox-casters still functioning in a worthwhile capacity?'

A chorus of negatives came back over his vox-bead. Blood of the Emperor, they'd taken a beating. Thade's three hundred men had six of the powerful vox-casters between them. And now, down to just under two hundred soldiers, their high-end communications gear was either lost in battle or scrambled by interference to the point of uselessness.

'No more delays. Punch it, Janden.'

'Sending. If they launch immediately, they'll touch down at our western perimeter in just over two minutes.'

The western perimeter. Darrick was there, leading his remaining platoons. He'd encountered the least resistance in this latest consolidation, and Thade knew that made Darrick's zone the clearest for an orbital landing.

Thade wasn't lying with what he'd said to the commissar. He was as pious as any Imperial citizen, but he sometimes wondered if the Emperor manipulated certain events just to see him squirm out of them. This was one such time. Darrick's voice broke across the vox, distorted and shouting.

'Captain! Captain! Throne in flames! Captain! Primary threat contact. This one's the biggest bastard yet.'

'What the hell? Darrick, you told me you could keep your area clear.'

'And it was going great, sir. Until this dreadnought showed up.'

THE SECOND SHADOW trembled in its death throes. In the red-lit confines of a drop-pod, Brother-Captain Corvane Valar looked at nine of his brother Astartes, each one strapped into their descent seats, facing inward. They sat in silence, trusting their fates to the Cadians below.

Zauren had tried to contact the sanctioned psyker several times, not trusting the shattered Imperial vox-channels to convey the coordinates. The nearness of so many warp-tainted Chaos vessels was ruining his psychic strength. Each time he felt his concentration reaching out to Seth, the feeling of connection was lost almost immediately. He feared it was more than natural warp distortion from the Archenemy's proximity. The pressure on his sixth sense was warm and insidious, almost alive. It occluded his psychic sight like a blanket thrown over his true eyes.

So the Raven Guard waited for a vox transmission they knew might never come. Corvane had given orders to launch the pods no matter what if they were still aboard when the ship's destruction came. But they were holding on until the last moment. To die as a drop-pod careened off a building and exploded on the ground was no way for a warrior to perish. With the *Shadow's* scanners down, they needed those landing coordinates from the surface.

The ship shuddered with supreme violence. 'Throne,' said Zaur quietly. It was the first word spoken in the pod since the Astartes had boarded minutes ago.

'Initiating drop,' blared a mechanical voice over the pod's internal vox speakers.

'For the Emperor!' one of the Astartes cried. Dockings uncoupled, locks released, and five night-black pods slashed from the hull of the burning *Second Shadow*.

Aboard Corvane's pod, the world was reduced to darkness and heavy shaking as it fore down through the planet's atmosphere.

'Two minutes,' he called out to his men. In answer, nine of humanity's finest warriors, gene-shaped from the genetic material of the Emperor and His beloved primarch sons, made the sign of the aquila to their leader.

Above them, the strike cruiser went critical. The explosion sent wreckage slicing through space, wounding Chaos vessels that were, in their mindless eagerness to destroy the Raven Guard, too close to evade the blast radius. Even in death, the Raven Guard vessel claimed traitorous lives.

THE ARCHENEMY WAR machine was approximately four metres tall and almost as wide. Roughly humanoid in shape, it walked in a stomping, short-legged stride that would have been comical had the war machine not been one of the deadliest things Taan had ever seen in his life. The walker's arms were weapons: the left was a steel limb ending in a wide chainsaw fist the size of a grown man, the right was a long cannon with coils along its length that glowed with dull blue heat.

Dreadnought. A thickly-armoured shell bearing hideous weapons. Darrick had seen one, and only one, before. The Flesh Tearers Chapter had fielded one of these relic war machines during the Black Crusade three years before. Darrick had watched with wide eyes as it had torn a tank to pieces with its steel-rending claws, ignoring endless streams of small arms fire clattering off its hull. Not much in this galaxy had managed to unnerve Lieutenant Taan Darrick in his years within the Shock, but that had been one of them.

And it had been on his side.

This one was not. It had walked from the city, surrounded by a mob of howling Remnant as it strode through the graveyard.

Darrick looked left. He looked right. His platoon, taking cover from the Remnant in the garden of mausoleums, was armed almost entirely with their standard-issue lasrifles. The ground shook as the dreadnought stomped closer.

'It's firing!' someone cried. Darrick didn't need to be told that. The air tingled and made his teeth ache as the dreadnought's plasma cannon charged up. To Taan, it was like a great beast was drawing breath to roar. He took a breath, looking around over the top of the waist-high marble wall he'd been crouched behind. The Remnant was still advancing, supported by the Death Guard war machine.

It fired. A horrendous stream of retina-burning light flared from the plasma cannon's steaming nozzle, striking the side of one mausoleum and washing the white stone in superheated energy. The first stones touched by the kiss of the beam weapon were incinerated into nothingness, and the surrounding rock melted a heartbeat later. The wall ceased to exist, and the Cadians nearby broke cover and fled. Most were gunned down by the advancing Remnant.

'Oh, that's just got to die,' Darrick said. He clicked his vox live. 'Darrick to Enginseer Osiron.'

'Osiron here.'

'Plasma cannon, big one, and I've got nothing that can crack open a dreadnought. Alliance is very, very Broken.'

'The plasma technology used by the Traitor Legions is primarily Heresy-era grade. That means–'

'Enginseer,' Taan tried.

'...the sustained build up of ionised gas...'

'Osiron!' Another wall exploded in a gum-aching eyesore of charged air and melted rock. 'Time is a factor!'

'...requires a longer and more forceful venting period than current plasma technology. Use that time to move into cover.'

'Oh.' Darrick killed the vox and shouted to his men, 'Grenades at the dreadnought when that cannon is cooling down!' He glanced at the man crouching next to him. Farazien was clutching his grenade launcher. 'Any serious ammunition in that?'

'Just frags.'

'Maybe we can give it an itch. 88th, time to stop hiding! Show your faces and kill some Remnant. Anyone with grenades, get ready to offer them up nice and generous, like. Throw for the dreadnought's feet on my mark.'

Another mausoleum wall ceased to exist under the cannon's fury. This time, several of Darrick's platoon were caught in the blast, dissolved by the plasma washing over them. Trooper Jova howled as his arm disintegrated and he stumbled out of his shattered cover to be scythed down by Remnant las-fire. Trooper Haken and Sergeant Taine were half-smothered by the white-hot, splashing plasma – not enough to kill them instantly. As they lay thrashing on the ground, bodies dissolving, Taan's rifle sang out twice and head-shotted them out of their misery.

He looked over the wall again, sighting the dreadnought. Off-white steam was gushing from the holes bored into the edge of the cone nozzle, and the coiled energy rings layered like a spine across the back of the cannon were glowing bright.

'Now!' Darrick called. 'Fire!'

Taan's men rose and opened fire. Grenades flew to smack around the feet of the dreadnought, and las-fire sliced into the advancing Remnant. Heretics were punched from their feet by the volley.

The cluster of grenades – fragmentation bombs used to kill infantry and break up units of men – went off a moment later. The dreadnought stalked through the resulting smoke, its greenish hull a little blackened in places but otherwise unharmed.

'Damn it,' Darrick said, getting ready to order a fallback. He had nothing that could wound the accursed thing, and the dreadnought marched on.

Its stomping advance suddenly halted as a high-calibre autocannon round hammered into its chest. Shards of armour splintered and flew aside as several more impacts followed. Taan's men cheered as Dead Man's Hand stalked past them, wading into the enemy.

Vertain guided his Sentinel from the relative cover of the mausoleums, triggers held down. Red ammo warnings flashed on his control console.

'I'm firing hopes and prayers, here,' he voxed on the general channel. 'If anyone has a heroic plan, now's the time to make it happen.'

'It's *bleeding*,' Greer voxed. And it was. The dreadnought's adamantite armoured shell was, in many places, sheathed over in patches of foul grey flesh. As the autocannon shells tore chunks of armour away, fragments of bloody bone and rancid meat flew aside, too. Taan's men renewed their return fire, cutting down Remnant with lethal accuracy.

Thade ran into cover alongside Darrick. With him were Rax and Ban Jevrian.

'I heard you had a problem,' the captain said. Venator platoon and the Kasrkin squad were dispersing alongside Darrick's men. Thade rose, fired his pistol at the Remnant, but his gaze fell over the dreadnought.

One of Dead Man's Hand was down before it – the Sentinel's legs sheared off at the knees by the dreadnought's massive chainblade. Thade saw the pilot, Greer, burst the roof of his walker open and scramble to get away. The dreadnought's swinging chainblade put an end to that attempt. Greer's body fell in two gory halves.

Dead Man's Hand was backing away now, firing sporadically. Thade knew most of them needed to reload.

The enemy war machine was limping, dragging one leg while blood, pus and a black fluid streamed from the gaping holes in its semi-organic armour. Even at a distance of fifty metres and more, it reeked of filth and waste.

'That's got to die,' Thade whispered.

'My thoughts exactly,' Darrick said.

'Kasrkin, with me!' the captain shouted, gunning his chainsword. '88th, covering fire!'

'You're joking.' Taan grabbed Thade's wrist, feeling the tension of cables and steel under the sleeve. 'This is the stupidest thing you've ever done.'

With his free hand, Thade tapped the silver on his own helm.

'Point taken,' Darrick amended, letting go of Thade. 'This is the second-stupidest thing you've ever done.'

'Are we doing this, or what?' Jevrian snapped. 'There's a war going on, you know.'

'Watch it, glory boy,' Taan smirked.

'For the Emperor!' Thade shouted as he broke into a run. Jevrian and the Kasrkin sprinted after him, with Rax running alongside.

What followed took place in the span of half a minute. To Taan, watching as he and his men provided covering fire, it lasted a few seconds. To Thade, it felt like an hour.

The dreadnought was wounded. Dead Man's Hand had seen to that. He'd never have tried something this… this stupid, otherwise.

Thade led the Kasrkin across the open ground. The wounded dreadnought turned in a ponderous arc, seeking to bring its plasma cannon to bear, but the Cadians were already too close. Thade's chainblade sang at the back of the war machine's knee joints, ripping through cables slick with filth. On the backswing, as the dreadnought roared its anger, the whining sword slashed at a hip joint and dug in. Thade clenched his teeth as the blade bucked in his hands, the teeth ravaging the softer mechanics of the dreadnought's waist joint.

The Kasrkin fanned out, opening up with their hellguns and shooting into the surrounding Remnant, forcing them back from Thade's insane melee. Jevrian ran at the dreadnought's front, his power sabre gleaming with crackling energy as he activated it. He fired his hellpistol at point-blank range, spearing holes in the great, rotting hulk that towered above him.

'Hurry the hell up!' he yelled. Thade sawed, head turned from the outpourings of stinking, oily blood that gushed from the severed pipes and joint cables.

Jevrian threw himself to the side as the wailing dreadnought lashed out with its massive chainfist. Even prone, he was still in its arc, and at the last second his power sword clashed against the falling blade to block certain death. The impact was beyond jarring; he felt something snap in his shoulder and was thrown ten metres away, landing in a ragged heap of dented armour and Cadian oaths. He staggered to his feet, seeing stars and clutching the hilt of his shattered power blade. With a Kasrkin battle cry, he ran in again while still half-dazed and with a broken arm.

'Never fall! Never surrender!'

The Kasrkin ringing the duellists shouted as they fired at the Remnant daring to approach. 'Never outnumbered! Never outgunned!'

Thade heaved back on his chainsword to pull it free, and hammered it back into the mutilated hip joint with all his strength. The blade bounced for the ghost of a moment, then the whirring teeth snagged on the mechanics again, biting in with renewed ferocity. The dreadnought tried to spin on its waist axis, but its attempt amounted to little more than a grinding of broken gears and squealing, mutilated joints.

Thade felt the teeth bite solid metal, sawing into the core of the dreadnought's leg, eating through the machine's metal bones. It began to stumble, slashing its chainfist wildly and unleashing a torrent of plasma fire at the ground.

'Go!' Thade shouted, finally ripping his sword free. He ran back, clearing the dreadnought's immediate radius of destruction as it sagged and staggered, lower to the ground now.

Jevrian scaled the war machine one-handed. His broken blade, crackling with its power field unstable but still active, rammed into the staggering dreadnought's frontal armour and sank to the hilt. The Kasrkin sergeant's gloved right hand sought purchase, finding it in an oozing hole made by an autocannon shell. He hauled himself up with one hand, his boot on his impaled sword hilt for support.

As the Death Guard war machine flailed and staggered, half-crippled and trying to shake off the human that clung to its front, Jevrian jammed the muzzle of his hellpistol into the finger-thin vision slit on the dreadnought's ornate face and pulled the trigger.

It fell. The pilot of the dreadnought had once been an Astartes, interred within a walking adamantite tomb of ancient Mechanicus design. The pistol fire lanced into the withered husk that was all that remained of the warrior within, cutting the once-man to pieces and ending the dreadnought's last vestiges of life.

A low whine rang out as the hulking mass powered down. Jevrian leapt clear in case it toppled. It didn't; it merely stood slouched, arms hanging dead at its sides. Having seen their champion fall, the Remnant force was in full retreat. Cadian lasfire flashed after them, biting into exposed backs and sending more of the Archenemy's troops to the ground.

Thade and Jevrian walked back to Taan, both out of breath.

'Shitting hell,' Darrick said.

'Yeah,' agreed the Kasrkin sergeant. 'My arm's broken,' he said, just noticing. Thade smiled his crooked smile, absently patting the top of Rax's chrome head.

'I hope we never see another one of those.'

Seventeen seconds later, a tank-sized pod – painted black and scorched blacker from planetfall – smashed into the ground fifty metres from the 88th front line. A wave of dirt was thrown up with the impact, some of the smaller earthen debris clattering off the Cadians' helmets and shoulder guards. With a snarl of moving parts, the sides of the drop-pod opened like a flower facing the sun. The sides clanged onto the ground, becoming ramps by which the Raven Guard descended.

The ten giants came out, bolters up, seeking targets. After a moment, the ten Astartes lowered their weapons in unison. They gathered around the mangled, dripping hulk of the dead dreadnought. Faint vox-clicks reached Thade's ears – the Astartes were talking to each other about what they were seeing. One of them moved over to the exhausted soldiers. Thade recognised him from his armour and made the sign of the aquila. His men mirrored the salute.

'Victory or Death, brother-captain.'

The Astartes didn't reply at once. Then, in the most human gesture Thade had ever seen from one of the Emperor's chosen, Corvane Valar hiked a thumb over his massive shoulder plate, in the direction of the downed war machine.

'Impressive work, captain.'

Thade felt himself smiling as he spoke to the giant in black, 'Thank you. Incidentally, you're welcome to help out with the next one.'

CHAPTER XII
Alone

Solthane, Yarith Spire Graveyard,
Monastic sector

Two HOURS LATER, the Cadians abandoned their
dead.

'The Reclamation is over until reinforcements
come,' Inquisitor Caius had addressed the 88th
survivors as the skies darkened with the threat of
rain. 'I have spoken with the Raven Guard
commander and established limited contact with
what remains of the Imperial Guard force in
Solthane. The picture is grim. The Astartes have
departed to secure their own objectives in the city
and battle the Death Guard on their own terms.
That leaves the Imperial Guard regiments to create

whatever unified resistance they can forge from the ashes of this... this disaster.'

The Cadians, barely a hundred and fifty still standing, clustered around the speaking inquisitor.

'What about the rest of the regiment?' a trooper called. 'What about Colonel Lockwood?'

'We've lost contact with whatever remains of the colonel's forces,' Thade said. 'They were attacked by a force that far eclipsed the Remnant assaulting us. Odds of survival are unfavourable.'

'What about the colours?' Darrick asked. 'If I'm going to die here, I want to do it under the banner of the 88th.'

'He's right, sir,' Vertain said. 'If we're all that's left, we can't leave the standard in the mud.' A chorus of agreement met this. Thade crossed his arms and looked at the inquisitor with a raised eyebrow.

'I told you they'd say that,' he observed.

It was decided a short time later. The 88th under Thade's command would travel to the last known coordinates of Lockwood's men and look for survivors. The regimental banner had to be retrieved. They would do this on the way back to Reclamation headquarters.

'Are we going back for the tanks?' Ban Jevrian asked. The Kasrkin sergeant was a mess of bruises and cracked carapace armour.

Thade nodded. 'Count on it.'

'Good,' Darrick cut in. 'I'm tired of walking everywhere.'

'Platoon leaders, see to your wounded. We leave no one behind.' Thade scanned the crowd – all that remained of his regiment. 'On the way to Colonel Lockwood's last coordinates, we stop to load the Chimeras. Then scouts will enter the main Reclamation base and look for supplies. Priorities are water purifiers, anti-infection medication and ration packs. Any questions?'

Silence answered this. 'Good,' Thade finished. 'The Emperor protects. Now move.'

As the men moved out, Thade fell to the back of the column, walking with Inquisitor Caius. Once the two men were out of earshot from the others, Thade opened with a rueful smile.

'That business with Tionenji...'

'He'll see you all shot and be well within his rights to do it. But for now I need you, so you get to live.'

Thade nodded, expecting no less. 'That's not the reason I wished to speak with you. Don't make me beg for the answers I need, lord.'

Caius turned his head to face the captain, and his psycannon pivoted accordingly. 'Throne,' Thade complained, 'doesn't that ever shut down?'

'No. Now get to the point.'

'The Ordo Sepulturum. What are you looking for on Kathur?'

'Do not mistake me, captain, your recent defence was exemplary. You are a fine officer, and using that cluster of mausoleums as a firebase was inspired thinking. The Reclamation's restriction on heavy weaponry has proven a chore, but even with this disadvantage you have done well. But try to be realistic with your ambitions. You do not have the ear of the Holy Ordos of His Majesty's Inquisition.'

'You don't know, do you?'

'I am running out of patience with this course of conversation.'

'Listen to me.' Thade rested his augmetic hand on the inquisitor's shoulder. The psycannon hummed for a moment, powered up on instinct and quelled by the inquisitor's psychic command.

'I am listening.'

'We are trapped on this world for the next month or more without reinforcements. The main bulk of the ground forces' water purification was performed by recyclers aboard the orbiting fleet. While we have enough food and anti-ague medication on the surface, we'll lose all of it if the Death Guard or the Remnant take over the Reclamation's base – which, by all reports, they already have.'

'I am aware of the situation we face.'

'No, inquisitor. You're not. You're missing something rather vital.'

'Explain yourself.'

'Look at these soldiers,' Thade nodded to the marching column ahead. 'Take a long look. What do you see?'

'Your men.'

'Look harder.'

'The Cadian 88th.'

'Try again.'

'I am not obtuse, but I am far from patient. I asked you to get to the point.'

'Humour me.'

The inquisitor, curious now, looked at the soldiers up ahead. What did he see? Brain-dead servitors walked in their shambling gait around the red-cloaked form of Enginseer Osiron. The surviving Kasrkin kept together in their own dark-armoured pack, a little away from the others. Caius noticed, for the first time, a tattoo on the back of Ban Jevrian's bullish neck. 'Unbroken' it read, in stylised Gothic script. Seth Roscrain walked alone, leaning heavily on his black staff. While the Kasrkin kept their distance, the soldiers seemed to instinctively avoid the sanctioned psyker.

The main bulk of soldiers were ragged, dirty, but straight-backed and alert with their weapons at the ready. The formation was orderly and efficient, with the stretcher bearers carrying the wounded – each pair surrounded by a fire-team of men from their platoon. The Sentinels, the four still in working order, stalked in a ceaseless patrol around the marching column.

Caius's psychic sense picked up on what his natural senses did not. The air around the Cadians was powerfully grim – every man's thoughts turned to the trials of surviving the next few hours, let alone the next five weeks until reinforcements reached orbit. The sense of defeat was palpable now.

'I see...'

'Yes?'

'...your point, captain.'

'I thought you would. Our regiment was a thousand strong. Just over a hundred remain alive, and we're looking at the prospect of dying of starvation or Chaos-tainted infection unless we can secure our conquered base. Now I know what you want. You want to continue your search, seeking whatever it is that brought the Curse of Unbelief to this world. I'm telling you in cold honesty that without answers, without *hope*, that's not going to happen with us at your side. And now we face execution if Tionenji wishes it.'

Thade drew a breath and continued, 'This is not about Inquisitorial authority, lord. This is about war, and this is about Cadia. Every single man here expects to die today. I expect to die today. And we want to die, because one last charge against the Death Guard and killing as many of them as we can is one hell of a way to go. Since childhood, we've all known we were born to die in war. Walking across a plague planet for days on end until starvation sets in is not the way any Cadian wants to die. Nor is a firing squad because of one overzealous otherworlder seen as a prime way to meet the God-Emperor in the afterlife.'

'You're wrong. This *is* about authority, Thade. And I hold it. I demand that you serve me.'

'Ah, now we come to the crux of the matter. I could disobey this order and never suffer punishment, as being dead in the coming battle would leave me far from harm's way. So let me be clear, lord. I'm charged with leading my men into battle and ensuring above all that they fight and die for the Golden Throne. So convince me. Convince me that one last charge against the enemy and killing a horde of them isn't the best way to serve the Throne. Convince me the God-Emperor wants more from us, or we die in battle for Him tonight.'

Caius smiled. 'This is an amusing little blackmail, is it not? But I take your point. You will obey because I demand it, but I will throw you the bone you and your men need in order to be... motivated.'

'You've a generous soul, lord.' Thade grinned back.

'You ask much of me. I already gave you permission to recover your regimental banner, did I not?'

'That coin spins two ways. It's tactically sound to seek out the survivors of the 88th. I am, after all, the current commanding officer. But let's cut to the point. What is it I should know, inquisitor?'

'And what if I say that what I know for certain is little more than what I already told you?'

'Then I would ask you to guess what's going on, because the educated assumptions of a servant of the Ordo Sepulturum are more than good enough for me.'

'Very well. I am tasked with visiting the various shrines of true merit within Solthane, seeking the source of the taint.'

'That much I know.'

'Unlike any other outbreak in recorded Scarus history, no Archenemy vessel brought the disease from orbit, no sightings of the Herald's flagship were registered before the plague struck, nothing of the conventional kind occurred here. We reasoned that something already present on the planet was responsible.'

'This is still not news to anyone, lord.'

'The Ordo Sepulturum has its suspicions of what caused this plague.' That caught Thade's attention. 'We have a theory. It matches the records I have of a cultist interrogation before the Curse of Unbelief struck. And now, with hindsight, it matches the sudden appearance of the *Terminus Est* and the Herald's fleet.'

'Tell me.'

'First you tell me, captain. What do you know of Kathur's achievements before his glorious ascension to sainthood?'

Thade shrugged. 'Nothing. Just what's stated in the shrineworld's scrolls. A file of them was attached to our initial briefing reports on planetfall.'

'And what glorious picture of sainthood did these holy texts paint?'

'He was a crusader. An Imperial Army commander thousands of years ago. He worked with the old Astartes Legions to reclaim the lost worlds of mankind.'

Inquisitor Bastian Caius smiled. The patronising curve of his lips made Thade's skin crawl.

'So, he was a leader within the fledgling Imperium, allegedly during the Great Crusade. And how did he die?'

'He was killed in battle on this world, the last planet his armies brought into compliance with the Imperium. I've heard it said even the Raven Guard primarch honoured him by speaking at his funeral.'

'And what of his remains? Where do the bones of this great hero rest?'

'They are interred across Solthane in various shrines.'

'A perfect recital of common knowledge, captain. And almost entirely incorrect.'

Thade shrugged again. He wasn't surprised.

'So enlighten me,' he said.

'Kathur did not die in the Great Crusade. He died in the Horus Heresy itself. And his bones, may the God-Emperor bless them, do not rest on this world. This shrineworld does not honour his final resting place. It honours his memory.'

'So where did he die?'

'That's not the vital question, but I'll answer it.' Caius slowly raised a finger. At first Thade thought the inquisitor wanted silence. Then he realised the other man was pointing. Pointing up.

'He died in space?'

'In orbit. Aboard the flagship of his fleet, the Emperor-class battleship *In Purity Protected*. The vessel was lost with all hands, and the wreckage rained down to the planet below.

'What destroyed his ship?'

'Now that, captain, is the vital question. The truth is a strange beast. It appears differently to each soul seeing it. The mists of time will shroud any truth, because truth changes with age. Events become memories, memories become history, and history becomes legend.'

'I see,' said Thade. He resisted the urge to roll his eyes, guiltily hoping the inquisitor hadn't picked up on that thought.

'Ten thousand years before this Reclamation, when our newborn Imperium almost tore itself apart in the Horus Heresy, the galaxy burned in countless battles across countless systems. Unknowable numbers of stories from this era are no longer recounted in their entirety. But this one... This one we know is the truth. An enduring core of truth behind a lie that has grown around it like a pleasant shell.'

'So what destroyed Kathur's ship? Was it the *Terminus Est*? My sanctioned psyker has learned that the Herald's vessel destroyed the flagship of the Raven Guard in the Horus Heresy.'

'No, captain,' Caius smiled. 'The grudge held by the Raven Guard is their own weight to bear – though I am not blind to the fact Fate seems to have brought us all together against the XIV Legion on this world.'

'Throne, just answer the bloody question. What destroyed Kathur's ship? What was he fighting here?'

'The Death Guard battleship *Aggrieved*. After the failed Siege of Terra, when the Traitor Legions turned tail and fled to the warp, not all of them made it to the blossoming *Occularis Terribus* here in Scarus Sector. Many were damaged from the assault on Holy Terra, and their warp drives threw them back into realspace far short of their daemonic haven. Lord Admiral Kathur and his vessel, *In Purity Protected*, chased the *Aggrieved* here and engaged it above the world that would one day be named for him.'

'So your theory is that the *Aggrieved* left something here after it destroyed Kathur's ship? Something that has lain silent until now?'

'That is a possibility. But I believe otherwise.'

'The *Aggrieved* never left.' Thade said, swallowing as it all fell into place. 'The *Aggrieved* remained here, hidden somewhere on the planet.'

'That is what I believe. *In Purity Protected* was the cream of the Imperial Navy, even were it damaged in the hell of Terra's Siege. The Death Guard vessel would have suffered under its assault. I suspect the *Aggrieved* was forced into a crash landing. It struck the surface and remained undiscovered since the days of the Heresy. Ever since I came to this world, I've heard a voice calling out, screaming into the warp, pleading for aid. Your sanctioned psyker has heard it, too. I've read his mind several times to be sure. I believe he even tried to tell you once. The voice is weak, but the screamer was at least strong enough to leave a beacon for its brethren to find.'

'The Curse of Unbelief.'

'Yes, the plague. All the suffering, all the disease, all the death. A sickening sign that lights up in the unseen world, saying: "I am here. Come to me".'

The thought staggered Thade. To consider such pain reaching out into the warp, acting as a beacon. All those lives lost, just to send a message. It was blasphemy on a scale he couldn't fully comprehend.

'But why now?' he asked. 'If you're right, the *Aggrieved* has been here for a hundred centuries, silent as a tomb. Why now?'

'Because something aboard the ship's wreckage has finally woken up. Something powerful enough to cause the plague that killed this world, and so important to the Death Guard that the Herald himself has come to meet it.'

'Where is it? Throne, *what* is it?'

'If we knew the answers to those questions, this war would already be over. I had planned to visit each truly holy site within Solthane's cathedral district and perform various rituals of scrying. It's my belief that the first colonists and city-builders will have sensed the slumbering malice from the crashed vessel. Imperial records are full of similar incidents – cultures unknowingly raising their holiest sites over places of great darkness to nullify the touch of evil. A subconscious defence, if you will.'

'There's a lot of "maybe" sticking out of this plan, lord.'

'Do I have your support now, Captain Thade? Have I convinced you the Emperor wants more from you and your men than some vainglorious last charge?'

Thade took a long time before answering. Finally, with a rueful smile and a strange gleam in his violet eyes, he said 'We have to reach the wreck of the *Aggrieved* before the Herald.'

'That is impossible at this stage. They will be landing as we speak. They likely know exactly where it is. We do not.'

'Yes, we do.' Thade clicked his vox live and ordered Seth to join him at the back of the column.

'I've already spoken with your sanctioned psyker. He was unable to confirm anything of use. He could be no more precise than first sensing it upon entering the cathedral district several nights ago. We are already in the cathedral district, captain. We still have hundreds of square kilometres to search.'

'Count the Seven,' Thade whispered with a dawning smile. 'Count the Seven. The clarity of our scanners at the monastery... The vox-ghosts... We heard them trying to speak with it, trying to wake it up. We caught them voxing Death Guard battle mantras on every frequency. They were scanning for it. They were *calling* to it. Blood of the God-Emperor, it's under the monastery. It has to be.'

'It might be,' the inquisitor allowed. 'But it's far from certain. Yours was not the only regiment to encounter scanner clarity in the monastic sector in the past week; merely the first. I intended to visit each reported site. And I remind you that "under the monastery" means no more than "under a building the size of a small city".'

The captain took a breath, watching the shuffling form of Seth Roscrain making his way back through the marching soldiers. Once more, he remembered the sanctioned psyker's words in the Shrine of the Emperor's Unending Majesty – at the heart of the monastery before they'd faced the first Death Guard warrior. Seth had never spoken of the voice before. It started that night, on that mission, when everything had really started to foul up beyond repair. It had happened in the monastery's heart.

'Seth only heard the voice as he grew nearer to it. But you… The Astartes… You both heard it before and hear it now. But Seth is weaker than you. He heard it only as he drew nearer to it. You can't track it yourself because the voice is ever-present. But you can track it by watching its influence within him.'

The inquisitor's gaze remained unbroken as Thade finally said, 'I've been blind.'

'Yes, you have.'

'You were planning all along to use us – use Seth – as the bloodhound to track this voice.'

'As soon as his sensitivity to the psychic scream became apparent, yes. Before that, well, the fact the 88th was the finest regiment involved in the Reclamation was just good fortune. I needed soldiers, Thade. I needed to scour this city.'

'The Traitor Legion may know exactly where the *Aggrieved* is. But we have a chance if we can track the voice to its source.'

The inquisitor was impressed. Not at Thade's deduction, but at his ruthlessness. To use Roscrain as an open conduit for the warp-voice would almost certainly kill the sanctioned psyker. He didn't need to say it. Thade knew, anyway. The Cadian wasn't blind to his role in the Imperium, nor the roles of his men.

'I can see in your eyes that you've sensed the truth of the matter. This search will still likely take days or weeks, but you are right. We will play this game, with your psyker as the pawn.'

Both men looked to the towering spires and domes of the monastery a few kilometres away. Entire sections of the palatial monument were blackened, fire-touched from battle and darkened from the smoke of funeral pyres when the world's population had first begun to die, and the incinerators still functioned. There it stood: the scorched heart of a fallen city.

The sight made Thade smile.

'In a stunning break with tradition, I think we actually have a shot at this,' he said. 'In fact, to the Eye with your doomsaying, Caius. All we've done on this planet since we landed is retreat. No more. If we're destined to die here, we'll die fighting, doing our duty to the Emperor. And I'm willing to bet we're close enough to beat the Herald to the prize.'

'There's one matter you've not considered, Thade.'

'I don't appreciate you spoiling my uplifting speech with an addendum, but enlighten me nevertheless.'

'The *Aggrieved*, and whatever has awoken within its wreckage, is likely under the monastery's foundations. The Mechanicum supplied me with heavy digging equipment in case I had to seek my prey under the earth. That equipment, obtained at massive cost I might add, is now dust in the atmosphere.'

Thade looked at the inquisitor with a clash of bemusement and despair on his face.

'Sacred Throne, it's one thing after another with you. I'm glad we're only seconded to you for one mission.'

'If we survive, I could make it permanent.'

'If you tried, I'd shoot you myself,' Thade said. 'Uh, lord,' he added several seconds later.

Part III
The Last Day

CHAPTER XIII
For Home and the Throne

Solthane, Monastic sector.

IT RAINED AS the Death Guard made planetfall.
Ancient winged craft drifted through the grim
clouds, descending to the surface in juddering landing arcs while rain streamed from their rotting
hulls. It was the first rain Solthane had seen in
weeks, and the thirsty soil drank its fill.

Typhus set foot on Kathur. His armour was hot to
the touch, radiating heat the way a man gripped by
sickness runs a fever, and the greenish plate steamed
gently as the cold rainfall hissed against it. In his fist
was his Manreaper scythe, deactivated and silent.

'That smell,' breathed Typhus, his helmet vox
speakers adding a crackle to the wet drawl of his
voice. 'That scent on the air…'

Solthane reeked of death. It had reeked of death
for months, but the rain hammering down on
mouldering corpses – both those that moved and
those that did not – was adding a thick, sick smell
to the already corrupt air.

'The smell of divinity,' Typhus growled. 'The smell
of the Disease God's gift to mortal flesh.'

The warriors of the XIV Legion had touched down
within Solthane itself, in an expansive city park
large enough to accommodate the landing craft of
a hundred Traitor Astartes. Thousands of cultists in
Remnant uniforms emerged from the dark places of
the shrine-city, clustering around the disembarking
Death Guard like worshippers greeting their gods.
For the most part, the Astartes ignored the mortal
scum milling about and chanting praises.

'Lord! Lord, have you come to deliver us? Lord!'

Typhus turned to the screaming woman. She was
wretched in every way imaginable: filthy from head
to toe with encrusted grime, half her face was blackened by a flesh-eating disease, and her raised hands
were mutilated from where she'd eaten her own fingers to stave off starvation.

To the Herald, she was beautiful. Typhus watched
her for several moments before she was lost in the
press of ravaged humanity surrounding the Death
Guard. It was becoming difficult to move through
the dense crowd. People so diseased they had no
right to be alive pressed in from every direction.
The god's blessing kept them alive and ripe with
sickness, on the edge of deaths that would take

years of pain to come unless they were put out of their misery first.

+Clear a path.+ Typhus's words wormed into the minds of the Death Guard. A hundred bolters were raised at once, unleashing their fury into the crowd. The crowd dispersed like a tide, fleeing in every direction as the guns of the fallen Astartes reaped scores of lives. Bolt shells detonated in bodies, showering the Death Guard in gobbets of bloody flesh.

The park was soon clear. Typhus was loath to destroy any soul sworn to his master, but this rabble barely counted. Most had pledged their devotion out of panic and confusion. If they died, little was lost. The Herald's mission meant so much more than the lives of a handful of half-faithful peasants.

AMONG THE BUILDINGS nearby, tall figures in black armour moved quietly, watching the advancing Death Guard. They observed in near silence, watching as the rain slashed from the Traitor Astartes' greenish armour and cleansed the plate of heretic blood.

'We see them,' voxed Brother-Captain Corvane Valar.

'Good hunting,' replied Captain Thade's voice in his internal helm speakers. 'Victory or Death.'

'Not today, Cadian. Today, it shall be both.'

* * *

THE CHIMERAS SAT at the edge of the graveyard, lined up in neat rows along a wide avenue. The rain was heavy now, scything into soil that was quickly becoming thick mud. Thade led the column of men, leaving the graveyard through the towering marble archway they'd entered by only hours before.

The squads spread around the tanks, rifles up. No one was there. The street was deserted.

'No guards,' said Darrick. 'Anyone get Valiant on the vox?'

Thade had left fifteen men, Valiant squad, to watch over the thirty troop transports. The possibilities were uniformly unpleasant. Either Valiant had met its end too fast to vox for assistance, or any cries for help had been lost in the maelstrom of the broken vox network.

'I've got blood over here,' said Corrun, his laspistol drawn. Thade came over to him, his own pistol out and held low in both hands. Thade's command Chimera, black where the others were a mix of black and grey, had a scarlet smear up one side.

'No bodies.' Thade's skin prickled.

'Tick-tock,' Darrick reminded him.

'Perimeter sweep, and make it fast,' Thade ordered. The squads checked the immediate area, finding nothing more than a few bloodstains on the ground.

'I can't reach Valiant,' Janden admitted, slinging his patched-up vox-caster on his back. He came over to where Thade stood by the tracks of the command Chimera. 'Though this isn't exactly working at peak performance.'

'I've got them,' a voice crackled over the vox. 'Throne, they're in pieces.'

Horlan's squad found the fifteen men of Valiant several hundred metres from the Chimeras, within a small enclosed street chapel made of inexpensive white stone that poorly imitated marble. A pilgrim trap, set up by fake relic traders, and now the tomb of almost twenty Guardsmen.

Valiant were indeed in pieces. Their bodies lay limbless and desecrated in a heaped pile, their armour and flesh alike showing evidence of blade wounds and las-fire.

'Sir,' Horlan was backing out of the chapel, voxing the captain. 'All dead. The Remnant did this.'

'Damn it,' breathed Thade. 'Mount up, we're leaving. The Raven Guard is engaging the XIV Legion. Astartes or not, there's no guarantee they can buy us much time.'

The Cadians boarded, and the ramps slammed closed as they made ready to move out. When the tanks rolled away, almost half of them remained behind, uncrewed and unmoving. Once they were underway, Thade joined Corrun in the front of the command Chimera.

'You know the way to link up with Colonel Lockwood?'

Corrun didn't take his eyes from the vision slit, watching the buildings speed past.

'You know I do.'

'No harm in checking. Vox to the other drivers – when we arrive, we're going to disembark and be back on board within thirty seconds.'

'Thirty seconds? What about survivors?'

Thade fixed him with a look that spoke volumes. 'Just vox it, Corrun. Thirty seconds. We deploy, we reclaim the banner, and we go.'

Corrun complied, and the tanks trundled on. Through wide avenues and slender, winding streets; through abandoned barricades that had stood untouched since the planet's Enforcers deserted them weeks before. All the while, the vox chattered with intermittent howls of static and indecipherable whispers.

'We're getting close, sir,' Corrun said, pulling into an expansive concourse. The transport started to jostle, treads clawing the tank over mounds of the slain. 'This was some battle…'

'I want to see for myself,' the captain said.

Thade climbed the short ladder to the cupola and pushed it open. He peered out of the hatch, pistol in hand, and activated his vox. The scene resembled a marketplace of detritus and abandoned traders' carts. As the tanks slowed, Thade emerged to stand on the Chimera's rain-slick roof, scanning the scene around. The bodies of slain Guardsmen were strewn across the marble-tiled ground, staining the mosaic patterns across the floor dark and unrecognisable with blood. The bodies of Remnant were spread in far greater numbers, punctuated here and there by the hulking form of a slain Traitor Astartes.

He took it in with a tactician's eye. There was little order here, hardly any signs of how the battle had ebbed and flowed. It had been fast. The 88th had been encircled from the outset and cut down in the ranks they formed to repel the assault. Thade knew the colonel's Sentinels would be out of sight, almost certainly destroyed as the enemy first came upon them before engaging the main force.

'Thade to 88th,' he said as his eyes sought every detail of the scene, drinking it all in. Faces he recognised, drawn in death, bodies and uniforms soaked in blood and the rain. 'Be ready to deploy, weapons hot, on my order. Venator squad will go for the prize. Everyone else, stand ready.'

Corrun drove through the mess of dead soldiers, the Chimera's treads hissing as they splashed through the thin, orange fluid of rainwater and blood. There it was. The banner. Thade's gaze fixed on the fallen banner atop a small mound of slaughtered soldiers, the fabric itself stained and soaked through.

A burned-out husk of a Chimera, as black as Thade's own, sizzled in the rainfall. The nuance was not lost on Thade: it was a blunt premonition of things to come.

And the banner was on the ground only twenty metres from it. Ragged, ruined and filthy. It lay like a blanket across the body of the last man to carry it, its rain-darkened surface distorted by the lumps of the corpse it covered.

'Corrun, kill the engine. Venator squad, deploy. The banner is by Colonel Lockwood's transport, twenty steps north. Go.'

The men spilled out.

'Courage, Adamant, Defiance and Liberation,' Thade named the squads he knew were suffering with low ammo. 'Deploy and scavenge for what you need.'

The other squads deployed. Thade watched them taking magazines from the dead. His attention remained mostly on Kel and his Whiteshields. They didn't balk at the duty. That was something, at least.

'Can you see Lockwood?' voxed Darrick.

'Don't ask,' Thade replied. He recognised Lockwood's corpse by the silver trim on the charred corpse's shoulder armour. It was lying half out of the destroyed Chimera's turret hatch, a pistol and sword on the transport's roof out of reach of its blackened, outstretched hands.

Thade moved to the edge of the roof and leaped down to the ground. His boots splashed filthy water in a spray as he landed.

'Sir,' crackled the vox to the percussion of clanking feet in the background.

'Copy, Greer.' Then he swallowed. Greer was dead; he'd seen him die.

'This is Vertain, sir.'

'My apologies. Interference and... Thade here. Go.'

'Enemy sighted. We'll need to make this fast. Looks like plague-slain coming down the avenue to the west.'

'Numbers?'

'Hundreds. We've got a few minutes, they're just shambling.'

Thade ran over to the wrecked Chimera, near where his command squad were reverently lifting the banner, squeezing the water from the thick fabric and furling it for retrieval. He climbed the side ladder to the tank's roof, kneeling to pick up Colonel Lockwood's bolt pistol.

Lockwood watched him perform this indignity, rapt with an eyeless stare, blackened face locked in a wide-jawed and silent scream.

'Need the clips, sir?' Tasoll asked as he finished rolling the banner up. Thade didn't answer. He looted Lockwood's burned corpse the way the other squads were looting their slain brethren, adding Lockwood's unspent bolter magazines to his own dwindling supply. Using a spare holster from his webbing, he strapped the colonel's pistol to his other thigh.

Thade moved back to his Chimera alongside Venator. Throne, did he ever want to leave. It wasn't that the carnage-rich site of this last stand unnerved him. It was that he didn't want to join the rest of the regiment here.

'Let's get out of here,' he said to his squad. He voxed the same words to everyone still alive in the regiment once he was back on board.

'Vertain, maintain the mobile perimeter. We're rolling.'

'Copy, sir.'

Darrick voxed again. 'Private channel. Horlarn said you took the colonel's gun.'

Thade glanced down at the second bolt pistol at his hip. It was ornate for Cadian wargear, edged in shining bronze with an ivory grip. The whole regiment knew the story behind how Lockwood had come by it. Like Thade's silver medal, it was a point of pride for the 88th – one of their symbols.

'I took it, yes.'

'Good,' Darrick said, and left it at that.

Thade gripped the overhead handrail and moved to where Janden and Tasoll were cleaning the banner as best they were able. Zailen was near them both, on his back, looking up at the roof. His breathing came in doglike pants through purpling lips. Thade clicked his fingers to get Tasoll's attention, and flicked a glance at Zailen. Tasoll shook his head.

'Zailen,' Thade said, crouching by the wounded man.

'Cap,' he said. Blood flecked his lips. Not a good sign.

'I'm sorry, but the formal record of the Reclamation is going to say how you got gutshot just to have some time off.'

Zailen managed a grin, blinking his eyes three times to focus. He was doped-up nicely, Thade knew, but the fact he wasn't screaming with the pain of the belly wound was the best evidence of that.

'Darrick already used that line on me, sir.'

'Well, forget Darrick. I outrank him. My threats mean more.' He turned to Tasoll and Janden, watching them rinse the banner, fighting an uphill battle to dry it out. The decking floor of the transport was wet with the bloody water they had squeezed from the flag so far. Thade ordered Trooper Iaun, who was performing a whispered Rite of Maintenance on his lasrifle, to sweep the water out using spare uniforms from the supply trunks under the seating benches.

Tasoll fingered a hole in the banner. It was a lasburn, scorching the surrounding fabric black.

'No respect, eh?'

'Hold it up,' Thade said. 'Let's see the damage.'

The banner's background was quartered grey and black, with the edges decked in silver rope. The centre symbol was the traditional emblem representing the Cadian Gate, an angular arch detailed in silver thread, with the fortress-world itself in the centre. A golden corona framed the top of the arch. Beneath it were the words 'CADIAN 88th – FOR HOME AND THE THRONE, FOR CADIA AND THE EMPEROR.'

A smaller banner hung attached to the bottom right corner – the banner of the Kasrkin of Kasr Vallock who were traditionally seconded to the regiment. It mirrored the larger crest on the main banner, though the Cadian gate was done in dark grey instead of silver, and it had an additional message: 'NEVER FALL, NEVER SURRENDER, NEVER OUTNUMBERED, NEVER OUTGUNNED.'

It was, by the standards of most Imperial Guard banners, rather muted and subtle.

It was also ruined, scored by a dozen small holes from las-fire, ripped in several places, discoloured and stinking from both bloodstains and rainwater, and missing most of the silver rope that had decorated the edges. It had seen many better days, and few worse ones.

'Still looks proud, though,' Tasoll said, guessing the captain's thoughts easily enough.

'For Home and the Throne,' Thade smiled, then turned to Zailen again. 'You're not getting out of work just yet.'

'Fine by me... it means I'm still getting paid.' Zailen smiled. His face was so pale and drawn he looked like a skull. Thade refrained from mentioning that to him.

'We'll lock you in here,' the captain said, 'with Janden's vox-caster.'

'I understand, sir.'

Thade nodded. Zailen wouldn't survive an hour, but at least he'd die doing his duty.

'Coming up on the monastery,' Corrun called over his shoulder.

'Copy. Dead Man's Hand, any problems ahead?'

'Looks clear, sir,' Vertain voxed. 'Clear all the way to the monastery's grounds.'

'Let's pray it stays that way.'

It didn't.

The plague-slain were out in force that night. A massive horde of the walking dead milled around the front grounds of the monastery; some quiet and still, others weeping and raving into the night sky.

The 88th hit them with the force of a thunderclap. Seventeen Chimeras tore into the garden grounds, laser turrets wailing and chopping the dead to pieces. Heavy bolters on the front of the transports – cautiously unused for so much of the campaign – opened up with barking chatter, no longer silenced by Reclamation protocol. The explosive bolts scythed the plague-slain down in droves, and filled the cold air with sprays of even colder gore.

Thade rode his Chimera as he had stood on it before, atop the roof, both bolters drawn. He held the colonel's weapon in his human hand, clenching his own pistol in his augmetic fist. No sign of the Death Guard – neither the advance elements already on the planet, nor the Herald's own warriors who had landed hours before. There was still a chance the 88th had made it here first. The Raven Guard had presumably delayed the XIV Legion, but no contact had been established with Valar and his Astartes since they'd first engaged the Herald.

The tanks bumped and jostled as they crushed fallen curse victims. Thade kept his balance, voxing on the general channel.

'88th, deploy as ordered.' As he spoke the words, Thade holstered one of his pistols and crouched, gripping a handrail with one hand, firing with the bolter in the other.

It was as close to perfect as they were ever going to be able to do in the circumstances. With too many tanks and too little room to manoeuvre, the drivers wrenched their vehicles into a near-perfect performance of Opening the Eye. Tracks rumbled, gang-ramps slammed down, and the last surviving platoons of the Cadian 88th disembarked with rifles up and firing.

The horde of plague-slain was rent apart less than a minute after the first Chimera entered the grounds.

The Chimeras were locked and sealed, left parked in their star pattern. The 88th formed up. At the head of the formation, Thade drew both his pistols again.

'Thade to Zailen.'

'Here, sir,' came the vox-reply from the wounded man still aboard the Chimera.

'Begin.'

Every vox-bead in the regiment clicked live. Zailen's voice was strained and distorted, but all the more earnest for those facts as he spoke the Litany of Courage into Janden's vox-caster.

'...forever in defiance, we stand true to Him on Earth...'

Thade spoke over the continuing litany, using it as a quiet backdrop as he voxed his orders. At the last, as his remaining squads stood to attention, steeling themselves before entering the monastery, Thade spoke again.

'We've got one chance to do this right. One chance to make sure every soul that died aboard the lost fleet, every soldier that died in the city today, and every citizen that died in the plague weeks ago… didn't die in vain.

'One chance.' He let the words hang.

'We're going into the catacombs. Then deeper, into the foundations. Then, if we can, we're going deeper still. The XIV Legion killed this world, this holiest of planets, and we failed to make them pay. Something under this monastery has been calling to the Herald. The Herald has answered. He comes now.

'We have one chance to beat him to the prize he seeks, one chance to kill whatever he's come to find. You know what we seek: the Heresy-era battleship *Aggrieved*. You know what we risk: everything and nothing, for all we have left to give is the breath we draw, and the blood in our veins.

'This is our one last chance to stand together before we die how we knew we always would – in service to Cadia and the God-Emperor.'

'For Home and the Throne!' the soldiers chorused. Zailen's recital of the Litany of Courage continued, muted but audible, in the background of the general vox channel.

'For Home and the Throne,' Thade echoed. 'The Emperor protects. Now move out.'

THE MONASTERY WAS cold and dead, which surprised no one. Yet the silence was still unnerving. Booted footfalls echoed strangely through the cavernous halls, all sound bouncing from the skeletal architecture while stern-faced and disfigured statues of saints, angels and Astartes peered down from their alcoves.

Thade had given the four remaining members of Dead Man's Hand a choice: remain outside with the tanks or abandon their Sentinels and join the rest of the regiment. To a man, they'd voted to remain in their walkers. Thade had given them a final salute before entering the monastery's towering double doors. The regiment knew the chances of the Sentinels surviving out there alone were too slim to contemplate. Only the fact every man knew he was marching to almost certain death under the monastery prevented them from seeking to dissuade the walker pilots.

'I'll let them die how they wish,' Thade had said. 'They'll kill more of the Archenemy's host if they're sat in their Sentinels.'

'We need everyone that can still carry a weapon!' Tionenji insisted.

'Four pistols will make no difference,' Thade shook his head. 'They stay and die how they wish to die. They stay and fight however they choose. This conversation is over.'

Now the 88th advanced through the ruined cathedral, the occasional gunshot blasting out to silence a stray plague-slain that shambled through the empty halls. Over the vox, Zailen spoke on, now reciting the Litany of Defiance in the Face of the End. His voice grew fainter as time passed.

'The vox-link is getting weaker. And choppy. I can barely hear Zailen,' Darrick said.

Thade nodded. He didn't have it in him to play along with the lie. Neither did Master Sergeant Jevrian, but he didn't stay silent on the matter.

'He's breathing his last, joker. Don't shine it up for smiles.' The Kasrkin leader tossed aside an empty glass vial, and tensed his hand into a fist a few times. 'That's better.'

'Did you just gland something?' Darrick asked, his irritation rising. Cadian regulation discouraged all use of combat drugs, and Thade was especially hard on those he found indulging. With the temporary boost to reflexes and strength from most combat narcotics, came unreliability and dangerous side-effects. Stimm abuse might be common in other regiments, but it was rare in the Shock.

'Shut your whine-hole.'

'Go to hell, stimm junkie,' Darrick snapped.

'Ban,' Thade turned to him and stopped walking. 'Is that frenzon?'

'Like it matters if it is?'

There was a click and the nearby hum of a charged weapon. Jevrian flicked his glance to the left, where Commissar Tionenji was holding his laspistol to Ban's temple.

'Be a good little soldier and answer the captain, you shaved ape,' Tionenji warned. Thade shared a look with the commissar. He was pleased; this was almost the first thing Tionenji had said in the hours since their confrontation, and the first signs of the atmosphere thawing between them. Still, this was hardly ideal...

'Naw, it's not frenzon,' Jevrian growled.

'This isn't some penal legion, and you're not a Catachan jungle thug who gets to gland combat drugs that are forbidden in the Primer.' Thade was as close to angry as Darrick and the others had ever seen him.

'Is this a Ten-Ninety, sir?' asked the commissar.

'That depends. Is that frenzon, Jevrian?'

'A Ten-Ninety? For glanding stimms? I already said it wasn't bloody frenzon.'

'So what is it?' Thade asked. 'I won't have that crap in my regiment, Kasrkin. We're all better than that.'

'Dying with dignity is awfully important to the Cap,' Darrick interjected.

'Shut up, Taan.'

'Shutting up, sir.'

'Listen,' Jevrian said, reaching up to lower Tionenji's pistol with his brutishly large hand. 'It's not frenzon or satrophine, we clear? Throne in flames, don't we have a job to do? There's still a war on, last time I checked. It's just a cocktail of 'slaught with a little downer to stay sharp. Reflex juice.'

The captain let it slide. As the command team moved on, Jevrian walked next to Thade.

'That was some fine loyalty you showed me there, hero. Next time the Garadeshi has his gun pointed at your face, I might not leap to your defence.'

'Get over it,' Thade said. 'You were in the wrong then, too.'

'I'll remember that.' Jevrian fell back into line with his Kasrkin. 'I'll remember that, captain.'

SETH WAS HEARING the voice with astonishing clarity now.

And that was the problem. It was coming from everywhere now, from the dust on the ground, from the bloodstains on the walls, from the pores of his sweating skin.

The inquisitor trailed his every step now. Seth knew what this was about – they needed him to find the source of the voice. It was obvious. But as Thade's small army descended down the wide stone stairs into the undercroft, he knew they were setting their hopes on a false path. He couldn't make out any sense of place or direction in the voice's ululating scream. Even with his senses opened wide to the hidden world, all he could feel was the illusory sensation of unseen fingernails scratching lightly at his mind.

He began to wonder after a while if the feeling was really just an illusion. A taste appeared in his mouth, raw and rancid and tingling on his tongue like burning copper. He was stronger than this. He knew it. He could listen for the voice and remain untainted. Caius did, didn't he? Zaur had?

Seth placed one foot in front of the other, at times shambling forward like one of the plague-slain and remaining upright only by gripping his black staff. He felt their eyes on him... Thade's, Caius's, the bastard Jevrian's.

They didn't care if he died. Whatever it took to get their prize. Whatever it took to reach the crashed ship. Here he was, swallowing the taste of blood and trying not to choke on it, while they silently willed him on with smiles on their faces.

He could, he realised, kill them if he wished. Within that realisation was a flare of shame, quickly quenched in Seth's rising anger. Cadian Blood, the fuel of the Imperium... Born to die in service to the Throne. It was laughable, Seth realised. Laughable and grossly wrong.

Damn the Throne. The Throne was a meat-grinding engine feeding on the souls of those that wasted their lives worshipping it. *Damn the Throne. To the Eye with all of them for wishing me dead.*

They were in a vault with a ceiling so low many of the taller soldiers had to slouch as they walked. It helped the popular opinion that the entire cathedral, raised over several decades of toil by tens of thousands of workers, was thrown together more by faith than sensible design.

As Seth passed between rows of stone sarcophagi, each one adorned with golden decoration and bearing long-faded names carved into the stone, the Cadians detected a curious noise.

'You hear that?' Thade asked Caius.

The inquisitor nodded, gesturing to the sarcophagus closest to Seth's trailing coat. As Thade passed it, he heard…

– something inside, something made of dry bones, furiously scratching to get out –

…SOMETHING WITHIN. An eerie sound, like vermin running over stone.

'Tell me that's the rats,' he said to Caius, loudly enough for the men nearby to hear.

'It's the rats,' the inquisitor replied, not looking back.

From that point on, Tionenji followed Seth with his laspistol drawn.

The Cadians had been within the monastery for approximately three hours when the voice addressed Seth by name.

'Why are you smiling?' Thade asked him immediately. Seth blanked his face and looked at the captain while they walked. The false pity on Thade's face sickened him so powerfully he had to tense his stomach and force it not to rebel.

'Nothing,' he said at last.

'You're looking bad, Seth. Do you need to rest for a while?'

'No rest.' Caius shoved Seth forward with the palm of his hand on the psyker's spine, right between the shoulder blades. Seth drooled as he staggered on. He'd been about to say yes. Been about to mention that the voice was calling his name now.

Thade moved closer to Caius as the troops walked through a tunnel lit by dim strip lighting running off one of the forgotten power generators in the city-sized monastery. This, too, was unnerving. The Cadians were used to Solthane as a city devoid of power.

'This is killing him,' the captain whispered.

'This will kill us all,' Caius replied in a tone that brooked no further comment. The inquisitor wondered if Thade had really considered the sanctioned psyker's chances of survival after all. Either way, now was not the time for sentimentality. Now was the time to shut up and serve.

From up ahead, where the tunnel branched into a T-junction, Lieutenant Horlan voxed back to the main force.

'We've got some chanting up here. The tunnel splits north and south and leads into attached chambers. We've got chanting coming from the south side. Silence from the north.'

Caius stared at the back of Seth's head as the sanctioned psyker shivered in the cold air. He seemed to be listening to something only he could hear.

'We go south,' the inquisitor said. Thade voxed the order to Horlan, and the units closed together once more, catching up with their scouts.

The chanting turned out to be the dregs of some plague cult lost in the darkness of the catacomb maze. The 88th squads stormed in, opening fire and cutting down the handful of heretics as they crouched down for their evening meal.

Several soldiers spat on the corpses as they passed on once the fighting was done, disgusted to see how the heretics had been feasting on the bodies of their own dead. They were but the first of several splintered, isolated gangs of mindless pilgrims lost down in the dark. Each one fell before the guns of the Imperials, and the 88th ventured deeper and deeper through subterranean burial vaults, storage chambers, habitation wings and abandoned ritual halls. None of these had been used in thousands of years except for the recent deprivations of the scavenging heretics.

'We're in the real catacombs now,' Thade said at one point, running his metal hand across the wall of a chamber.

'How do you know?' asked Caius.

Thade tapped the wall with his knuckles. 'Stone. Not marble. This is cheap and serviceable, probably never meant to be seen by any pilgrims even when the temple was still growing. What? Don't look at me like that. Just because I'm a soldier doesn't mean I'm an idiot.'

'I'm beginning to forget what sunlight feels like,' muttered Darrick. He held a lamp-pack in one hand, panning it around the dark chamber. Power was sporadic in the undervaults, and the ceiling lightglobes were off more often than on.

'It's only been six hours,' Jevrian said. 'Grow a backbone.'

'It's been nine,' Thade said, holding his wrist chronometer within Darrick's circle of illumination.

'I count seven hours and fifty,' Kel piped up. More responses came. Not a single chron agreed with another.

'This can't be good,' Darrick commented.

'Move,' called Caius. 'Time displacement is a common effect of warp distortion. Just keep moving.'

'Oh,' Darrick muttered. 'Well, that's fine, then. Silly me for worrying.' Grin in place, Darrick expected Thade to tell him to shut up. He found the fact the captain remained silent to be more disconcerting than time itself playing around.

TYPHUS WRENCHED HIS scythe clear and the Raven Guard sank to the ground. It had been a brief fight: brief but deliciously satisfying. Blood hissed and bubbled on the Herald's blade, cooking black on the surface of the psychically-charged metal.

Brief. Satisfying. But costly. The Raven Guard had swooped down all too literally, striking from the air as they descended on jump-packs with howling thrusters. Chainswords sang and bolters barked at close range as the Astartes butchered one another in a savage brawl.

The black-armoured Astartes had been outnumbered three to one, but the advantage of surprise counted for much. Typhus stared through the Y-shaped visor of his gory, horned helm. Death Guard, their cracked armour the colour of gangrene, lay across the landing site. Men (or beings that had once been men and still maintained roughly human form) that had stood alongside the Herald for millennia, lay cleaved by Imperial chainblades or burst open by bolter fire.

Typhus felt no emotion at seeing this. He was capable of no emotional sensation that even vaguely approached something a human would comprehend. What he felt was hollow, the absence of emotion. His thoughts plumbed this vacant space within his mind, searching the void, finding it chilling and almost fascinating where his emotions once resided.

A plague on these accursed sons of Corax in their black armour. Their guerrilla assaults had held the Death Guard's advance for too long.

The momentary introspection passed, and Typhus took a Raven Guard head with a sweep of his scythe. Picking up the black helm, he shook the head free and stamped on it, crushing it to blood-and-bone paste under his boot.

'We honour our enemies,' the Herald growled, and vomited a stream of bloated, sticky flies through his narrow visor into the empty helmet in his hands. He tossed the writhing mass onto the headless corpse at his feet, letting the flesh-eating flies spill across the body and seek openings in the deactivated power armour.

The final insult. The gene-seed of these fallen Astartes could never be recovered by the Imperium. This last thought stirred something deep and sludge-thick within the recesses of the Herald's mind. The Raven Guard still suffered today from their near extermination ten thousand years before. To deny them the genetic legacy of their primarch now brought a smile to the Herald's lips. His emotions might have decayed long ago, but he was forever delighted by both vengeance and cruelty – especially when the two mixed.

The Death Guard, minus half their initial landing force, moved on shortly after, leaving the flesh-flies of the Destroyer Hive to finish their meal.

THE VESSEL, WHAT remained of it at least, was an Astartes battle-barge. This ancient spaceborne fortress lay in pieces, the largest sections of hull still bone white and emerald green in the XIV Legion's original colours, unstained by the years of warp-corruption that had tainted the *Terminus Est* and the armour of the Death Guard themselves. The taint was insidious rather than obvious, but no less true.

Here and there on ridged sheets of exposed hull metal, black marks showed where the ship had ploughed through the atmosphere on its death dive, before gouging this savage cleft in the rock of the world soon to be named Kathur.

Silence reigned within the shattered ship. The crew, Astartes, servitors and Legion serfs alike, had long since mouldered to bone and dust.

Only a single soul claimed anything akin to life here.

It waited in the silence, screaming soundlessly, knowing its hour of freedom had finally come.

CHAPTER XIV
Cadian Blood

Beneath the catacombs

IT DEFIED THEIR expectations.

Seven hours of trekking through the monastery, and they'd found it. Seth no longer even needed to lead the way; Caius was all too aware of the force of the voice's pull as he made his way through the catacombs. Impossible to ignore, its intensity made it increasingly difficult to reach out of his own mind, and he felt inexorably drawn deeper into the subterranean labyrinth.

All notions of needing excavator equipment were banished from thought. All images of the great ship blown to a million pieces and seeing the impressive wreckage in an underground cavern were purged from imaginations. The truth was both much more logical to understand and much more uncomfortable to behold.

The *Aggrieved* wasn't buried in the rock of Kathur's crust beneath the foundations of the monastery. It *was* the foundations of the monastery.

The Cadians became aware immediately when the deepest tunnels of the catacombs all appeared to be walled with metal instead of stone. It was strikingly obvious, as the carved rock passageways gave way to corridors of riveted iron and black steel; it was clear to all who laid eyes upon it that they were entering the halls of an Imperial ship.

A very old Imperial ship, it had to be said. But one of Standard Template Construct design, and therefore, timeless – the design still in use in new vessels today.

Osiron could scarcely believe what his photoreceptors were showing him.

'They made the lowest levels of their fledgling cathedral link to these corridors,' his metallic voice rang out, echoing weirdly down the spaceship's wide hallways. 'This is… blasphemous. Such a violation of the Mechanicum's treasured lore. Such an unholy waste of power and knowledge.'

'The blasphemy was committed before the vessel even crashed, tech-priest,' Caius said softly. 'And after.'

'The blasphemy against the Emperor, yes. I speak of blasphemy against the Cult Mechanicus of Mars, and the Omnissiah.'

'The Omnissiah? I thought your Machine-God *was* the God-Emperor,' Darrick cut in. 'You just dressed him differently.'

Osiron's crimson hood moved in a gesture that may or may not have been indicative of a nod. 'All this knowledge,' he said again, stroking metal fingers across the vessel's internal skin. 'All this stolen power.'

'Tainted by heresy,' Caius said.

Now Osiron definitely nodded, conceding the point. The vessel may have been close to the peak of Mechanicus ingenuity, but the tech-adepts of forge world Mars wished no truck with the touch of Chaos. Tainted was tainted. Lost was lost.

'I'd expected an Archenemy vessel to be more… obvious,' Darrick said. 'This is bad enough – and how in the Great Eye are these wall lights still on? – but it looks just like one of our ships.'

'We are in the upper decks and have not penetrated far,' Osiron reminded them all. 'And when the *Aggrieved* fell to the surface, its corruption from its crew's heresy was still fresh. This ship died before Chaos could worm all the way through it.'

'No,' Caius said, goading Seth forward. 'This ship is riddled with the Archenemy's touch. I feel it clearly.'

'As do I,' Seth spoke for the first time in hours. His tongue was thick in his mouth, and slimy strings of saliva stretched between his chattering teeth.

'Seth,' Thade began.

'Seth,' the psyker replied, 'has been dead for some time now.'

THE ENTITY DWELLING within the wreckage of the *Aggrieved* had reached out to the sanctioned psyker as the Cadians descended. It was a trifling matter to stir Seth's thoughts into dwelling on rebellion, bitterness and disloyalty.

At least, at first. Before the final blow that killed Seth and allowed the entity to wear the psyker's body, there had been much to do and a surprising amount of resistance to doing it.

The entity had stirred these dark thoughts within the thin, weak, mortal soup that formed Seth's consciousness. And at first it had been easy, the suggestions of emotion and thought blending seamlessly with Seth's own brain function. He was an outcast among his people – thoughts of this forever rode high in his consciousness – and amplifying his loneliness and hatred of rejection was a simple matter, the merest of psychic tweaks. The entity probed with invisible fingers, tasted the surface pain, and flavoured it a touch darker, a touch angrier, minute by minute.

Disguising this gentle manipulation from the other psychically-gifted member of the Imperial coterie was no difficult feat. The entity at the edge of Seth's mind knew that its own psychic beacon, the endless silent scream, was clouding the other human's perceptions.

It did not know Caius was an inquisitor, and had no frame of reference for the term, as the title had not been coined in any significant way in the age when the entity had truly existed in the flesh. Even had it known the meaning of the title and the formidable skills of those that bore it, the entity would not have been troubled. Its powers far eclipsed those of the approaching mortals.

What it needed now was flesh. It could not rebuild itself without flesh; lots of flesh, blood, sinew and the other meats that made up the human form. It had woken, and the psychic pangs of its rebirth manifested as the plague, a cry for aid from its distant brethren. But now... now it needed flesh. Birthing the curse had left it weak and lingering on the edge of slumber. Finally, after weeks of regeneration, it was ready once more.

Yet its manipulations of Seth's mind began to snap back, repressed and refused by the mortal whose skull the entity was trying to claim.

What are you doing? the mortal had asked. Seth melted back into his own thoughts, reaching for the cancerous taint taking hold behind his eyes.

What intrusion is this? Who are you?

The entity saw how the mortal manifested itself out of its meaty shell: a being of silver light with eyes of violet fire.

'I am the death of Kathur,' the entity had replied. It also took psychic form now, within the human's psychic perception. A bulky, swollen figure with white armour that somehow writhed in a million little movements. Seth looked closer – the armour, despite being Astartes in shape and style, was formed of fat, wriggling maggots.

You are Death Guard, Seth had said.

'I was. For my loyalty to the Grandfather and the pain I inflicted upon the servants of the False Emperor, I was raised above the Legion.'

As was the Traveller. Seth was serene as he spoke, as though he were idly contemplating some matter of minor curiosity rather than the presence of a daemon within his mind. *You are kin to the Traveller.*

'I know no Traveller,' it said.

The Herald. Typhus.

'The First Captain. The Host. My brother in arms, Typhon. I am a prince of daemons and deservedly so. But the Herald's blood is avataric and thrice-blessed by the Plague Lord.'

I understand nothing of what you say.

'You are human. If you understood the words, the knowledge would kill you.'

The Herald, he comes for you.

'We were friends once. Battle-brothers. We will slay Scarus together.'

I cannot let you do this. We will stop you.

'No. You are already dying. You have turned within for too long, and I am now the force animating your mortal bones.'

I will warn Thade.

'Your hive-brother sees you move and thinks you still live. He does not see the truth.'

I will fight you here, then.

'You will not win.'

Even in death, we serve Home and the Throne.

'You will not win,' the entity said again, and launched at the psyker, its writhing claws extended. The Cadian steeled himself for the assault, and for the last time in his life, Seth Roscrain went to war.

It was cripplingly intimate, fighting on a battlefield that existed only within Seth's mind. As his flesh and blood body walked on, drooling and whispering to itself in the darkness beneath the monastery, his consciousness and power was utterly focused within, fighting the daemon inside his head.

The ethereal Astartes lashed out with bleeding claws that tore shreds from the silver light that formed Seth's psychic projection. Where the talons fell and rent corposant psy-flesh, they left trails of ravenous maggot-things that bored into his silver skin.

Seth screamed into the depths of his mind as his eyes blasted back with violet flame in a vicious reply. The squirming mass covering the Astartes burned away in a wave of black smoke, revealing the bloated, corrupted armour beneath.

'Your defiance is laughable. I cannot feel pain,' the Astartes said, readying for another attack.

I will be glad to teach you. Seth smiled through clenched teeth as the worms burrowed into his form. With a surge of concentration, his staff flared into existence, held in his hands. He pointed the aquila motif at the Death Guard.

Pain. It feels a little like this.

Golden arcs of coruscating energy leapt the distance between the double eagle symbol and the Astartes. Seth felt a moment of heated satisfaction as the daemon shrieked and writhed in the holy fire.

The mind of the Astartes-thing was a union of daemonic and once-human perceptions, and this heady clash of conception struggled to grasp just why it was feeling agony for the first time in ten thousand years. It was strong, *immortal*.

But it was still disembodied, and that made it weak. Most of its true strength was in its physical form, and even that was massively depleted in the wake of calling the plague.

It had been a fool to let the mortal bait it like this, and as it glared at Seth's ghostly form, gleaming with golden light and a halo of violet flame, it saw the psyker knew it, too. Their telepathic closeness within this internal battleground sent their thoughts flashing back and forth to one another.

Are we done? Seth sneered, the eagle atop his black staff wreathed in blinding fire. *I had more.*

'You die for this, human.'

I was born ready for that.

'You will greet that death now!'

True... The two wraiths met, claws against flesh and holy eagle against armour. Both souls caught fire and began to dissolve in the psychic fury of their meeting, but only one of the souls screamed. Seth managed a smile as his psychic body immolated, and he looked into the daemon's shrieking visage. He'd never had a chance of winning. Even now his form was dissipating in the blink of an eye compared to the slow erosion of the daemon Astartes. And still the Astartes howled.

…but death is worth it, he hissed as the violet light faded from his eyes, *just to see that look on your face.*

'Seth,' it had said, 'has been dead for some time now.'

The daemon wearing Seth turned to face the Cadians. Already, it swelled and grew, bulges of contorted muscle tearing through the oversized bad weather jacket Seth had owned for years. Blood ran in trails from the sockets in his head and neck, and the aquila atop the psyker's staff shattered in a hail of shards that killed three men.

Tionenji fired first, blowing the insides of Seth's head out the back of his skull. Thade and the others opened fire a moment later, shredding their psyker's stolen flesh in a hail of las-fire. Thade's bolters pounded once each, hammering explosive rounds into Seth's chest and sending the psyker back against the wall in a mess of blood and bone.

It wasn't dead. It wasn't even annoyed. Still it grew, for now it had flesh, but it needed more for a true rebirth. Clawed hands of thickening yellow flesh reached out for the closest two men in the confines of the corridor. The manifesting daemon tore the throat from the first and pulverised the spine of the second in its vice-like grip.

Corrun's head rolled back on his neck and he collapsed, fingers spasming as they touched the gaping wound where his throat had been. The second man stayed in the daemon's grip, wielded like a flail to hammer more soldiers from their feet and bludgeon them to death against the decking and walls.

The 88th fell back to a wider part of the corridor, the front ranks crouched so those behind could fire. Thade's pistols roared alongside the inquisitor's psycannon, these heavier weapons ripping chunks from the mass of warty flesh rising before them. The daemon, hunched in the hallway, regarded the fragile Cadians with one bloodshot violet eye the size of a human hand. The air reeked of burning meat and the ozone of las-weapons discharging at close quarters. More soldiers died as the beast swung left and right with its corpse flail.

'Purge the unclean!' Caius shouted, chanting a screed of chastisements as his shoulder cannon fired. Each bolt landed like a spray of acid, biting hard and making steaming wounds in the daemon's flesh.

The creature began to back away, retreating from the carnage it had caused. In the space of a handful of heartbeats, fifteen men lay dead. Thade's cry to pursue broke off in his mouth as those fifteen men, in various states of dismemberment and ruin, all began to move again. As Seth had done moments before, they too started to swell and discolour.

'Flesh!' the daemon roared, and clutching two corpses in each giant fist, it turned and moved

down the corridor in a hunchbacked run. The Cadians heard its pounding footsteps even as they
turned their guns on the rising bodies of their own
comrades.

Corrun and the other slain Cadians were similarly resistant to injury as their bodies thickened
and bloated in imitation of Seth's corrupted form.
Thade aimed his pistols at the wet, blinking orb in
the centre of Corrun's forehead, formed from his
eyes merging as he mutated. The shells rammed
into the soft tissue and detonated a moment later,
leaving the daemon without half of its head.

Thade backed away. The thing that had been Corrun seemed untroubled by the myriad injuries it
was sustaining in the onslaught.

'We have to get through!' Caius cried.

'Hold ranks!' Thade called. The corridor was illuminated in the flickering redness of mass las-fire.
The sharp tang of ozone even smothered the reek of
the monstrous beings stalking towards the Imperials.

'Don't let them touch you!' Caius yelled to the
men. No one asked why. The order was enough;
details were irrelevant. You could tell just by looking at them that touching them was going to kill
you somehow.

'Advance!' Thade ordered. The survivors of the
Cadian 88th fell into step, unleashing fire in a
relentless torrent as the daemons advanced down
the narrow corridor towards them.

* * *

OUTSIDE THE MONASTERY at last, Typhus and his Death Guard escort stood at the open doors of the Shrine of the Emperor's Unending Majesty. Although he had linked up with XIV Legion forces already on Kathur, his warband was devastated.

The Death Guard had come across the seventeen Chimeras left by the 88th in the monastery grounds.

'Abandoned,' Typhus hissed over the vox as he gestured to the tanks. 'I sense only trace echoes of life.'

'I hear the puling creed of an Imperial tongue,' one of the Traitor Astartes had voxed as they surveyed the scene. 'He chants.'

Typhus heard it, too. A lone man, whispering Imperial litanies across a vox-channel. The benedictions in the Emperor's name hurt the Herald's ears, and he deactivated the channel with a blink-click directed at an icon on his helmet's internal display.

+Find him+, Typhus pulsed to his brethren. The Death Guard moved closer to the tanks, which was when they started to die.

Nine of the turrets spun on cue, as Osiron's servitors – hardwired into the weapons systems of the Chimeras under Thade's orders – opened fire on the Traitors. Multi-barrelled laser turrets emitted their high-pitched whines, slicing through Astartes plate while heavy bolters mounted on the tank's hulls boomed their own angry chorus.

No once-mortal being, even those granted immortality by the Ruinous Powers, was without weakness. The Death Guard had survived dozens of centuries as the hosts of supernatural plagues, but their incredible resilience to torments of the flesh also made them cumbersome – at least relative to their skills in life as true Astartes. They sought cover with lumbering slowness, several of their number being cut down and pain-filled lives lasting ten thousand years ending forever in a storm of ambushing fire.

Dead Man's Hand waited until the Death Guard had advanced fully into the monastery grounds and surrounded the tanks. Vertain licked his lips as he watched the green-armoured heretics taking refuge behind smaller buildings in the estate gardens. He picked his targets, sent a series of vox-clicks to the other three pilots alongside him so they would know not to waste ammunition by overlapping his fire arc, and ordered the attack.

Vertain had smiled as he heard Zailen still chanting.

Typhus's rage was boundless. He had ordered his men to destroy the tanks and pull the walkers apart. Half of this plan met with success. The servitors aboard the Chimeras offered little threatening resistance when the Traitor Astartes tore into the hulls and attacked them with roaring chainblades.

The Sentinels, however, retreated back into the powerless, empty night-time city, leaving only a vox echo of laughter for Typhus to sneer over.

The Herald's forces had taken a punishing beating throughout their short commitment to this campaign, but by the Grandfather, he was here now.

And now he would…

And now…

'No,' Typhus breathed, feeling the hive in his intestines writhe and clench.

'Lord?' voxed a nearby Death Guard.

In the recesses of his mind, the eternal scream from beneath the monastery fell silent. Typhus clenched his teeth, shattering two of them and swallowing the wave of carrion-eating flies that threatened to leave his lips.

'No!' he roared within the confines of his horned helmet.

+NO!+ his mind's voice shrieked, a thousand times louder despite its physical silence.

FROM A THOUSAND, barely a hundred remained.

Bloodstained, battered, wounded, the last hundred entered the circular bridge of the *Aggrieved*.

Jevrian's broken arm was set, but he'd picked up a limp from one of the cyclopean creatures' claws gashing his thigh. The wound was smeared with anti-ague gel but it still stung, in Jevrian's own words, like an army of bastards.

Osiron's breathing rattled in and out of his rebreather and he held his axe low in tired hands. Rax stalked alongside the tech-priest, jaws spread for battle, its armoured body filthy with enemy blood.

Thade and Darrick were unharmed but exhausted, and Thade's sword was clogged with gore, preventing any function. Caius had expended all of his sacred ammunition on the warp-beasts, and simply let his heavy psycannon fall to the floor, ignoring it now that it was useless.

The 88th fanned out around the circular room, looking in at the centre of the chamber where the raised control throne jutted from the floor on a grand stepped platform. Chains hung from the ceiling of the chamber, decorated by the old mark III helms of long-dead loyalist Astartes. The cogitator banks and consoles by the walls sat in ruin, many still with their operators close to their stations, wasted away to loose piles of bone on the ground.

A hundred rifles raised to cheeks as Thade pointed his fouled sword at the figure in the throne. The entity was reborn. Its reserves of strength might have been exhausted by both the plague it unleashed and the invisible, draining wounds inflicted by Seth's final assault, but it sensed the nearness of Typhus, and that nearness made the entity bold.

It was clearly once an Astartes. Time, and the favour of its hateful god, had changed that. What sat upon the throne now was club-limbed and twisted, like something half-formed from a psyker's nightmare and wrapped in ill-fitting Astartes armour. Its flesh was liquefied in places, melting and reforming like hot candlewax. Blisters and buboes covered its skin where bleeding rashes did not.

'Hello,' it said.

'In the name of the God-Emperor,' Caius intoned, and the daemon recognised the only true threat in the room. Power roiled from Caius. In the moment the entity sensed it up close, it knew fear.

'Die,' it said to the inquisitor.

Caius died. Not instantly, but within a few short seconds. The veins stood out on his face, dark and ugly, as he mustered his psychic might to repel the horrendously powerful telepathic invasion. It was more thorough and disgustingly more tender than any physical violation. Bastian Caius, who had come all this way to serve the Throne, drew his power sword and activated it, feeling an alien force eating his mind. He would have been at least a little consoled to learn of the immense effort the daemon had used in this command. He would have been proud to learn the daemon had feared him so much that it risked further psychic drain to ensure Caius's demise.

The Cadians never saw the inquisitor's death. By the time Caius had obeyed the terrible command and plunged his aquila-hilted blade into his own belly, the Guardsmen had opened fire on the daemon.

'Have you come to bring me back into the False Emperor's light?' Grotesquely, it spoke with Seth's voice even though it no longer wore his features, masked as they were under its reformed power armour. 'To show me my sins in the light of your dead god?'

Something like that, Thade thought as his broken sword fell in a chop, and a hundred rifles fired in anger.

ALL TOLD, THE final battle between the survivors of the Cadian 88th Mechanised Infantry and the daemon responsible for the Kathurite Scourge lasted under one minute, yet it cost the lives of forty-six loyal Cadian-born servants of the Throne.

The volleys of las-fire did almost nothing to the creature, and it rampaged through the bridge, its claws tearing soldiers limb from limb, while it paused only to vomit acid on those too slow or too proud to retreat.

Thade and Horlan, both armed with ruined chainswords that sported stilled teeth, ran in to engage the daemon. They were joined by the wounded Ban Jevrian with his malfunctioning and half-snapped power sabre, and twenty men using their pistols and bayonets. With Thade was Rax, leaping at its master's side.

This swarm assault also did almost nothing, except cost lives. Horlan was decapitated by a sweep of the daemon's claw. Thade was saved from the same fate at the last moment by a grinding metal hand blocking the falling claw's arc.

Osiron, his back-mounted powerpack and additional servo-arm sparking as its joints gave way under the pressure, held the creature at bay long enough for Thade to get to his feet again.

The tech-priest's last action in the battle was to
swing his two-handed axe with all his machine-
enhanced strength, ramming it solidly into the
daemon's body. This, at last, did something. The
blade bit hard, snagging within the beast's spine,
dropping it to its knees. Its return strike smashed
Osiron to the side of the chamber, where he would
die several minutes later from blood loss and internal haemorrhaging.

Renewed las-fire slashed into the prone daemon,
every beam now carving its burn lines into the fatty
flesh of the thing's face. Thade came at it from the
side, both pistols hammering until their clips ran
dry. Rax leapt at the horror, its jaws ripping head-
sized chunks of spoiled meat from the beast's
bones.

It was weakening, but hardly out of the fight,
even without the use of its legs.

'Thade!' Commissar Tionenji cried as he ran at
the creature, hacking into its neck with his slender
chainblade. His own strike was a distraction, as the
sword he'd taken from Inquisitor Caius's body
flashed through the air in Thade's direction. The
captain caught it, reversed it in his hands, and
plunged it two-handed into the daemon's neck.
Black blood flowed from a legion of wounds now.

And it still wouldn't die.

There was no glorious final blow, though the
soldiers of the 88th – those that survived – would
say over the years that it was Thade's last strike
which assuredly saw the daemon dead. The truth

was altogether less glorious, and because Taan Darrick was involved, consisted of much more swearing than the saga would say.

'Run, you idiots!' Darrick cried from his position by the side consoles with the remains of his squad.

Thade and the others in their desperate melee saw a rain of black incoming, clattering all around.

Grenades.

As Thade threw himself aside, his world exploded in light.

'Let this world rot.' The Herald's voice was a savage whisper. He still stood at the gates of the monastery, listening as the psychic death scream faded from his sixth sense. 'I am done with this place.'

The Death Guard formed around their lord and master, unsure of his meaning.

'We are leaving, Great One?' a plague-ridden Astartes asked.

Typhus chuckled. The things living within his windpipe writhed at this rare mistreatment.

'Yes. I have real business to attend to beyond this petty distraction. Tell me, do you remember Brother-Sergeant Arlus?'

'No, lord,' replied the closest Death Guard.

'Do any of you?'

'I do, lord. I was Brother Menander. I served Arlus in life. We were Seventh Company. He was greatly blessed by the Grandfather when we made war upon Terra.'

'He was. But he squandered his gift. And this shall be the last time I allow the whining of distant fools to distract me from my duty. Come. We return to *Terminus Est*.'

'And then, lord?'

'And then… to Cadia. Take me to the Warmaster.'

'MEDIC!'

Thade knelt by Osiron, flinching back as sparks flared from the tech-priest's sundered body armour.

'Sir,' Tasoll looked awkward as he held his narthecium kit, staring down at the torn red robe now revealing an entirely augmetic body. 'W-what should I do? He's not even bleeding blood.'

'It… is a synthesised compound…' Osiron wheezed '…of haemolubricant qualities… and…'

'Shut up, you idiot,' Thade looked at the oily black fluid covering his hands. 'Just shut up, and tell us what to do!'

Tech-priest Enginseer Bylam Osiron said nothing more.

AMONGST THE STINKING fallout and moans of the injured, Commissar Tionenji leaned against the door arch leading from the bridge. He caught his breath away from the men, not willing to let them see how exhausted he was. It was his duty to be inspiring at all times. Not for Commissar Tionenji were the aches and woes of mortal tiredness. The men shouldn't see such things.

A smile crossed his lips. He was alive. Life! After all they had witnessed and all they had endured.

He was a man whose intelligence was both ruthless and restless. Already he planned stratagems for the remains of the regiment to survive on Kathur long enough to greet the main Reclamation forces. The incident with Thade and his command team pulling their weapons on a commissar would have to be addressed, but...

'Hey.' Ban Jevrian of the Kasrkin limped up to the commissar, his right trouser leg soaked with red. 'One hell of a fight.'

'Greetings, master sergeant,' Tionenji grinned – all white teeth set in his dark face. 'The Emperor smiles on us, I think.'

'Oh, you think?'

The knife came from nowhere. One moment Jevrian had been leaning against the wall with Tionenji, cradling his broken arm and favouring his bad leg. The next moment, Jevrian's fist was at the commissar's ear and his hand-length boot knife was sticking clean through Tionenji's skull.

Blood barely even had time to spurt before the commissar dropped to the decking. Jevrian reclaimed his knife several seconds later, wincing as he needed to bend down. His leg really did ache like an army of bastards.

'The Emperor smiles upon me,' Jevrian raised himself back up, wiping his knife, the blade clearly stamped with the regiment's insignia, on the sleeve of his fatigues.

'But you? I doubt he'd piss on you if you were on fire.'

Jevrian returned to the main area. Taan Darrick met his eyes from across the bloody bridge, and the Kasrkin officer nodded once.

In the earpiece of every soldier still standing, a single vox-click sounded. Several men nodded. Some smiled. Most pretended not to hear it, but only one never knew what it meant.

'What was that?' asked Thade, tapping his vox-bead.

'Nothing, sir,' Darrick replied. 'Just a glitch.'

EPILOGUE
Home

I

TWENTY-SEVEN DAYS LATER, the Reclamation fleet arrived in full force.

The Herald's fleet was gone – had been gone for weeks – leaving only the faintest echoes in the warp to mark their departure. They left a dead world behind them, marking their failure.

The first troops to walk the surface encountered fewer threats than the Reclamation's initial spearhead had faced. Never concerned with reinforcing the world for conquest, no Archenemy vessels arrived to save the heretics of the Remnant and its splinter cults drawn from the treasonous populace. With all global production shut down and off-world imports utterly ceased, the still-living humans of Kathur began to die of thirst and starvation before long. Those that maintained supplies of food and water eked out an existence as territorial warbands until the Imperial Guard's main force annihilated them completely in what scholars came to know as the 'True Reclamation'.

The Guard units arriving at the headquarters of Overseer Maggrig and the fallen regiments he commanded, encountered a fortified base of jury-rigged prefab structures and salvaged tank cannons mounted on scratch built fortress walls.

As the gates to this rather humble fortress opened, General Millius Rylo of the Hadris Rift 19th descended from his command tank – a pristine Leman Russ Demolisher – and was greeted by a man in ragged Cadian-pattern armour painted black with grey fatigues.

'Welcome to New Solthane,' said the man with a captain's stripes on his shoulder. He scratched at a black beard that had been growing for the past few weeks at least. Water rations apparently hadn't allowed for luxuries like shaving. 'I sincerely hope you've brought us some ammunition.'

The man next to him, equally filthy, raised his hand.

'I wouldn't say no to some food, either.'

'Shut up, Taan,' the captain said.

'Shutting up, sir.'

The general observed these scruffy examples of Guard discipline, clearly less than thrilled at the sight before his eyes.

'You look like death, both of you,' he said, his lip curling. And that wasn't even the worst of it. The captain – and the men joining him from the buildings around – all stank to high heaven.

Evidently bathing hadn't been on the cards, either.

■

My Lord Castellan,

I recommend First Lieutenant Parmenion Thade for the highest citation in our world's defence. Despite grievous injury and a shattered chain of command, he assumed leadership of Shock and Interior Guard forces stationed in the recent retreat at Kasr Vallock, arranging for the evacuation of seventy-one per cent of citizenry even as the fortress-city fell. All survivors bolstered the defences at nearby Kasrs, including the wounded governor-militant and his family.

I also have reports from over fifty eyewitnesses that First Lieutenant Thade duelled and slew a Traitor Astartes of the Thousand Sons Legion with the assistance of his command platoon.

As a final note, I offer the eyewitness reports listed in the attached file, listing Mechanicum personnel who will testify to the destruction of the enemy Titan (Reaver-class) designated 'Syntagma' at the fall of Kasr Vallock. Thade's sappers and tech-priest contingent were responsible for the overloaded generatoria within the city's industrial sector that led to the Syntagma's immobilisation. The following deployment of Interior Guard and Shock forces storming the crippled Titan resulted in the war machine's destruction.

Creed, I heard about the new medals. Give one to Thade. Too many are being given posthumously, and we've little to be proud of since the Despoiler set foot on Home. He deserves this, and with the losses sustained to our regiment, I'm making him a captain immediately.

We will march together again, Lord Castellan, under Cadian skies. Until that day, may the God-Emperor watch over you.

Colonel Josuan Lockwood
Cadian 88th Mechanised Infantry

* * *

III

THADE LOWERED THE dataslate.

He'd never read his citation before, and Colonel Lockwood's words to Lord Castellan Creed sat uncomfortably in his mind. Melancholy at the disaster of Kathur months ago mixed with the bitterness of Kasr Vallock still less than a year before. It had always seemed ridiculous to him – earning a medal and a priceless sword for the first time in his life he'd ever had to run from a battle. The first battle he'd ever lost. In failure, he was rewarded. Promoted, even.

He'd told Lockwood the truth once. The truth behind Kasr Vallock.

'I wanted to stand and fight,' he'd said. 'It was Osiron who talked me down, gave me a long speech about fighting the good fight when it counted most for Cadia and not when it counted for my pride.' He'd clenched his fists; one familiar and warm, the other – freshly implanted – unfamiliar, still numb to most sensation beyond a sense of aching cold.

'Throne, I wanted to die there. It was home. We left our own home to burn. Now we're being shipped off-world while the enemy pisses on the rubble of the city where we were born.'

'Stop whining, Thade,' the colonel had said. 'Slap a smile on your miserable face tomorrow when the Lord Castellan gives you that sword, and get over yourself. We're all hurting. Half of Home has fallen, son. Cadian Blood, eh? Ice in your veins.'

Thade had chuckled then, and forced a smile. Lockwood was right, of course. He'd always had that damnable ability and Thade admired him for it.

'You win.'

'Of course I do. You gave the Warmaster one hell of a black eye, and you've every right to be proud instead of wallowing in this self-pitying nonsense I'm seeing right now. But shake Creed's hand at the ceremony tomorrow and remember: this isn't all for you, you selfish bastard. It's for the 88th. The men need some inspiration to take with them after all this. Home still needs a lot of our sweat before it's all ours again.'

Thade drifted back to the present, feeling the shiver of the ship around him.

'Colonel?' asked a voice nearby. Thade looked out of the porthole, comfortable in the flight seat, staring out into the void of space. The troop carrier *Infinite Faith* rumbled onward, and a planet slowly hove into view. A planet of blue oceans and silver cities, a planet that Thade knew better than any other, ringed by a colossal war fleet that looked like twinkling stars from this distance.

'Colonel?' Darrick repeated. Thade turned his head.

'That's "warden-colonel" to you.' He grinned and turned back to the window, looking out at the planet as they slowly drew closer. The night side of the world showed glints of flame flaring on the surface, like distant candles in the blackness. War, viewed from orbit, had a beauty all its own. Darrick moved around Rax, who sat polished and oiled by his master's side, and he nodded to the porthole.

'How does Home look, Par?'

'Same as always, Taan.' He stared at the planet below, watching parts of it burn.

'Unbroken.'

Coming in Spring 2010: Soul Hunter, *the first Night Lords novel from Aaron Dembski-Bowden*

ABOUT THE AUTHOR

Aaron Dembski-Bowden is a British
author with his beginnings in the
videogame and RPG industries. He was
the Senior Writer on the million-selling
MMO Age of Conan: Hyborian Adventures.
He's been a deeply entrenched fan of
Warhammer 40,000 ever since he first
ruined his copy of *Space Crusade* by
painting the models with all the skill
expected of an overexcited nine-year-old.

Aaron lives and works in York, UK. His
hobbies generally revolve around reading
anything within reach, and helping
people spell his surname.

Beneath the sands, something is stirring...

DESERT RAIDERS
Lucien Soulban

ISBN 978-1-84416-492-9

An Imperial Guard Novel

ICE GUARD
Steve Lyons

UK ISBN 978-1-84416-672-5   US ISBN 978-1-84416-609-1

An Imperial Guard Novel

GUNHEADS
Steve Parker

UK ISBN 978-1-84416-587-2   US ISBN 978-1-84416-698-5